A LITTLE FRIENDLY
INTERROGATION

Gleeson laughed nervously. "You're a terrible fraud," he said as cheerfully as he could. "You couldn't fool a child with that act."

"Unlike yours, old buddy," I said, "mine ain't an act." Then I grabbed his wrist and squeezhe heavy silver bracelet into his soft flesh. "Intellectual discourse is great, man, but in my business, violence and pain is where it's at."

"My God," he squeaked, squirming, "you're breaking my arm."

"That's just the beginning, man," I said. "Keep in mind the fact that I like this, that I don't like you worth a damn."

"Please," he whimpered, sweat beading across his scalp.

"Let's have the rest of it," I whispered.

"There's nothing, I swear . . . Please . . . you're breaking . . ."

"Listen, old buddy," I said pleasantly, "the U.S. Army trained me at great expense in interrogation, filled my head with all sorts of psychological crap, but when I got to Nam, we didn't do no psychology, we hooked the little suckers up to a telephone crank—alligator clips on the foreskin and nipples— and the little bastards were a hundred times tougher than you, but when we rang the telephone, the little bastards answered."

"All right," he groaned, "all right." I released his wrist. "Can't you get this off?" he grunted as he struggled with the bent bracelet.

"Sure," I said, then straightened the silver. His face wrinkled and his eyelids fluttered. He rubbed his wrist as I fixed him a drink. "You had something to tell me."

JAMES CRUMLEY

THE LAST GOOD KISS

PUBLISHED BY POCKET BOOKS NEW YORK

The lines from "Degrees of Gray in Philipsburg" are reprinted from *The Lady in Kicking Horse Reservoir* by Richard Hugo with the permission of W. W. Norton & Company, Inc. copyright © 1973 by Richard Hugo.

 POCKET BOOKS, a Simon & Schuster division of
GULF & WESTERN CORPORATION
1230 Avenue of the Americas, New York, N.Y. 10020

Copyright © 1978 by James Crumley

Published by arrangement with Random House, Inc.
Library of Congress Catalog Card Number: 77-90286

ISBN: 0-671-82813-4

First Pocket Books printing January, 1981

10 9 8 7 6 5 4 3 2 1

POCKET and colophon are trademarks of Simon & Schuster.

Printed in the U.S.A.

for Dick Hugo,
grand old detective of the heart

You might come here Sunday on a whim.
Say your life broke down. The last good kiss
you had was years ago. You walk these streets
laid out by the insane, past hotels
that didn't last, bars that did, the tortured try
of local drivers to accelerate their lives.
Only churches are kept up. The jail
turned 70 this year. The only prisoner
is always in, not knowing what he's done . . .

—Richard Hugo, *Degrees of Gray in Philipsburg*

THE LAST
GOOD KISS

1 ••••

WHEN I FINALLY CAUGHT UP WITH ABRAHAM TRAhearne, he was drinking beer with an alcoholic bulldog named Fireball Roberts in a ramshackle joint just outside of Sonoma, California, drinking the heart right out of a fine spring afternoon.

Trahearne had been on this wandering binge for nearly three weeks, and the big man, dressed in rumpled khakies, looked like an old soldier after a long campaign, sipping slow beers to wash the taste of death out of his mouth. The dog slumped on the stool beside him like a tired little buddy, only raising his head occasionally for a taste of beer from a dirty ashtray set on the bar.

Neither of them bothered to glance at me as I slipped onto a stool between the bulldog and the only other two customers in the place, two out-of-work shade-tree mechanics who were discussing their lost unemployment checks, their latest DWI conviction, and the probable location of a 1957 Chevy timing chain. Their knotty faces and nasal accents belonged to another time, another place. The dust bowl '30's and a rattletrap, homemade Model T truck heading into the setting sun. As I sat down, they glanced at me with the narrow eyes of country people, looking me over carefully as if I were an abandoned wreck they planned to cannibalize for spare parts. I nodded blithely to let them know that I might be a wreck but I hadn't been totaled yet. They returned my silent greeting with blank eyes and thoughtful nods that seemed to suggest that accidents could be arranged.

Already whipped by too many miles on the wrong roads, I let them think whatever they might. As I ordered a beer from the middle-aged barmaid, she slipped out of her daydreams and into a sleepy grin. When she opened the bottle, the bulldog came out of his drunken nap, belched like a dragon, then heaved his narrow haunches upright and waddled across three rickety stools through the musty cloud of stale beer and bulldog breath to trade me a wet, stringy kiss for a hit off my beer. I didn't offer him any, so he upped the ante by drooling all over my sunburnt elbow. Trahearne barked a sharp command and splashed a measure of beer into the ashtray. The bulldog gave me a mournful stare, sighed, then ambled back to a sure thing.

As I wiped the dogspit off my arm with a damp bar rag that had been used too lately and too often for the same chore, I asked the barmaid about a pay telephone. She pointed silently toward the gray dusty reaches beyond the pool table, where a black telephone hung from ashen shadows.

As I passed Trahearne, he had his heavy arm draped over the bulldog's wrinkled shoulders and recited poetry into the stubby ear: "The bluff we face is cracking up . . . before this green Pacific wind . . . this . . . The whale's briny stink . . . ah, christ . . . dogged we were, old friend, doggerel we became, and dogshit we too shall be . . ." Then he chuckled aimlessly, like an old man searching for his spectacles.

I didn't mind if he talked to himself. I had been talking to myself for a long time too.

That was what I had been doing the afternoon Trahearne's ex-wife had called me—sitting in my little tin office in Meriwether, Montana, staring across the alley at the overflowing Dempster Dumpster behind the discount store, and telling myself that I didn't mind if business was slow, that I liked it in fact. Then the telephone buzzed. Trahearne's ex-wife was all business. In less than a minute, she had explained that her ex-husband's health and drinking habits were both bad and that she wanted me to find him, to track him down on his running binge before he drank himself into an early grave. I suggested that we talk about the job face to face, but she wanted me on the road immediately, no time wasted driving the three hours up to Cauldron Springs. To save time, she had already hired an air-taxi out of Kalispell, which was at this very moment winging its way south toward Meriwether with a cashier's check for a retainer, a list of Trahearne's favorite bars around the West—particularly those bars about which he had written poems after other binges—and a dust-jacket photo off his last novel.

"What if I don't want the job?" I asked.

"After you see the size of the retainer, you'll want the job," she answered coolly, then hung up.

When I picked up the large manila folder at the Meriwether Airport, I glanced at the check and decided to take the job even before I studied the photograph. Trahearne looked like a big man, a retired longshoreman maybe, as he leaned against a pillar on the front porch of the Cauldron Springs Hotel, a drink shining in one hand, a cigar smoking in the other. His age showed, even through his boyish grin, but he clearly hadn't gone to Cauldron Springs for the waters. Behind him, through the broad darkened doorway, two arthritic ghosts in matching plaid bathrobes shuffled toward the sunlight. Their ancient faces seemed to be smiling in anticipation of dipping their brittle bones into the hot mineral waters.

In the years that I had spent looking for lost husbands, wives, and children, I had learned not to think that I could stare into a one-dimensional face and see the person behind the photograph, but the big man looked like the sort who would cut a wide swath and leave an easy trail.

At first, it was too easy. Back at my office, I called five or six of the bars and caught the old man up in Ovando, Montana, at a great little bar called Trixi's Antler Bar. Trahearne had left, though, by the time I drove the eighty miles, telling the bartender that he was off to Two Dot to check out the beer-can collection in one of Two Dot's two bars. I chased him across Montana but when I reached Two Dot, Trahearne had gone on to the 666 in Miles City. From there, he headed south to Buffalo, Wyoming, to write an epic poem about the Johnson County War. Or so he told the barmaid. As it turned out, Trahearne never made a move without discussing it with everybody in the bar. Which made him easy to follow but impossible to catch.

We covered the West, touring the bars, seeing the sights. The Chugwater Hotel down in Wyoming, the Mayflower in Cheyenne, the Stockman's in Rawlins, a barbed-wire collection in the Sacajawea Hotel Bar in Three Forks, Montana, rocks in Fossil, Oregon, drunken Mormons all over northern Utah and southern Idaho—circling, wandering in an aimless drift. Twice I hired private planes to get ahead of the old man, and twice he failed to show up until after I had left. I liked his taste in bars but I was in and out of so many that they all began to seem like the same endless bar. By the middle of the second week, my expenses were beginning to embarrass even me, so I called the former Mrs. Trahearne to ask how much money she wanted to pour down the rolling rathole. "Whatever is necessary," she answered, sounding irritated that I had bothered to ask.

So I settled back into the bucket seat of my fancy El Camino pickup for a long siege of moving on, following Trahearne from bar to bar, down whatever roads suited his fancy, covering the ground like an excited redbone pup just to keep from losing him, following him as he drifted on, his tail turned into some blizzard wind only he felt, his ear cocked to hear the strains of some distant song only he heard.

By the middle of the second week, I had that same high lonesome keen whistling in my chest, and if I hadn't needed the money so badly, I might have said to hell with Abraham Trahearne, stuck some Willie Nelson into my tape deck, and tried to drown in a whiskey river of my own. Taking up moving on again. But I get paid for finding folks, not for losing myself, so I held on his trail like an old hound after his last coon.

And it made me even crazier than Trahearne. I found myself chasing ghosts across gray mountain passes, then down through green valleys riddled with the snows of late spring. I took to sleeping in the same motel beds he had, trying to dream him up, took to getting drunk in the same bars, hoping for a whiskey vision. They came all right, those bleak motel dreams, those whiskey visions, but they were out of my own drifting past. As for Trahearne, I didn't have a clue.

Once I even humped the same sad young whore in a trailerhouse complex out on the Nevada desert. She was a frail, skinny little bit out of Cincinnati, and she had brought her gold mine out West, thinking perhaps it might assay better, but her shaft had collapsed, her veins petered out, and the tracks on her thin arms looked as if they had been dug with a rusty pick. After I had slaked too many nights of aimless barstool lust amid her bones, I asked her again about Trahearne. She didn't say anything at first, she just lay on her crushed bed-sheets, hitting on a joint and gazing beyond the aluminum ceiling into the cold desert night.

"You reckon they actually went up there on the moon?" she asked seriously.

"I don't know," I admitted.

"Me neither," she whispered into the smoke.

I buttoned up my Levis and fled into the desert, into a landscape blasted by moonlight and shadow.

Then in Reno I lost the trail, had to circle the city in ever-widening loops, talking to bartenders and service-station attendants until I found a pump jockey in Truckee who remembered the big man in his Caddy convertible asking about the mud baths in Calistoga. The mud was still warm when I got there, but his trail was as cold as the eyes of the old folks dying around the hot baths.

When I called Trahearne's ex-wife to admit failure, she told me that she had received a postcard from him, a picture of the Golden Gate and a cryptic couplet. *Dogs, they say, are man's best friend, but their pants have no pockets, their thirst no end.* "Trahearne has this odd affinity for bar dogs," she told me, "particularly those who drink as well as do tricks. Once he spent three weeks in Frenchtown, Montana, drinking with a mutt who wore a tiny crushed officer's cap, sunglasses, and a corncob pipe. Trahearne said they discussed the Pacific campaign over shots of blackberry brandy." I told her that it was her money and that if she wanted me to wander around the Bay Area looking for a drinking bar dog, I would surely comply. That's what she wanted, so I hooked it up, headed for San Francisco, a fancy detective hot on the trail of a drinking bar dog, a fool on her errand.

I should have guessed that the city of lights would be rife with bar dogs—dancing dogs and singing dogs, even hallucinating hounds—so it wasn't until three days later, drinking gimlets with a pink poodle in Sausalito, that I heard about the beer-drinking bulldog over by Sonoma.

The battered frame building was set fifty yards off the Petaluma road, and Trahearne's red Cadillac convertible was parked in front. In the days when the old highway had been new, back before it had been rebuilt along more efficient lines, the beer joint had been a service station. The faded ghost of a flying red horse still haunted the weathered clapboard walls of the building. A small herd of abandoned cars, ranging from a russet Henry J to a fairly new but badly wrecked black Dodge Charger, stood hock deep in the dusty Johnson grass and weeds, the empty sockets of their headlights dreaming of Pegasus and asphalt flight. The place didn't even have a name, just a faded sign wanly promising BEER as it swung from the canted portico. The old glass-tanked pumps were long gone—probably off to Sausalito to open an antique shop—but the rusted bolts of their bases still dangled upward from the concrete like finger bones from a shallow grave.

I parked beside Trahearne's Caddy, got out to stretch the miles out of my legs, then walked out of the spring sunshine into the dusty shade of the joint, my boot heels rocking gently on the warped floorboards, my sigh relieved in the darkened air. This was the place, the place I would have come on my own wandering binge, come here and lodged like a marble in a crack, this place, a haven for California Okies and exiled Texans, a home for country folk lately dispossessed, their eyes so empty of hope that they reflect hot, windy plains, spare, almost Biblical sweeps of horizon broken only by the spines of an orphaned rocking chair, and beyond this, clouded with rage, the reflections of orange groves and ax handles. This could just as easily

7

have been my place, a home where a man could drink in boredom and repent in violence and be forgiven for the price of a beer.

After I had thought about it, I stuck my dime back in my pocket, walked back to the bar for another beer. I had found bits and pieces of Trahearne all along the way and I felt like an old friend. It seemed a shame not to enjoy him, not to have a few beers with him before I called his ex-wife and ended the party. Whenever I found anybody, I always suspected that I deserved more than money in payment. This was the saddest moment of the chase, the silent wait for the apologetic parents or the angry spouse or the laws. The process was fine, but the finished product was always ugly. In my business, you need a moral certitude that I no longer even claimed to possess, and every time when I came to the end of the chase, I wanted to walk away.

But not yet, not this time. I leaned against the bar and ordered another bottle of beer. When the barmaid sat it down, a large black tomcat drifted down the bar to nose the moisture on the long neck.

"The cat drink beer too?" I asked the barmaid.

"Not anymore," she answered with a grin as she flicked the sodden bar rag at the cat's butt. He gave her a dirty look, then wandered down the bar past the bulldog and Trahearne, his tail brushing across Trahearne's stolid face. "Sumbitch usta drink like a fish but he got to be too much trouble. He's like ol' Lester there," she said, nodding toward the shade-tree mechanic with the most teeth. "He can't handle it. He'd get so low-down, dirty-belly, knee-walkin' drunk, he start up tom-cattin' in all the wrong damn places."

The barmaid gave ol' Lester a hard, knowing glance, then broke into a happy cackle. As he tried to grin, ol' Lester showed me the rest of his teeth. They weren't any prettier than the ones I had already seen. "One night that crazy black bastard started up a-humpin' ever'thing in sight—pool-table legs, cues, folks' legs, anything that didn't move fast enough—and then he did somethin' nasty on a lady's slacks and somebody laughed and damned if we didn't have the biggest fistfight I ever seen. Ever'body who wasn't in the hospital ended up in jail, and they took my license for six weeks." She laughed, then added, "So I had that scutter cut off. Right at the source. He ain't wanted a drink since."

"Is that Lester or the tomcat?" I asked.

The barmaid cackled merrily again, the other mechanic brayed, but ol' Lester just sat there and looked like his teeth hurt.

"Naw," she answered when she stopped laughing. "Ol' Lester there, he don't cause no trouble in here. He's plumb terrified of my bulldog there."

"Looks like a plain old bulldog to me," I said, then leaned back and waited for the story.

"Plain," Lester squealed. "Plain mean. And I mean *mean*. Hell, mister, one mornin' last summer I come in here peaceful as could be, just mindin' my own business, and I made the mistake of steppin' on that sumbitch's foot when he had a hangover, and damn if he didn't like to tore my leg plumb off." Lester leaned over to lift his pants' leg and exhibit a set of dog-bite scars that looked like chicken scratches. "Took fifty-seven stitches," he claimed proudly. "Ol' Oney here, he had to hit that sucker with a pool cue to get him off'n my leg."

"Broke that damned cue right smack in two," Oney quickly added.

"Plain old bulldog, my ass," Lester said. "That sumbitch's meaner'n a snake. You tell him, Rosie."

"Listen, mister," the barmaid said as she leaned across the bar, "I've seen that old bastard Fireball

9

Roberts come outa dead drunks and blind hangovers and just pure-dee tear the britches off many a damn fool who thought he'd make trouble for a poor woman all alone in the world." When she said *alone*, Rosie propped one finger under her chin and smiled coyly at me. I glanced over her shoulder into the ruined mirror to see if my hair had turned gray on the trip. An old ghost with black hair grinned back like a coyote. Rosie added, "He don't just knock'em down, mister, he drags 'em out by the seat of their britches, and they're usually damn glad to go."

"Well, I'll be damned," I said, properly impressed, then I glanced at the bulldog, who was sleeping quietly curled on his stool. Trahearne caught my eye with a glare, as if he thought I meant to impugn the courage of the dog, but his eyes lost their angry focus and seemed to drift independently apart.

"'Course now, if'n Fireball can't handle all 'em by his own damn self," Lester continued in a high, excited voice, "ol' Rosie there, she ain't no slouch herself. You get her tail up, mister, she's just as liable to shoot your eyes out as look at you."

I nodded and Rosie blushed sweetly.

"Show him that there *pistole*," Lester demanded.

Rosie added a dash of bashful reluctance to her blush, and for an instant the face of a younger, prettier woman blurred her wrinkles. She patted her gray curls, then reached under the bar and came up with a nickel-plated .380 Spanish automatic pistol so ancient and ill-used that the plate had peeled away like cheap paint.

"Don't look like much," Lester admitted gamely, "but she's got the trigger sear filed down to a nubbin, and that sumbitch is just as liable to shoot nine times as once." He turned to point across the bar to a cluster of unmended bulletholes between two windows above a ratty booth. "She ain't had to touch it off but one damn

10

time, mister, but I swear when she reaches under the bar, things do tend to get downright peaceful in here."

"Like a church," I said.

"More like a graveyard," Lester amended. "Ain't no singin' at all, just a buncha silent prayers." Then he laughed wildly, and I toasted his mirth.

Rosie held the pistol in her rough hands for a moment more, then she sat it back under the bar with a thump.

"'Course I got me a real pistol at home," Lester said smugly.

"A German Luger," I said without thinking.

"How'd you know?" he asked suspiciously.

The real answer was that I had spent my life in bars listening to war stories and assorted lies, but I lied and told Lester that my daddy had brought one back from the war.

"Got mine off'n a Kraut captain at Omaha Beach," he said, his nose tilted upward as if my daddy had won his in a crap game. "Normandy invasion," he added.

"You must have been pretty young," I said, then wished I hadn't. People like Lester might tell a windy tale now and again, but only a damn fool would bring it to their attention.

Lester stared at me a long time to see if I meant to call him a liar, then with practiced nonchalance he said, "Lied about my age." Then he asked, "You ever been in the service?"

"No, sir," I lied. "Flat feet."

"4-F, huh," he said, trying not to sound too superior. "Oney here, he's 4-F too, but it weren't his feet, it was his head."

"Ain't going off to no damn army," Oney said seriously, then he glanced around as if the draft board might still be on his tail.

"Ain't even no draft no more," Lester said, then snorted at Oney's ignorance.

"Yeah," Oney said sadly. "By god they oughtta go over there to San Francisco and draft up about a hunnert thousand a them goddamned hairy hippies."

"Now, that's the god's truth," Lester said, and turned to me. "Ain't it?" His eyes narrowed at the three-day stubble on my chin as if it were an incipient beard.

For a change, I kept my mouth shut and nodded. But not emphatically enough to suit Lester. He started to say something, but I interrupted him as I excused myself and walked over toward Trahearne. Behind me, Lester muttered something about *goddamned gold-brickin' 4-F hippies,* but I acted as if I hadn't heard. I reached over and tapped Trahearne on the shoulder, and his great bald head swiveled slowly, as if it were as heavy as lead. He raised an eyebrow, wriggled a pleasant little smile onto his face, shrugged, then toppled backward off the bar stool. I caught a handful of his shirt, but it didn't even slow him down. He landed flat on his back, hard, like a two-hundred-fifty-pound sack of cement. Rafters and window lights rattled, spurts of ancient dust billowed from between the floorboards, and the balls on the pool table danced merrily across the battered felt.

As I stood there stupidly with a handful of dirty khaki in my right hand, Lester leaped off his stool and shouted, "What the hell did you do that for?"

"Do what?"

"Hit that old man like that," Lester said, his Adam's apple rippling up and down his skinny throat like a crazed mouse. "I ain't never seen nothin' as chickenshit as that."

"I didn't hit him," I said.

"Hell, man, I seen you."

"I'm sorry but you must have been mistaken," I said, trying to be calm and rational, which is almost always a mistake in situations like this.

12

"You callin' me a liar?" Lester asked as he doubled his fists.

"Not at all," I said, then I made another mistake as I stepped back to the bar for my beer: I tried to explain things. "Listen, I'm a private investigator, and this gentleman's ex-wife hired me to . . ."

"What's the matter," Lester sneered, "he behind in his goddamned al-i-mony, huh? I know your kind, buddy. A rotten, sneaky sumbitch just like you tracked me all the way down to my mama's place in Barstow just 'cause I's a few months behind paying that whore I married, and let me tell you I kicked his ass then, and I got half a mind to kick yours right here and now."

"Let's just calm down, huh," I said. "Let me buy you boys a beer and I'll tell you all about it. Okay?"

"You ain't gonna tell me shit, buddy," Lester said, and as if that weren't enough, he added, "and I don't drink with no trash."

"I don't want no trouble in here," Rosie interjected quietly.

"No trouble," I said. Lester and Oney might have comic faces, funny accents, and bad teeth, but they also had wrists as thick as cedar fence-posts, knuckled, work-hardened hands as lumpy as socks full of rocks, and a lifetime of rage and resentment. I grew up with folks like this and I knew better than to have any serious disagreements with them. "No trouble at all," I said. "I'll just leave."

"That ain't near good enough," Lester grunted as he took two steps toward me and a wild swing at my face.

I ducked, then backhanded him upside the head with the half-full beer bottle. His right ear disappeared in a shower of bloody foam, and he fell sideways, scrabbled across the floor, cupping his ear and cursing. Oney stood up, then sat back down when he saw the broken bottle in my hand.

"Is that good enough?" I asked.

13

Oney agreed with a nervous nod, but Lester had just peeked into his palm and found bits and pieces of his ear.

In a high, thin voice, he shouted, "Goddammit, Oney, get the gun!"

Behind me, I heard Trahearne stand up and dreamily wonder what the hell had happened. But nobody answered him. Oney and Rosie and I were locked into long silent stares. Then we all moved at once. Rosie dashed down the bar toward the automatic as Oney scrambled over it. I glanced at the bulldog, who still slept like a rock, then I lit out for open country. I would have made it, too, but good ol' Lester rolled over and hooked a shoulder into my right knee. We went down in a heap. Right on his ruined ear. He whimpered but held on. Even after I stood up and jerked out a handful of his dirty hair.

Behind the bar, Rosie and Oney still struggled for the pistol. Trahearne had sobered up enough to see it, but as he tried to run, he crashed into the pool table, then tried to scramble under it just as Oney jerked the pistol out of Rosie's hands and shoved her away. As she fell, she screamed, "Fireball!" I gave up and raised my hands, resigned myself to an afternoon of fun and games in payment for Lester's ear. But as Oney lifted the pistol and thumbed the safety, Fireball came out of a dead sleep and cleared the bar in a single bound like a flash of fat gray light. Still in midair, he locked his stubby yellow teeth into Oney's back at that tender spot just below the short ribs and above the kidney. Oney grunted like a man hit with a baseball bat, dropped his arms, and blanched so deeply that ancient acne scars glowed like live coals across his face. He grunted again, sobbed briefly, then jerked the trigger.

The first round blew off a significant portion of his right foot, the second wreaked a foamy havoc in the cooler, and the third slammed through the flimsy beaverboard face of the bar and slapped Mr. Abraham Trahearne right in his famous ass. The fourth powdered the fourteen ball, the fifth knocked out a window light, and the rest ventilated the roof.

When the clip finally emptied, Oney sank slowly behind the bar, the automatic still clutched in his upraised hand, and Fireball still locked to his back like a fat gray leech. During the rash of gunfire, the tomcat had come out of nowhere and shot out the front door like a streak of black lightning, while Lester had hugged my knees like a frightened child. Or a man whose war stories had finally come true.

"Goddammit, Lester," I said when the echoes had stopped rattling the old beams, "you're bleeding all over my britches."

"I'm sorry," he said quietly as if he meant it, then turned me loose.

As I handed him my handkerchief for his ear, Fireball came trotting around the end of the bar, his drooping jowls rimmed with blood. He scrambled onto the platform bar rail, a stool, then up on the bar. He worked his way along, tilting bottles, catching them in his muzzle, and drinking them dry. Then he lapped his ashtray empty, belched, then hopped down to the floor the same way he had gotten up. With a weary waddle that seemed to sigh with every step, he wandered over to the doorway and stretched out in a patch of sunlight, asleep before his belly hit the floor, small delicate snores rippling the dust motes around him.

"I don't believe I've ever seen anything quite like that," I told Lester.

"Goddamned sumbitchin' dog," Lester growled as he walked over to a booth to sit down.

I went behind the bar to check on Oney and Rosie. He had fainted and she lay on the duckboards like a corpse. Except that her hands were clasped to her ears instead of crossed on her chest.

15

"Anybody dead?" she asked without opening her eyes.

"Some walking wounded," I said, "but no dead ones."

"If you'd wait till I get my wits about me before you call the law," she said, "I'd surely appreciate it. We got to figure some way to explain all this crap."

"Right," I agreed. "You got any whiskey?"

She nodded toward a cabinet, where I found a half-empty quart of Old Crow. I did what I could for Oney's foot, took off his work shoe and cotton sock and poured some whiskey on the nubbins of flesh where his two middle toes had been, then wrapped the foot in a clean bar towel. After I washed out the dog bite with bar soap, I went over to help Lester clean slivers of glass out of the side of his head and tattered ear.

"Ain't no ladies gonna slip their tongues in that ear no more," I joked.

"Never much cared for that anyway," he said primly. "How's ol' Oney?"

"Blew off a couple of toes," I said.

"Big'uns or little'uns?"

"Medium sized," I answered.

"Hell, that ain't nothin'," Lester said as he gently touched his ear. "How 'bout Rosie?"

"I think she's taking a little nap."

"Looks like the big fella is, too," Lester said with a nod.

I thought it unkind to point out that "the old man" had somehow become "the big fella," so I went over to see why Trahearne still huddled under the pool table.

"Are you all right, Mr. Trahearne?" I asked as I knelt to peer under the table.

"Actually, I think I've caught a round," he answered calmly.

I didn't see any blood, so I asked where.

"Right in the ass, my friend," he said, "right in the

ass." Then he opened his eyes, saw the bottle, and took it away from me.

"You drink this pig swill?"

I didn't, or least hadn't, but he didn't have any trouble getting his mouth around the neck of the bottle. Not as much as I had trying to get his pants and a pair of sail-sized boxer shorts down so I could see the wound. The jacketed round had left a neat blue hole, marked with a watery trickle of blood, just below his left buttock. I had no way of knowing if the bullet had struck a bone or artery, but Trahearne's color and pulse were good, and I could see the lead nestled like a little blue turd just beneath the skin below the hump of fatty tissue hanging over his right hip.

"What's it look like?" he asked between sips.

"Looks like your ass, old man."

"I always knew I'd die a comic death," he said gravely.

"Not today, old man. Just a minor flesh wound."

"That's easy for you to say, son, it's not your flesh."

"In a few days, you won't have nothing but a bad memory and a sore ass," I said.

"Thank you," he said, "but I seem to have both those already," He paused for a sip of whiskey. "How is it that you know my name, young man?"

"Why, hell, you're a famous man, Mr. Trahearne."

"Not that famous, unfortunately."

"Yeah, well, your ex-wife was worried about your health," I said.

"And she hired you to shoot me in the ass," he said, "so I couldn't sit a bar stool."

"I didn't shoot you," I said.

"Maybe not," he said, "but you're going to get the blame anyway." Then he sucked on the bourbon until he curled around the empty bottle, adding his gravelly snore to Fireball's quiet drone.

17

2 ••••

As the official caravan, two ambulances and a deputy sheriff's unit, swept out of Rosie's parking lot in a cloud of dust, they all hit their sirens at once and wailed into the distance. From where Rosie and I sat on the front steps, it sounded like the beginning of the end of the world.

"Them boys sure do favor them sirens," she said quietly.

"It's just about the only fun they get out of life," I said.

"You speakin' from experience?" she asked with narrow eyes.

"I've ridden in the back seats of a few police cars," I said, and she nodded as if she had too.

As she and I had cleaned up the mess inside the bar, moved the wounded outside, and concocted a wildly improbable but accidental version of the shooting, Rosie and I had become friends. Now we were also bound by our mutual lies to the authorities. Lester and Oney would have lied for free, just to be contrary, but I doled out a generous portion of cash to help with medical expenses. Lester pocketed the money, then told me that he and Oney, by virtue of several trips to the drunk farm, were medical wards of the state of California. The middle-aged deputy who questioned us seemed to know we were shucking him but he didn't seem to care. He was more interested in ragging Oney about shooting himself in the foot. As he left, though, he mentioned that I should drop by the courthouse the next morning to sign a statement, and he and I both knew what that meant.

As soon as the sirens had faded away, Rosie said, "Reckon we should have us a beer?"

"Whiskey," I said, then went over to my pickup for the road pint in the glove box. When I got back to the steps, Rosie had found two whole bottles of beer for chasers. After we drank silently for a bit, I said, "Sorry for the trouble."

"Wasn't your fault," she answered waving with a tired hand. "It was that damned worthless Lester. Truth is, when that there private detective caught him down in Barstow, Lester smartmouthed him, and that boy proceeded to whip the living daylights outa Lester right there in his momma's front yard, whipped him till Lester just begged to pay some back childsupport."

"Thought it might be something like that," I said.

"How come you were after that big fella, anyway?" she asked. Then she quickly added, "'Course you don't have to tell me if it ain't none of my business."

"I was supposed to find him before he drank himself into the hospital," I said. "Or into the grave."

"That's a fool's errand," Rosie said with authority.

"I was just supposed to find him," I said, "not take the bottle out of his hands."

"Is that what you do for a living?" she asked. "Find folks?"

"Sometimes," I said. "Other times I just look."

"You do okay?"

"Fair to middling," I admitted, "but it ain't steady. I end up tending bar about half the time."

"How come?"

"Beats the hell out of standing around Monkey Wards watching out for sixteen-year-old shoplifters."

19

"I reckon so," she said, then laughed and hit the pint. "How long you been trackin' the big fella?"

"Right at three weeks," I answered.

"Get paid by the day, huh?"

"Usually."

"This job oughtta do you nicely," she said.

"Hope so," I said. "They might feel unkindly, since the old man got shot, and decide that I'm overpriced, unworthy of my hire."

"Sue 'em."

"Ever try to sue rich folks?" I asked.

"Hell, boy, I don't even know any rich folks," she said, then paused to stare at the ground. "What you reckon that old boy was runnin' from?"

"Maybe he just needed a high lonesome," I said, "or a running binge. I don't really know." And I didn't. Usually, after I had been after somebody for a few days, I had some idea of what they had in mind. But not with Trahearne. During some of my less lucid moments, I had the odd feeling that the old man was running from me, running so I would chase him. "Maybe he just wanted to see what was over the next hill," I added.

"He musta got tired of lookin'," Rosie said quietly, "'cause he holed up here like chick come to roost."

"Well, if he's only half as tired as I am, he's plenty damn tired," I said, "'cause I'm worn to a frazzle. I could sleep for a week."

"But you probably won't, will you?"

"Probably not."

"What are you gonna do?" she asked, too casually to suit me.

"Hang around the hospital until he gets out," I said.

"How long would that be?"

"A week or so," I said. "Depends."

For a few minutes we sat silently again, watching the

20

soft spring sunshine spark green fire across the shallow hills, listening to the distant hum of traffic.

"Hey," she said suddenly, as if the idea had just come to her. "It might be that I could put you on to a piece of work while you're hangin' around. No sense in sittin' idle."

"I usually work one thing at a time," I said quickly. "That's my only advantage over the big outfits." When she didn't say anything, I asked, "What do you have? A bundle of bad checks?"

"Enough to paper a wall," she said, "but that ain't the problem." When I didn't ask her what the problem was, she continued. "It's my baby girl. She run off on me, and I thought maybe you might spend a few days—whatever time you got—lookin' around."

"Well, I don't know . . ."

"I know this place don't look like much," she interrupted, "but it's free and clear and it turns a dollar now and again—"

"It's not that," I interrupted her. "I just need some time off the road."

"You wait right here," she said as if she hadn't heard me, then flounced back into the bar.

As I waited, what had earlier seemed a fine spring haze clearly became Bay Area smog, which reminded me that this wasn't some country beer joint down in Texas on a spring afternoon in the '50's. The maze of San Francisco lay just across the bay, a haven for runaways, and although the '60's were dead and gone too, young girls still ran there to hide. That hadn't changed, though everything else had. The flower children had gone sour and commercial or middle-class, and even the enemy was tired and broken, exiled to San Clemente. I didn't want to hear what Rosie had to tell me—I didn't want to stare at another picture of a lost child. Whichever wise Greek said that you can't step

21

into the same river twice was right, even though he forgot to mention that nine times out of ten, you'll get your feet wet. Change is the rule. You can't go home again even if you stay there, and now that everyplace is the same, there's no place to run. But that doesn't keep some of them from trying. And that didn't stop Rosie either.

"Here," she said as she sat down and handed me a photograph. "Look here."

I glanced at the picture just long enough to see that it was a wallet-sized school photograph of a fairly pretty girl. Then I looked back and saw the dates: 1964–65.

"She was a pretty girl," I said as I tried to hand the picture back to Rosie.

"Smart as a whip, too," she answered, holding her hands between her knees.

I had to look at the picture again. It could have been a picture from my high school days in the '50's. The face was pleasant, no more, though she seemed to have good bones beneath a soft layer of baby fat. The wide mouth seemed pinched, almost sullen, and the thick cascade of blond hair looked fake. The nose was straight but slightly too bulbous at the end to be pretty. Only the eyes were striking, darkly fired with anger and resentment, a redneck rage more suited to a thinner face. She wore an old-fashioned, high-collared lace blouse with a black ribbon threaded through the collar to hold a small cameo to her throat. As I looked at the face again, the blouse seemed oddly defiant, the face so determined not to be laughed at that it seemed sad, too sad.

I knew the story: a nearly pretty girl, but without the money for the right clothes or braces or confidence, the sort of young girl who either lurked about the fringes of the richer, more popular girls, and was thought pushy for her efforts, or who stood alone and avoided the high school crowd, and for her lonely troubles was thought stuck-up, stuck on herself without good reason. Ah, the sad machinations of high school. As I stared at the picture, I was once again pleased that I had missed most of those troubles. I lived in the country and worked, and although I hadn't exactly planned it that way, I had joined the Army three weeks before I was supposed to graduate. Somehow the GED I had earned in the Army seemed cleaner than a high school degree. Less sad, somehow.

"How long ago did she take off?" I asked Rosie, the photograph dangling from my fingers like a slice of dead skin.

"Ten years ago come May," she answered as calmly as if she had said *a week ago come Sunday.*

"And you haven't heard from her since?" I asked.

"Not a single solitary word."

"Ten years is too long," I said, still trying not to sound shocked. "Even a year is usually too long, but ten years is forever."

Once again, though, Rosie acted as if she hadn't heard me. "She went over to San Francisco one Saturday afternoon with this boy friend of hers, and he said she just stepped out of the car at a red light and walked off without sayin' a word or even lookin' back. Just walked away. That's what he said."

"Any reason to think he might have lied?"

"No reason," Rosie said. "I've known him all his life, and his momma's a friend of mine. She's been fixin' my hair once a week for nearly twenty years. And Albert, he was torn up by it something terrible. He kept lookin' for Betty Sue for years after I give up. His momma says he still asks about her every time she sees him."

"Did you report it to the police?" I asked.

"Well of course I did," Rosie answered angrily, her

wrinkled eyes finding an old spark. "What kinda mother would I be if I hadn't? You think I'd let a seventeen-year-old girl wander around that damned city fulla niggers and dope fiends and queers? Of course I told the police. Half a dozen times." Then in a softer voice, she added, "Not that they did diddly-squat about it. I even went over there my own damned self. Twenty, maybe thirty times. Walked up and down them hills till I wore out my shoes, and showed pictures of her till I wore them out. But nobody had seen her. Not a soul." She paused again. "I just hate that damned city over there, you know. Wish it would have another earthquake and fall right into the sea. I just hate it. I was raised Church of Christ, you understand, and I know I ain't got no right to judge, runnin' a beer joint like I do, but I swear if there's a Sodom and Gomorrah in this wicked, sinful world, it's a-sittin' over there across the bay," she said, then pointed a finger like a curse across the hills. When she saw an amused grin on my face, she stopped and glared down her sharp nose at me. "You probably like it over there, don't you? You probably think it's all right, don't you, all that crap over there?"

"You don't have to get mad at me," I answered.

"I'm sorry," she said quickly, then looked away.

"That's all right."

"No, it ain't all right, dammit. Here I am askin' a favor of you and hollerin' at the same time. I'm sorry."

"It's okay," I said. "I understand."

"You got any children of your own?"

"No," I said. "I've never even been married."

"Then you don't understand at all. Not even a little bit."

"All right."

"And don't go around pretending to, either," she said, hitting me on the knees with her reddened knuckles.

"All right."

"And goddammit, I'm sorry."

"Okay."

"Oh hell, it ain't a bit okay," she complained, then stood up and rubbed her palms on her dusty slacks. "God damn it to hell," she muttered, then turned around and gave Fireball a fierce boot in the butt, which knocked the sleeping dog off the steps into the skim of dust on the concrete. "Goddamned useless dog," she said. "Get outa my sight."

Fireball must have been accustomed to Rosie's outbursts. He slunk away without glancing back, not hurrying exactly, but not waiting around either. At the corner of the building, he stumbled over the black tomcat, who was curled asleep in the deep grass below the eaves, and they had a brief but decisive and probably familiar encounter, then went their separate ways, the cat beneath the building, and Fireball right back to his place in the sunshine warming the steps. As he lay down, he gave Rosie one slow glance, then shut his eyes, sighing like an old husband saddled with a mad wife. But Rosie was watching the breeze weave through the hillside grass.

"How about another beer?" I asked.

"I'd like that just fine," she answered without turning. Sadness softened her nasal twang, that ubiquitous accent that had drifted out of the Appalachian hills and hollows, across the southern plains, across the southwestern deserts, insinuating itself all the way to the golden hills of California. But somewhere along the way, Rosie had picked up a gentler accent too, a fragrant voice more suited to whisper throaty, romantic words like *wisteria*, or humid phrases like *honeysuckle vine*, her voice for gentleman callers. "Just fine," she repeated. Even little displaced Okie girls grow up longing to be gone with some far better wind than that hot, cutting, dusty bite that's blowing their daddy's crops to hell and gone. I went to get her a beer, wishing it could be something finer.

"It was the damndest thing," she said when I came back, "when I was looking for Betty Sue over there." Rosie still stood upright, her wrists cocked on her hips, still stared southwest across the gently rounded hills toward the cold, foggy waters of the Bay. "I never had no idea there'd be so many folks lookin' for their kids. Musta been a hundred or more walkin' up and down too, holding out their pictures to any dirty hippie that would look at it. Some of the nicest folks you'd ever hope to meet, too, some of them really well-off. But, you know, not a single one of them had the slightest idea how come their kids run off. Not a one. And the kids we asked *why,* they didn't seem to know either. Oh, they had a buncha crap to say, but it sounded like television to me. They didn't even know what they were doing there. Damndest mess I ever did see, you know."

"I know," I said.

And in my own way I did, even though I had no children to run away. In the late '60's, when I came back from Vietnam in irons, in order to stay out of Leavenworth I spent the last two years of my enlistment as a domestic spy for the Army, sneaking around the radical meetings in Boulder, Colorado, and when I got out, after a brief tour as a sports reporter, I headed for San Francisco to enjoy the dope and the good times on my own time. But I was too late, too tired to leave, too lazy to work, too old and mean to be a flower child. I found a profession, of a sort, though, finding runaways. For a few years, Haight-Ashbury was a gold mine, until I found one I couldn't bear. A fourteen-year-old boy decomposing into the floorboards of a crash pad off Castro Street, forty-seven stab wounds in his face, hands, and chest. The television crew beat the police to the body, and none of it was any fun at all. Not anymore. I knew. I had seen Rosie in her best double-knit slack suit and a pair of scuffed flats wandering those hills, staring into each dirty face that came down the street, then back into the photograph in her hand, just to be sure that it wasn't her baby girl hiding behind lank hair, love beads, a bruised mouth, and broken eyes.

"It's been so long," I said to Rosie, "so long. Why start looking again now?"

"She's all I got left, son," she answered softly. "The last child, the only one I ain't seen in a coffin. Lonnie got blown up in Vietnam right after she run off, and Buddy, he got run over by a dune buggy down at Pismo Beach last summer. Betty Sue's all I got left, you see."

"Where's their daddy?" I asked, then wished I hadn't.

"Their daddy? Their wonderful, handsome, talented daddy?" she said, giving me another hard, accusing look. "Last I heard he was down in Bakersfield sellin' aluminum cookware on time to widow-wimmen." She let that stand for a moment, then added, "I run the worthless bastard off when Betty Sue was a junior in high school."

"You mind if I ask why?"

"He thought he was Johnny Cash," she said, and stopped as if that explained it all. "Damn fool."

"I'm not sure I understand."

"Ever' other year, he'd get drunk and clean out the bank account and take off for Nashville to find out if he could make the big time as a singing star. Only thing the damned fool ever found out was how long my money would last, then he'd drag-ass home, grinnin' like an egg-suckin' dog. Last time he done that, he showed up and found himself divorced and slapped in jail for nonsupport. That's the last I seen of him," she said with a grin. "He was sure enough a good-lookin' devil, but like my daddy told me when I married him, he's as worthless as tits on a boar hog."

"He's never heard from Betty Sue either?"

"Not that I know of," Rosie said. "Betty Sue was always stuck on her daddy, but Jimmy Joe was stuck on himself and he did favor the boys too much, so I don't know if she ever forgave him for that, but I think he'd told me if he heard from her. He knows I been lookin' for her, and he's plumb scared I'll dun him for all that back support, so I think he'd mentioned it." Then she paused and looked down at me. "So what do you think?

"You want the truth?"

"Not a bit of it, son. I want you to spend a few days lookin for my baby girl," she said, then handed me a wad of bills that had been clutched in her fist all this time. "Just till the big fella gets out of the hospital, that's all."

"It's a waste of my time," I said trying to hand the sodden bills back to her, "and your money."

"It's my money," she said pertly. "Ain't it good enough to buy your time?"

"What if she doesn't want to be found?"

"Did that big fella ask you to come huntin' for him?" she asked.

"She might be dead, you know," I said, ignoring the point she had made. "Have you thought of that?"

"Not a day goes by, son, that I don't think of that," she answered. "But I'm her mother, and in my heart I know she's alive somewhere."

Since I had never found any way to argue with maternal mysticism, I shook my head and went over to the El Camino for my note-and receipt books, carrying the wad of bills carefully, as if the money were a bomb. Then I went back, asked questions, took notes, and counted the money—eighty-seven dollars.

Rosie gave me the name of the boy friend, who was a lawyer over in Petaluma now, Betty Sue's favorite high school teacher, who still taught drama in Sonoma, and her best girl friend, who had married a boy from Santa Rosa, named Whitfield, divorced him and married a Jewish boy from Los Gatos, named Greenburg or Goldstein, Rosie wasn't sure, divorced him, and was supposed to be going to graduate school down at Stanford. Details, details, details. Then I asked what sort of girl Betty Sue had been.

"You'll see," she answered cryptically, "when you talk to folks. I'll let you find out for yourself."

"Fair enough," I said. "Why did she run away?"

After a few moments thought, Rosie said, "For a long time I blamed myself, but I don't now."

"For what?"

"I live in a trailer house behind here," she said, "and one time after I divorced Jimmy Joe, Betty Sue found me in bed with a man. She took it pretty hard, but I don't think that's why she run off anymore. And sometimes I used to think she run off because she thought she was too good to live behind a beer joint."

"Did the two of you have a fight before she left?"

"We didn't have fights," Rosie said proudly. "Nothin' to fight about. Betty Sue did as she pleased, ever since she was a little girl, and I let her 'cause she was such a good little girl."

"Could she have been pregnant?"

"She could have. But I don't think she would have run away for that," Rosie said. "But then, I don't know." Then, in a shamed voice, she added, "We weren't close. Not like I was to my momma. I had to run the place 'cause Jimmy Joe wouldn't, most of the time, and when he did, he'd give away more beer than he sold. Somebody had to make a living, to run things." Then she paused again. "I guess I still blame myself but I don't know what for anymore. Maybe I blame her too, still. She always wanted more than we had. She never said anything—she was a sweet child—but I could tell she wanted more. I just never knew what it was she wanted more of. If you find her, maybe she'll be able to tell me."

"If I find her," I said, then handed her a receipt for the eighty-seven dollars.

"Is that enough?" Rosie asked. "I didn't get a chance to count it."

"That's plenty."

"You give me a bill if it's more, you hear," she commanded.

"It's already too much," I said. "I'll talk to this Albert Griffith over in Petaluma and this Mr. Gleeson here, and see if I can get in touch with Peggy Bain, then I'll bring back your change. But I'm telling you up front, it's a waste of money."

"Fair enough," she said, then glanced at the receipt again. "What's that name? Sughrue?"

"Right."

"My momma had some cousins back in Oklahoma, lived down around Altus, I think, name of Sughrue," she asked. "You got any kin down that way?"

"I got kin all over Texas, Oklahoma, and Arkansas," I admitted.

"Hell, we're probably cousins," she said, then stuck out her hand.

"Could be," I said, then shook her firm, friendly hand.

"Folks don't understand about kinfolks anymore," she said.

"World's too big for that," I said. "I guess I'd best head for town to see if my other client is still alive and kicking."

"Want a road beer?"

"Sure," I said, then went to the john to make room for it.

30

When I came back, she leaned over the bar to hand me the beer and said, "You're a drinking man yourself."

"Not like I used to be."

"How come?"

"Woke up one morning in Elko, Nevada, emptying ashtrays and swabbing toilets."

"But you didn't quit," she said.

"Slowed down before I had to quit," I said. "Now I try to stay two drinks ahead of reality and three behind a drunk." She smiled with some sort of superior knowledge, as if she knew that the idea of having to quit drinking scared me so badly that I couldn't even think about it. "Would you keep an eye on Mr. Trahearne's Cadillac?" I asked.

"Get the rotor," she said, "and I'll let Fireball sleep in it after I close nights." After I removed the rotor from the distributor and closed the hood, Rosie nodded at my Montana plates and asked, "Don't it get cold up there?"

"When it does, I just drift south," I said.

"Must be nice."

"What's that?"

"Goin' where you want to," she said softly. "I ain't been more'n ten miles from this damned place since I went to my momma's funeral down in Fresno eleven years ago."

"Footloose and fancy-free ain't always all it's cracked up to be," I confessed.

"Neither's stayin' home," she said, then smiled, the wrinkles etched into her face softened and smoothed, some of the years of hard living fell away like happy tears. "You take care, you hear."

"You too," I said. "See you the first of next week."

As I climbed into my El Camino, a carload of construction workers in dirty overalls and bright yellow hardhats skidded into a rolling stop beside me, the transmission clanking loudly as the driver jammed it into park. The men scrambled out, laughing and shouting at Rosie, goosing each other in the butts, happy in the wild freedom of quitting-time beers, and they charged into Rosie's open arms like a flock of baby chicks.

I knew the men were probably terrible people who whistled at pretty girls, treated their wives like servants, and voted for Nixon every chance they got, but as far as I was concerned, they beat the hell out of a Volvo-load of liberals for hard work and good times.

3 ••••

WHEN I ARRIVED AT HIS HOSPITAL ROOM, TRAHEARNE HAD been sedated into a deep rumbling sleep from which it would have been a crime to awaken him. I found the emergency-room doctor who had treated him, and the doctor suggested that Trahearne would live in spite of himself. He wasn't as sure about Oney and Lester, though. After their wounds had been cleaned and bandaged, they had split, heading back to Rosie's for another beer or two. As the doctor walked up the hallway, shaking his head, I finally used my dime to call the former Mrs. Trahearne collect. As usual, she sounded distantly reluctant to accept the charges.

"Well," I said more brightly than I meant to—I blamed it on the whiskey—"I finally ran the old devil to the ground."

"Finally," she said coldly. "In San Francisco?"

"No, ma'am," I said. "In a great little beer joint outside of Sonoma."

"Isn't that quaint," she murmured. "In what condition did you find him?"

"Drunk," I said, not specifying which of us.

"I assumed that, Mr. Sughrue," she said sharply. "What is his physical condition?"

"Right."

"Yes?"

"Yes, ma'am," I stalled. "He's fine, he's all right, he should be out of the hospital in three or four days, and he'll be as good as new."

"It may seem presumptuous of me to ask," she said smoothly, "but if he is in such wonderful shape, why then is he in the hospital?"

"It's a long story," I said.

"Isn't it always?" she said.

"Yes, ma'am."

"You're being unnecessarily obtruse, Mr. Sughrue," she said. Her voice sounded pleasant and refined, but accustomed to command.

"Yes, ma'am."

"So?"

"Well, he had a little accident."

"Yes?"

"He fell off a barstool and strained his back," I said quickly.

"How absolutely delightful," she said. "Perhaps that will teach him a much-needed lesson." Then she laughed, deep and elegant, like the rich susurruses of a mink coat being casually dragged down a marble staircase. "But nothing too serious, I hope."

"A minor sprain," I said.

"I'm glad to hear that," she said. "I expect you to remain by his side until he is released from the hospital, and then stay with him during his postmortality binge."

"Ma'am?"

"Violated flesh will insist upon wallowing in flesh," she said. "Particularly in Trahearne's case."

"Ma'am?"

"He will insist on a drunken debauch as soon as he is released from the hospital," she said. "You know—wine, women, and song—expensive whiskey, high-class hookers, and finally the same old sad song of regret. I expect you to take care of him during those few days."

34

"I'll do my best," I said.

"I'm sure you will," she said. "And when he is ready to return home to lick his wounds, I expect you to see that he does so."

"Yes, ma'am," I said, hoping Trahearne was supposed to lick his wound only figuratively.

"Perhaps if you inform him that his beloved Melinda is once again in the fold, throwing pots or whatever it is she does all through the night, then he may want to cut his debauch short."

"Yes, ma'am," I said, though I didn't have any idea who or what she was talking about. I didn't have any idea what Trahearne would think about my presence after his accident. Or my accident. The accident.

"Also, I'll expect a full report upon your arrival," she said. "Thank you and good night."

"A report of what?" I asked. But she had already hung up the telephone. "Only a crazy man works for crazy people," I told the dead wire, and a harried nurse hurrying past agreed with a quick nod.

Since it wasn't my money, and since I knew where I would probably spend the next night, I checked into the best motel in Sonoma, ordered a huge steak and some of that expensive whiskey the former Mrs. Trahearne had mentioned. Then I drove back out to Rosie's, got stupid drunk with Lester and Oney, and slept on the pool table.

"Where in the hell have you been?" Trahearne growled as I stepped into his room at ten o'clock two mornings later.

"A guest of the county," I said.

"Huh?"

"Jail."

"Why?"

"After the sheriff took my statement yesterday, he held me as a material witness. Just to see if I had a

35

different version of the shooting after a night in a cell," I said.

"Can they do that?"

"No," I said. "But if I had complained or called a lawyer, they would have found some minor crap to charge me with."

"Bastards."

"It's okay, I've been in jail before." Jails are jails, and there's never much to talk about when you get out.

"Well, now that you're here," he said, "You can run some errands for me." I reached into my hip pocket and pulled out a half-pint of vodka. "Oh my god," he whispered as he took the bottle from me. "You're a saint, my friend, an absolute saint." But before he could break the seal, a tall, nicely rounded nurse came briskly through the door.

"That will not do," she said as she snatched the bottle from his huge, trembling hands. "This will be returned upon your release."

"Now, see there, Mr. Trahearne," I said quickly. "I told you they didn't allow drinking in the hospital." Then to the nurse: "I'm really sorry, ma'am, I told him I shouldn't do it, but you know how it is, since I'm just a hired hand." Trahearne's face glowed red and greasy with sweat, and his chest rose half out of bed. He looked like a man intent on murder.

"Just so it doesn't happen again," the nurse said.

"No, ma'am, it won't," I said as I touched her lightly on the arm. "And if he gives you any trouble, just give me a call. I'm at the Sonoma Lodge." She smiled, nodded, and thanked me again, then carried her nicely molded hips out the door with quick, efficient steps. "Anytime," I said to her back.

"Son, I don't mind you making time, but not on my time and not at my expense," Trahearne grumbled. I lifted another halfpint out of my windbreaker pocket and handed it to him. "You're not a saint, boy, you're prepared for emergencies," he whispered, then had a quick snort. "My god, it's even chilled," he said, and had another. "You may be worth all the money you're costing me."

"I was under the impression I was working for your ex-wife."

"It's all the same pocket, boy," he said, staring at the clear liquor.

"One a day?"

"Two."

"Yes, sir."

"You certainly don't look like any of the others," he said as he looked me over.

"Others?"

"They all looked like unsuccessful pimps," he said, "pastel leisure suits and zircon pinky rings. You look like a saddle tramp."

"I see you've had dealings with other members of my profession," I said.

"You're the first one who ever found me before I wanted to be found," he said. "How'd you do it?"

"Professional secret."

"The damned postcard, huh?"

"You have no idea how many dogs hang out in bars," I said, and he grinned.

"You mind if I ask you a personal question?"

"What's a good ol' boy like me doing in a business like this?"

"Something like that," he said.

"I'm a nosy son of a bitch," I said.

"Me too," he said, and grinned again. "Maybe we'll get along."

"I'm supposed to keep an eye on you, Mr. Trahearne, not be your faithful Indian companion," I said.

"Horseshit."

37

"And gunsmoke?"

"You'll do," he said.

"How's your ass?"

"Getting better," he said. "I've survived worse. Of course, I was a younger man at the time. But the Marine Corps didn't have vodka deliveries."

"Glad to be of service," I said.

"It's the boredom that's hard," he said. "I need a couple of favors."

"I'm yours to command."

"I'd rather it be a favor."

"Whatever," I said.

"Get me some reading material," he said. "Paperback novels and popular magazines by the pound—I go through them like a kid through potato chips—whatever you pick up off the shelf will be fine. Also, it would be wonderful if you could arrange to have my dinners delivered. I don't care if it comes from McDonald's, just so it isn't hospital food."

"Okay," I said. "What about the dancing girls and a marching band?"

"I like a man who knows how to entertain," he said. "If I'm stuck here too long, maybe you can arrange for a working girl interested in oral gratification. But no bands. Maybe a string quartet."

"I'll look into it," I said, "but I can't promise anything. I'm out of my territory."

"If you can't work that foot-shuffling, hayseed, ma'am routine," he said, "I've got several interesting telephone numbers in San Francisco."

"Okay," I said. "I've got a favor to ask of you." He stopped grinning. "It won't interfere with your errands."

"What sort of favor?" he asked quietly.

"Seems that Rosie has this runaway daughter," I said, "and I told her I'd look into it while you were in the hospital, if it was all right with you."

After a moment, he said, "It's all right with me. I like to see a young man trying to get ahead in the world."

"I don't know if I qualify as a young man anymore," I said, "and I don't give a shit about getting ahead. I like the old lady and I said I'd do her the favor. If you don't mind."

"I don't mind," he answered.

"Probably a waste of money and time," I said.

"How much money?"

"Eighty-seven dollars," I answered, and he grinned again.

"Hell, how much time can you waste for eighty-seven dollars?"

"Whatever time I spend will be wasted," I said.

"Why?"

"The daughter ran away ten years ago, and that's too—"

"By god, I seem to have some drunken recollection of Rosie telling me that," Trahearne said quickly, then shook his head. "I'm afraid this is my fault."

"How's that?" I asked.

"I'm afraid that I told her that a private eye would come sniffing down my cold, cold trail," he said, then hit the bottle, "and suggested that she hire him. Thought that it might divert whomever Catherine sent for a few more days." He laughed. "So how can I mind?" he added. "How do you go about this missing person business?"

"Depends on who's missing and how long," I said, "but mostly I just poke around."

"Doesn't sound like much of a method."

"If you want method, you hire one of the big security outfits," I said. "They're great at method. Straight people don't know how to disappear, and crooks can't because they have to hang out with other crooks."

"And where do you fit in?"

"I'm cheaper," I said, "and my clients usually still

believe in the small, independent operator. They're usually romantics."

"You must be working all the time," Trahearne said with a chuckle.

"And every year I have to tend bar more often," I said.

"By god, boy, I knew right away that there was something I liked about you," he said.

"Everybody likes bartenders," I said. "By the way, your ex-wife asked me to tell you that Melinda was home, throwing fits or something."

"Pots."

"What?"

"My wife," he explained. "She's a potter and a ceramic sculptor."

"Oh."

"I can see by your face, boy, that you aren't aware of my situation," he said grimly. Since I wasn't, I didn't say anything. "We all live together—or nearly together—my mother, my ex-wife, my present wife, and me on a little ranch outside Cauldron Springs." Trahearne stared at the institutional beige wall as if it were a window overlooking the mountains, as if he could see himself standing in a crowded postcard scenic view. "One little happy family," he said quietly.

I knew I would have to listen to the story of his life eventually, but I preferred later to sooner, so I excused myself. As I turned to leave, his large hand wrapped around the small bottle as if it were his only hope of salvation.

There's no fool like a fool who thinks he's charming. On the way out, I stopped by the nurses' station to say hello to the tall nurse again. I asked her about having Trahearne's meals delivered, and although she didn't seem pleased about it, she promised to check with the doctor.

"And what are you doing about dinner tonight?" I asked.

"Fixing it," she said as she held up a banded finger.

"I'm not," a perky voice said behind me.

Before I picked up the line, I turned around to see who had dropped it. She was shorter than the other one but rounder, with a pert, snub-nosed face framed by curly blond hair and a solid, muscular body. She had bowlegs, but what the hell, so did I.

"Is that a date?" I asked her.

"Only if you want it to be," she answered quickly, her blue eyes brightly smiling.

"Eight o'clock," I said, "in the bar at the Sonoma Lodge?" I'm not a monster but I've got a beer gut and a broken nose, and strange women never pick me out of a crowd for blind dates, but gift horses and all that. Also, she had a small mobile mouth, and the straight-forward approach of a bedroom lady.

"Wonderful," she said, then extended a square, no-nonsense hand. "Bea Rolands," she added. "Are you a writer too? Like Mr. Trahearne?"

"Not exactly like Trahearne," I admitted, holding on to the hand as things became clearer. The only writer around was out of action, and I had read enough books on bored afternoons in Army gymnasiums to fake it, maybe even pick up Trahearne's slack. "I do research for him, sometimes, and take care of his affairs," I said with a leer.

"Isn't he a wonderful writer?" she gushed. "I just love his books. I have them all, you know. Hardbacks. Even his poetry. And I've seen all the movies, three or four times, and I just love them, too. Do you think he'd mind if I asked him to autograph them for me?"

"Well, I don't know," I said. "He's really shy, you know, and that sort of thing embarrasses him, but why don't you bring them along tonight, and I'll ask him tomorrow."

"Oh thank you," she bubbled, bouncing on her heels. Her small firm breasts bounded about quite nicely in the thin bra she wore beneath her uniform.

"See you at eight," I said, finally releasing her hand. "And thanks for saving me from a solitary dinner."

"Oh the pleasure's all mine," she answered, giggling.

Walking out of the hospital, I decided that Trahearne was all right. At least he wasn't boring. Things happened around him: blood, gunfire, a night in jail, and now a devoted fan with sexily bowed legs. I found myself hoping he would run away again. Soon. And often. Once every five or six months. Maybe he could just stop by and pick me up on the way, then we wouldn't have to waste all that party time while I busted my ass hunting for him.

4 ●●●●

AT THE SUPERMARKET, I ASKED THE CHECK-OUT LADY FOR a receipt for the fifteen pounds of magazines and paperbacks, then flashed a deputy sheriff's badge—obtained under extremely suspicious circumstances—from Boulder County, Colorado. I told her I was investigating the material for hidden pornographic meanings. She didn't turn a single artfully tousled hair. Which was one of the things I had always liked about California: Everybody's so crazy, you have to be really weird to get anybody's attention.

When I delivered my load to Trahearne's room, he was sleeping like a grizzly gone under for the winter, curled on his unwounded hip, spitting out snores that seemed to curse his sleep, great phlegm-strangled, whiskey-soaked, cigar-smoked, window-rattling roars. I wondered how he slept in all that racket, how his wives, past and present, ever got any sleep. I hid his afternoon ration of vodka between something called *The Towers of Gallisfried* and a thin Western, *Stalkahole,* then tiptoed out quietly, trying not to awaken the·monster.

At the nearest pay telephone, I found the high school drama teacher's number listed. When I called Mr. Gleeson and told him why I wanted to talk to him, he sounded vaguely amused rather than surprised. He didn't have to thumb through his memory to recognize

43

the name, though, which was a good sign. He agreed to talk to me as soon as I could drive out to his house, but only for a short time, since he had a student appointment later that afternoon. Then he proceeded to give me a set of directions so confusing that it took me thirty minutes to drive the ten miles out to his house at the base of the Oakville Grade. By the time I found it, I had stopped myself twice from driving on over the Grade into the Napa Valley and a wine tour.

Charles Gleeson lived in a cottage in a live oak glade, a small place that looked as if it had been a summer retreat once, with a shake roof and unpainted walls that had tastefully weathered to a silver gray. Some sort of massive vine screened his front porch and clambered like crazy over the roof, as if it feared it might drown among the large flowering shrubs that cluttered the yard. He came to the screen door before I could knock, a small man with a painfully erect posture, a huge head, and a voice so theatrically deep and resonant that he sounded like a bad imitation of Richard Burton on a drunken Shakespearean lark. Unfortunately, his noble head was as bald as a baby's butt, except for a stylishly long fringe of fine, graying hair that cuffed the back of his head from ear to ear. He must have splashed a buck's worth of aftershave lotion across his face, and he was wearing white ducks, a knit polo shirt, and about five pounds of silver and turquoise.

"You must be the gentleman who telephoned about Betty Sue Flowers," he emoted as he opened the door. A cruising fly, hovering like a tiny hawk, banked in front of me and sped for the kitchen. Gleeson swatted at it with a pale, ineffectual hand and muttered a mild curse.

"I'm sorry I'm late," I said.

"The directions, right? I must apologize, but my conception of spatial relationships is severely limited.

Except on stage, of course. My god, I can block out a monster like *Morning Becomes Electra* in my head but I can't seem to tell anyone how to find my little cottage in the woods," he prattled as he twisted the heavy bracelet on his wrist. Then we shook hands, and he patted my forearm affectionately and drew me into his Danish Modern, Neo-Navajo living room. "It's lovely out," he suggested, touching the squash-blossom necklace, "so why don't we sit on the sun deck? I fear the house is a disaster area—I'm a bachelor, you see, and housekeeping seems to elude me." He waved his hand aimlessly at some invisible mess. We could have lunched off the waxed oak floorboards or performed an appendectomy on the driftwood coffee table. I didn't mind going outside though. His sort of house always made me check my boots for cowshit. Unfortunately, this time they were innocently clean.

The sun deck, built out of the same silvered planks as the house and threatened by the same heavy vine, was done in wrought iron and gay orange canvas. At least it was outside. With a deep, throbbing sigh, Gleeson collapsed into a director's chair and genteelly offered me the one facing him.

"It's a bit early for me, but would you care for a *cerveza?*" he said, idly swirling the ice cubes in the blown Mexican glass he had picked up from the neat little table that matched his little chair. "A beer?" he added, just in case I hadn't understood.

"Right," I growled, "it's never too early for me." Then I chuckled like Aldo Ray. If I had to endure his *l'homme du monde* act, he had to suffer my jaded, alcoholic private eye.

"Of course," he murmured, then reached into a small refrigerator on the other side of his chair and came out with a can of Tecate, a perfect pinch of rock salt, and a wedge of lime already gracing the top of the can. He had prepared, the devil. "Do you like Mexican beer?"

"I like beer," I said, "just like Tom T. Hall."

"I see," he said, trying to hide a superior smile with a supercilious eyebrow. "Mexican beer is quite superb. Perhaps the best in the world. I'm quite fond of it myself. I summer in Mexico, you see, San Miguel de Allende, every year. Takes me away from the mundane world of high school," he said as he handed me the beer.

"Must be fun," I said, guessing that he spent his summers wearing a three-hundred-dollar toupee which looked like a dead possum and boring hell out of everybody for forty miles in every direction.

"A lovely country," he sighed, meaning to sound wistful and longingly resigned to a life unworthy of his talents. Then he glanced up and said, "A touch of salt on the tongue, then sip the beer, and bite the lime."

"Right," I said, then gobbled the salt, chug-a-lugged the whole beer, ate the lime wedge, rind and all, and tossed the empty can onto the lawn. Gleeson looked ready to weep, and when I belched, he flinched. "Got 'nother wunna them Mexican beers?" I said cheerfully. "That weren't half bad."

"Of course," he said, the perfect host, then doled me another can as if it were rationed. Before I had to destroy that one too, I was saved by the bell. Or the chirp. His telephone chirped like a baby bird. "Oh damn," he said. "Please excuse me."

After he went back inside, I stood up to let the heavy beer lie down. Out of an old nosy habit, I checked Gleeson's glass. Cranberry juice and a ton of vodka. He was either a secret tippler, a pathological liar, or more nervous about my visit than he cared for me to know. I sidled up to the kitchen window but I couldn't hear anything except the distant throb of his voice and the insane buzz of a frustrated fly. I opened the back door to let the poor starving devil out, then sat down to watch a hummingbird suck sugar water from Gleeson's feeder. I couldn't believe the little bastard had come all the way from South America for that. Or that I had come all this way to talk about a girl who had run away ten years before.

Gleeson came back muttering gracefully about the foibles of his simply, simply lovely students. "Now," he said as he leaned back in his chair and clasped his hands around his knee with a soft clink of silver rings. "What can I do for you?"

"Betty Sue Flowers."

"Quite." A brief frown wrinkled his forehead up toward the fragrant, glistening expanse of his scalp. "Betty Sue Flowers," he sighed, then shook his head and smiled ruefully. "I haven't thought about her in years."

"What comes to mind?"

"Such a gauche name for such a lovely, talented child," he said. "When it became apparent that she was more than just a good amateur actress, I advised her to change her name immediately, discard it like so much childhood rubbish."

"I sort of like the name," I said. I didn't like women who changed their names. Or men who wore jewelry before sundown.

"Quite," he said. "What exactly was it you wanted to know? I haven't seen or heard of her since the Friday before she ran away. What was that? Six, seven years ago?"

"Ten."

"How time does fly," he whispered with a dreamy lilt, mouthing the cliché like a man who knew what it meant.

"Quite," I said.

He glanced up, narrowed his eyes as if he was seeing

me for the first time. "It isn't polite to mock me," he suggested politely. He sounded half pleased, though, that I had taken the trouble.

"Sorry," I said. "A bad habit I have. What did she talk about that day?"

"I'm afraid I don't have the slightest notion," he said, then held up a finger. "Wait, I seem to remember that she stopped by my office to tell me that she had tickets at the ACT for the next night." He started to explain the initials, then stopped. "I'm afraid I don't remember what they were doing. It has been quite some time, you understand."

"Too long," I admitted for the tenth time.

"Do you mind if I inquire into your motives in this matter?"

"Her mother asked me to look for her," I said.

"Do you do this for a living? Or are you a member of the family?"

"Both," I said. "I'm a cousin on her mother's side and a licensed private investigator."

"Would you be insulted if I asked for some identification?"

"Nope," I said, and took out my photostat.

"I would have thought, from your accent," he said as he handed it back, "that you were from the Texas or Oklahoma branch of the family."

"Texas," I said. "But they let us live just about anywhere we want to nowadays."

"I see," he said. "Has there been some new information about Betty Sue that prompted her mother to hire you?"

"Nope," I said. "I was just handy. Down here on another case. And both Mrs. Flowers' sons are dead now, and she just thought she'd like to see her baby girl again."

"I don't imagine she's a baby anymore," he said, smiling at his own joke. "But if I were you I would get in touch with her father. For reasons I don't quite understand—perhaps because he withheld his affection from her—Betty Sue had an unhealthy fixation on him. I would think she would have been in touch with him. Yes, I would look for the father," he said, then leaned back in his chair, sipped his drink, and sighed heavily, like a detective who had just broken a big, sadly corrupt case in an existential movie.

My temper and my mouth had always gotten me in trouble. And occasionally prevented me from picking up the information I needed. I wanted to tell Gleeson to stuff his stupid advice. I also wanted to tell him to stuff his *Time* magazine analysis, and to explain what *fixation* meant, but instead of carping, I kept my mouth shut, my temper in hand.

"I never had a chance to meet Betty Sue when she was growing up," I said, changing directions. "What sort of girl was she?"

"One in a million," he answered, quickly but softly, then paused abruptly as if he had confessed to something. I knew I had him now.

"Why?"

"Why?" he whispered. "When I first saw her, she was playing in a grade school production of *Cinderella*, which I had to attend for reasons I don't even want to think about now. A simply dreadful production, even for grade school, and Betty Sue had been wasted in the fairy godmother role, but let me tell you, my friend, when that little girl, that mere child, was onstage, all the other children seemed like creatures of a lesser race. She had the best natural stage presence I had ever seen. Offstage, she wasn't anything special, a pleasant-looking child, no more, but onstage she was in charge. Such presence. Such a natural sense of character, too." He paused to chuckle. "Her fairy godmother was a queen, her gifts bestowed grandly on her inferiors. And even then, she had a frighteningly sexual presence. You could almost hear the middle-aged libidos in the audience whimpering to be unleashed.

"After the production, I went backstage to talk to her," he continued, "and found her staring with such awful longing eyes at the little girl who had played Cinderella that I gave her a lecture then and there about how good she had been. I'm afraid I quite lost control for a bit. When I finished, she looked up at me and said, 'It's just a prettier dress than mine, that's all. I wouldn't be Cinderella, anyway. I wouldn't stand for it.' She was nine, my friend, nine years old.

"After that, of course, I took her in hand, and whenever possible I arranged my high school and Little Theatre productions with a role for her in mind. I also tried to get that horrid mother of hers to allow me to enroll her in an acting class in the city—even offered to pay all the expenses out of my own pocket. Of course, she refused. 'Buncha damn foolishness,' I believe were her exact words." He paused again and clasped his hands together. "Her damned mother foxed me at every turn. I suppose she had been considered good-looking in her youth—though the idea escapes me now—and she resented Betty Sue. And who wouldn't, stuck on that horrid trailer house behind that sordid beer joint. Once, when Betty Sue was fifteen, I had a friend—a professional photographer—take a portfolio of photographs of her. They were lovely. Later, when I asked Betty Sue what she had done with it, she told me that it had been lost, but I remain convinced that her mother destroyed it.

"So sad," he said, sipped his drink, and hurried on. "At fifteen, she played Antigone in Anouilh's version, and at sixteen, Mother Courage. I wouldn't have believed it possible."

"Pretty heavy stuff for high school," I said.

"Little Theatre productions," he said. "We had a great company then. Even the San Francisco papers reviewed our productions favorably. She was so wonderful." He sounded like a man remembering heroics in an ancient war. "With a bit of luck, she might have made it on Broadway or in Hollywood. With a bit of luck," he repeated like a man who had had none. "The luck is nearly as essential as the talent, you know." Then he gazed into his empty glass.

I broke into his reverie. "How old was she when you seduced her?"

Gleeson laughed lightly without hesitation, his capped teeth gleaming in the sunlight. The hummingbird buzzed the sun deck like a gentle blue blur, pausing to check Gleeson's fragrance. But he wasn't a flower, so the bird flicked away. Gleeson rattled his ice cubes and stood up.

"I think I'll have that drink now," he said pleasantly. "Would you care for another Tecate?"

"I'd rather have an answer to my question," I said.

"My good fellow," he said as he fixed a drink, "you've been the victim of sordid rumors and vicious gossip."

"I got your name from Mrs. Flowers," I said, "and that's all. Except that I understand now why she gritted her teeth when she said it. Otherwise, I don't know a thing about you that you didn't tell me."

"Or that you surmised?"

"Guessed."

"You do the country bumpkin very well, my friend," he said as he handed me another beer. "But you slipped up when you didn't ask me to explain what ACT stood for, and you didn't learn about Brecht and Anouilh in the police academy or in a correspondence course for private investigators."

"I'm supposed to be the detective."

"I imagine you play that role quite well, too," he said, "and I suspect that it isn't in my best interest to continue this conversation."

51

"I don't live here," I said. "I couldn't care less how many adolescent hymens you have hanging in your trophy room. Better you here with candlelight and good wine than some pimpled punk in the back seat of a car with a six-pack of Coors."

"I'm not that easily flattered," he said, but I could see smutty little fires glowing in the depths of his eyes. "However, I do occasionally indulge myself," he added, smiling wetly. "Most of the simple folk in town think I'm a faggot, and I let them. A very nice protective coloration, don't you think?" I nodded. "But Betty Sue and I never had that sort of relationship. Not that I wasn't sorely tempted, mind you—she had a fierce sexuality about her—and not that she might not have been willing. Certainly, if I had known . . . known how things were going to work out, known that she wouldn't pursue a career in the theatre, I would have snatched her up in a moment. But I was afraid that a sexual relationship might interfere with our professional relationship."

"Professional?"

"That's right," he said. "I may be only a high school drama teacher now, but I have worked off-Broadway and in television, even taught in college, and I know the business. Betty Sue might have made it. And I confess that I intended to use her if she did." He sighed again. "Athletic coaches often rise on the legs of their star players, and I saw no reason why I shouldn't have the same chance. So I abstained. Betty Sue, as young girls so often do, might have grown bored with the older man in her life, and confused the sexual relationship with the professional one. So, my friend, I kept my hands off her," he said with just the right touch of remorse mixed with pride.

"I'm sorry," I said, trying to see his face behind the wistful mask. "You must still have friends in the theatre," I said, "and I assume that you have asked them about Betty Sue over the years."

"So often that I've become an object of some derision," he said ruefully. "But no one has ever seen or heard of her. That's a dead end, I'm afraid."

"Could she have been pregnant?"

"She could have, yes," he said. "I assumed that she wasn't a virgin much past her fourteenth birthday. But, of course, I had no way of knowing."

"You know," I said, still bothered about the earlier lie about his drink, "sometimes people confess a little thing—like your selfish intentions about her career—to cover up something larger."

"What could I possibly have to hide?" he said blandly.

"I don't know," I said, then leaned forward until our hands nearly touched. "I've got a little education," I said, "but I'm particularly sophisticated—"

"Still a country boy at heart?" he interrupted.

"Right. And, like you said, you're a professional—you know all about acting and lying, wearing masks," I said, "and if I find out that you've been lying to me, old buddy, I'll damn sure be back to discuss it with you." I crushed my empty beer can in my fist. An old-fashioned steel can.

Gleeson laughed nervously. "You're a terrible fraud," he said as cheerfully as he could. "You couldn't fool a child with that act."

"Unlike yours, old buddy," I said, "mine ain't an act." Then I grabbed his wrist and squeezed the heavy silver bracelet into his soft flesh. "Intellectual discourse is great, man, but in my business, violence and pain is where it's at."

"My god," he squeaked, squirming, "you're breaking my arm."

"That's just the beginning, man," I said. "Keep in

53

mind the fact that I like this, that I don't like you worth a damn."

"Please," he whimpered, sweat beading across his scalp.

"Let's have the rest of it," I whispered.

"There's nothing, I swear . . . Please . . . you're breaking . . ."

"Listen, old buddy," I said pleasantly, "the U.S. Army trained me at great expense in interrogation, filled my head with all sorts of psychological crap, but when I got to Nam, we didn't do no psychology, we hooked the little suckers up to a telephone crank—alligator clips on the foreskin and nipples—and the little bastards were a hundred times tougher than you, but when we rang that telephone, the little bastards answered."

"All right," he groaned, "all right." I released his wrist. "Can't you get this off?" he grunted as he struggled with the bent bracelet.

"Sure," I said, then straightened the silver. His face wrinkled and his eyelids fluttered. He rubbed his wrist as I fixed him a drink. "You had something to tell me."

"Yes, right. Once, some time ago," he babbled, "I thought I saw her in a porno flick over in the city. The girl was fat and awful, a pig, it might have been her, it looked like her, the print was bad, all grainy, and the lighting even worse, but it looked like her, except for this scar, this ugly scar in the middle of her belly." When he stopped talking, his ruined mouth kept moving like a small animal in its death throes.

"Why lie about that?" I asked, honestly amazed.

"I was . . . I am ashamed of my interest in that . . . that sort of thing," he said, then rushed into his drink. "And it was so sordid, that awful fat girl and all those old men . . ."

"You remember the name of it?"

"*Animal* . . . something or other. *Lust* or *Passion*,

54

something like that. I can't remember, it was so horrid," he moaned, then began to weep.

"And so exciting," I said, and he nodded. "That's all you had to tell me?" I asked, and he nodded again.

It didn't sound right, but I didn't know what sounded wrong. I did know that I couldn't push him anymore. I didn't have the stomach for it. The only interrogation I had seen in Vietnam had made me sick, but I didn't remember if I had vomited because of the tiny Viet Cong's pain, the Vietnamese Ranger captain's pleasure, or my own fatigue. I had been in the bush for twenty-three days, and I could sleep standing up with my eyes open, which was good, because I couldn't sleep lying down with them shut. A few days later, I made the mistake that got me out of Nam and two years later out of the Army. Those times seemed far away, usually, but listening to Gleeson sob into the clear sunlight, they seemed too close.

"Hey," I said, "I didn't mean to hurt you."

"Oh, I understand," he blubbered, "that horrid war twisted so many of you boys."

"I left Nam nine years ago," I said, "and I'm no boy, so don't make excuses for me."

"Of course," he said as sincerely as he could, "of course." Then he took his hands away from his face and wiped at the tears. "Will you do me one small favor?"

"What's that?"

"If you find her, will you call me? Please. I'll pay anything you ask. Please."

"You might have thought of that ten years ago."

"Ha," he said, rubbing his eyes. "Ten years ago I was still in my thirties, instead of nearly fifty, and I had no idea that I was going to be here ten more years, no idea that the peak of my career was going to be some little high school actress. No idea at all. I didn't know what she meant to me then. I do now. I'd just like to see her, talk to her again. Please."

"I won't find her," I said.

"But if you do . . ."

"I'll let you know for free," I said. "Sorry about your wrist, and thanks for the beers."

"My pleasure," he answered, a slight smile curling his lip, then his head dropped into his hands again.

I left him there on the sun deck, his huge head cradled in his arms like that of a grotesque baby. As I stepped out the front door, a young girl wearing a halter and cut-offs took that as her cue to push her ten-speed bike up the walk. I wanted to tell her that Gleeson wasn't home, but her greeting and smile were shy and polite with wonder, her slim, tanned thighs downy with sweat.

"Hello," she said. "Isn't it a lovely day?"

"Stay me with flagons," I said, "comfort me with apples, for I am sick of love."

"What's that?" she asked, sweetly bewildered.

"Poetry, I think."

Instead of taking her in my arms to protect her, instead of sending her home with a lecture, I walked past her toward my El Camino. Youth endures all things, kings and poetry and love. Everything but time.

5 ●●●●

Since it was getting on into Saturday afternoon, and since I didn't feel like Christian charity on the hoof, I hoped Albert Griffith wouldn't answer his telephone. No such luck. After I explained what I wanted, he agreed to meet me in his office at five. He even sounded anxious to talk to me. I drove to Petaluma and found an anonymous motel bar and dirge of a Giants game on the television with which to slay foul time until five.

After a couple of deadly dull innings and slow, carefully paced beers, the bartender drifted by and I asked him for a drink.

"Stay me with CC ditches, my friend, for I am bored shitless by all this."

"Hey, fella, take it easy, huh," he said, then walked away.

"That's Canadian Club and water, you turd," I shouted at his back. "But I'll have it someplace else."

"That's fine with me, buddy," he said.

For a tip, I left him the remains of a stale beer. When even the bartenders lose their romantic notions, it's time for a better world. Or at least a different bar. I found the local newspaper and the nearest bar.

Albert Griffith, though, had enough romantic notions to gag Doris Day. He kept an office in a restored Victorian house on a quiet side street just outside the downtown area, sharing the house with another lawyer and two shrinks. And he had dressed for the occasion. A dark-blue, expensively tailored, vested, pinstriped suit and a silk tie. As he ushered me into his office, he offered me a wing-backed gold brocade chair and a taste of unblended Scotch. I accepted them both. In my business, you have to buy everybody's act. For a few minutes. Usually lawyers are too devious to suit me. They seem to have the idea that justice is an elaborate game, that courtrooms are tiny stages, and clients simply an excuse for the legal act. They also have a disturbing habit of getting elected to political offices, or appointed to government commissions, then writing laws you have to hire a lawyer to understand. But Albert Griffith acted as if he were my best friend. For a moment.

As soon as I was settled, he leaned against the front of his massive desk, his arms crossed as he towered over me, smiling in a friendly way beneath sardonic eyes. After I had a taste of his great Scotch, he leaped into his act.

"All right, Mr. Sughrue," he said, "let's get something straight from the very beginning. I don't know how you persuaded Mrs. Flowers to hire you for this wild goose chase, and I don't know how much money you have managed to weasel out of that poor woman, but she's a personal friend of my mother's, and I intend to put an end to this nasty little gambit of yours."

"You want me to cut you in, huh?" I said. "Okay. There's enough for everybody."

"What?"

While he worked on his confusion, I stood up and walked around behind his desk, took a cigar out of a burled walnut box, lit it, sat down in his leather swivel chair, and propped my boots on his desk.

"What the hell are you doing?" he asked.

"Making myself comfortable, partner," I said, then blew smoke in his face.

"Get up from there," he sputtered. He couldn't have been any angrier if I had sat down on his wife's face.

"Listen, Buster Brown," I said, taking a fistful of his cigars for my pocket, "you've got a fancy setting here, but you're just another second-class creep. Your daddy, when he can stand up, holds a sign for the highway department, and your momma put you through law school with a beauty operator's tips. Your daddy-in-law is springing for this antique whorehouse decor, this whole lawyer scam, and you, Mr. Griffith, aren't only a failure, you're a courthouse joke, so get out of my face with this big-shot attorney crap."

"If you don't get out of my office this instant, I'm calling the police," he said in a voice on the verge of sobs.

"After you apologize," I said, "maybe we can start this whole thing over again."

At the moment, though, he didn't have anything to say. I watched his face change hues about four times and examined the shoddy dental work on his back lower molars. At the newspaper bar, I had found an AP stringer who, for the price of a 7&7, had given me Albert Griffith's life history.

"If it will improve your attitude," I said, "give Rosie a call. She's got eighty-seven bucks, two beers, and a smile into this, and I might take another beer or two, and I might only lose a hundred bucks on this, but she's paid all she's going to pay. So call her while I have another taste of this overpriced whiskey."

While I stiffened my drink, he called Rosie and spoke softly to her for a minute. Then he hung up, loosened his tie, and made himself a really stiff drink. I didn't have much of a picture of Betty Sue Flowers yet, but just the mention of her name seemed to drive grown men to drink.

"Let's sit on the couch," Albert said, and we sat at opposite ends of a long leather expanse. "Please accept my apology," he said. "I'm sure you've been in the business long enough to understand that most independent operatives are scumbags. Even the corporate security people are frighteningly ugly beneath that slick exterior they maintain."

"Thanks."

"For what?"

"For not thinking I have a slick exterior."

"You're welcome," he said, glancing at my faded Levis and worn work-shirt and laughing. A bit too long to suit me. "Rosie explained everything, Mr. Sughrue, and I am sorry for acting so hastily."

"That's okay," I said. "I'm used to it."

"Well, I am sorry," he repeated. I wished he would stop. "Rosie even said that you told her it was probably a waste of time and money," he said, then smiled sadly. "Let me tell you that it is definitely a lost cause."

"Why's that?"

"I was a student at Berkeley when Betty Sue ran away," he said, "and I spent all my spare time for two years searching for her in the city. Let me tell you, my transcript showed it too. I nearly didn't get into law school," he said dramatically. I wasn't impressed yet. "I never turned up a single lead. Not one. It was as if she walked away from my car that afternoon and off the edge of the world, off the face of the earth. I even had a friend from law school—he's in Washington—check her Social Security payment records, and there hasn't been a payment since she worked a part-time job the summer before she disappeared." He sucked on his whiskey glass, his hand trembling so badly that the lip of the glass rattled against his teeth. "I can only assume that either she doesn't want to be found or that's she's dead. Though if she is, she didn't die in San Francisco or any place in the Bay Area. At least not in the first five years after she ran away."

"How do you know that?"

"I checked Jane Does in county morgues for that long," he said softly, as if the memory made him very tired.

"You went to a lot of trouble."

"I was very much in love with her," he said, "and Betty Sue was a very special lady."

"So I've heard," I said, then regretted it.

"From whom?" he asked in a voice that tried to be casual.

"Everybody."

"Which everybody, specifically?"

"Her drama teacher, for one," I said.

"Gleeson," he snorted. "That faggot son of a bitch. He didn't know anything about Betty Sue, didn't care anything about her. He encouraged her acting so she would think he was a big man, that's all. She was good at it but she didn't even like it. She used to tell me, 'They just look at me, Albert, they don't see me.'"

"I thought Marilyn Monroe said that."

"Huh? Oh, perhaps she did," he said. "I'm sure it's a common psychological profile among actresses. Betty Sue was very sensitive about her looks. Sometimes when we would be having a . . . spat, she would cry and tell me, 'If I were ugly or crippled, you wouldn't love me.'"

"Was she right?" I asked without meaning to.

"Damn it, man," he answered sharply, "I haven't seen her in ten years and I'm . . . I'm still half in love with her."

"How does your wife feel about that?"

"We don't talk about it," he said with a sigh.

"Could Betty Sue have been serious enough about the acting to have run off to Hollywood or New York, something like that?"

"Do girls still do that?" he asked, glancing up at me.

"People still do everything they used to do," I said. "What about her?"

"Oh, I don't think so," he said, then asked if he could freshen my drink. When I shook my head, he got up and made himself a new one. "I don't think so at all," he said from the bar. "She enjoyed the work—rehearsals and all that—but for her, the play wasn't the thing." He sat back down. "She suffered from passing enthusiasms, you know," he said, as if it were a disease from which he had been spared. "One month it would be the theatre, the acting just a preparation for writing and directing, and the next month she would be planning to go to medical school and become a missionary doctor. Then she would want to be a painter or some sort of artist. And the worst part of it was that she could do damn near anything she set her mind to. For instance, I wasn't a great tennis player—though I nearly made the team at Cal—and when I could get her on the courts, she gave me a hell of a time, let me tell you." He paused to look at his drink, then decided to drink about half of it in a gulp. "And, you know, in spite of all the things she could do, she was the loneliest person I ever knew. That was the heartbreaking part of it, that loneliness. I couldn't help her at all. Sometimes it seemed my attempts just made it worse. I couldn't stop her from being lonely at all."

"Not even in bed?"

"You're a nosy bastard, aren't you?" he said quietly.

"Professional habit."

"Well, the truth is that I never laid a hand on her," he said with proper sadness. "Maybe if I had, I wouldn't still be carrying her around on my back."

"Did anybody else lay a hand on her?"

"I always suspected that she wasn't a virgin," he said with a slight smile. "But she wouldn't talk about it."

"Did you two fight about it?"

"I fought, but she wouldn't fight back," he said. "She'd just sit there, drawn into some sort of shell, and weep. Or else she'd make me take her home."

"Did you have a fight the day she walked away?"

"No," he murmured, shaking his head. "It was just a normal day. We drove over to San Francisco for dinner and a movie, and on the way she decided that she wanted to drive through the Haight to see the hippies. We got stuck in a line of traffic, and she just opened the car door, stepped out, and walked away. Without looking back. Without saying a word," he said slowly, as if he had repeated the lines to himself too many times.

"You didn't chase her?"

"How could I?" he cried. "I didn't know she was running away, and I couldn't just leave my car sitting in the street, man."

"I thought you had tickets for a play," I said.

"Hell, I don't know," he said. "It was ten years ago, ten goddamned years ago."

"Right."

"Need another drink," he either said or asked. When he stood up, I handed him my glass, but he paced around the office with it in his hand.

"Can you tell me anything else about her?" I asked.

He stopped and stared at me as if I were mad, then started pacing again, taking the controlled steps of a drunk man. But his hands and mouth moved with a will of their own; he waved his arms and nearly shouted, "Tell you about her? My god, man, I could tell you about her all day and you still wouldn't see her. Tell you what? That I had loved her since she was a child, that I couldn't just stop because she ran away? I tried to stop, believe me I tried to stop loving her." Then he paused. "It all sounds so silly now, doesn't it?"

"What?"

"That the disappearance of a damned high school chick that I'd never touched was the most traumatic experience of my life," he said. "And let me tell you, I know something about trauma, growing up with a drunken father. What do you want to know anyway?"

"Everything. Anything."

"That I married a safely dull woman and fathered two safely dull children that I can't bear to face and can't bear to leave and can't bear to love because they might all run away too," he said.

"Hey, man," I said, "take that crap upstairs to the shrinks. Don't tell me about it. I asked about her, not you." He stopped to stare at his feet. "You've already been upstairs, right?"

"I've been going for two years now," he said with that mixture of pride and shame people in analysis so often have. "And, in spite of the jokes, it's working. I meant to go to medical school, you know, but all those visits to the morgue, all those anonymous faces beneath the rubber sheets, were too much for me." He went to the bar to splash whiskey aimlessly into our glasses, then kept mine in his hand. "As you so aptly said, as a lawyer I'm not even a good joke. But I'm enrolled in next fall's medical school class out at Davis. Thanks to Betty Sue, it's taken me ten extra years to get started, but now I'm finally going to make it."

"Good luck," I said.

"Thank you," he muttered, not noticing my irony. "Anything else?"

"One more question," I said, "which I hate to ask, but I really would appreciate an answer."

"What's that?" he asked, then saw the two glasses in

his hands. He still didn't give me mine. "And why do you hate to ask it?"

"I heard a rumor that Betty Sue had made some fuck films in San Francisco."

"That's so absurd I won't even bother to answer," he said, and finally gave me my drink.

"You don't know anything about that, huh?" I asked as I stood up and put some ice in the warm whiskey.

"Don't be ridiculous," he said, facing me across an expanse of Persian carpet.

"Okay," I said. "Do you remember a girl named Peggy Bain?"

"Of course. She was Betty Sue's best friend. Only friend, I guess."

"You wouldn't know where she's living?"

"Actually, I might," he said. "I handled a divorce for her some years ago, and she sends me a Christmas card once in a while." He stepped over to the desk and thumbed through his Rolodex, then wrote an address and telephone number on a card with his little gold pen. The simple chore had restored some of his façade, but his knuckles were white around his glass when he picked it up. "Two years ago she was living at this address in Palo Alto. If you see her, please give her my regards."

"Thanks," I said, "I will."

"Say," he said too loudly, "let's sit down and have a drink. Pleasure instead of business."

"No thanks," I said, setting my unfinished Scotch on the coffee table. "I've got a date."

"Me too," he said sourly as he checked his watch. "With my wife." We shook hands as he led me toward the door, then he held my hand and asked, "Would you do me a favor?"

"What's that?"

"If you should, through some insane circumstance, find Betty Sue, would you let me know?"

"Not for love or money," I said, and took back my fingers.

"Why's that?" he asked, confused and nearly crying.

"Let me tell you a story," I said, which didn't help his confusion. "When I was twelve, my daddy was working on a ranch down in Wyoming, west of a hole in the road called Chugwater, and I spent the summer up there with him—my momma and daddy didn't live together, you see—and my daddy was crazy, had this notion, which he made up out of whole cloth, that he was part Indian. Hell, he took to wearing braids and living in a teepee and claiming he was a Kwahadi Comanche, and since I was his only son, I was too. And that summer I was twelve, he sent me on a vision quest. Three days and nights sitting under the empty sky, not moving, not eating or sleeping. And you know something? It worked."

"I'm not sure I understand what you're telling me," he said seriously.

"Well, it's like this," I said. "I had a vision. And I've been having them ever since."

"So?"

"You know, when you were telling me about those Jane Does and those rubber sheets, I had another one," I said.

"Of what?"

"I saw your face all scrunched up in disappointment every time you didn't find her under that rubber sheet," I said, and he understood immediately. After two years on the couch, he had begun to have visions of his own. "I know you're a nice person and all that and that you didn't mean to feel that way, but you did, and if I find her, you'll never hear about it from me."

"Why are you doing this to me?" he screamed, but I shut the door in his face. I didn't have a vision for that yet.

As I opened the outside door, I held it for a thin,

lovely woman with fragile features and a brittle smile. She thanked me with a voice so near to hysteria that I nearly ran to my El Camino. No visions, no poetry for her. Just a road beer for me. I sat for a bit, holding the beer from the small cooler sitting in the passenger seat like an alien pet, thinking about my mad daddy and those days and nights sitting cross-legged on a chalk bluff above Sybille Creek, sitting still like some dumb beast or a rock cairn marking a nameless grave. Of course I had visions. At first they were of starving to death, or being so bored I died for the simple variety of the act, then it was maybe freezing to death under the stars or finding myself permanently crippled, locked into my cross-legged stance like a freak on a creeper. Later, though, the visions came: a stone that flew, a star that spoke like an Oxford don, Virginia Mayo at my feet. I guess I wasn't a very good Comanche; I had seen too many movies, and besides, my crazy daddy had made the whole thing up. But, by god, I had visions. And none of the drugs, or combinations thereof, I had ingested as an adult had ever matched those first ones. But I had never gone back up Sybille Creek to that chalk bluff either. And never would.

6 ••••

As I DROVE BACK TO SONOMA, I WONDERED WHAT Gleeson and poor Albert had done to draw the meanness out of me. I had bullied Gleeson unmercifully and picked Albert open like a scabbed sore, left them both alone talking to empty drinks. Maybe I just had a natural-born mean streak. That's what the last woman I loved had told me when she refused to marry me. She said that she had two children to raise and that she didn't want them to learn about being mean from me. That, and other things. If it hadn't made me feel so mean, I would have tried to feel guilty about Gleeson and poor Albert. Maybe even the lady who wouldn't marry me. But I had washed her out of my system with the binge that had ended in Elko's ashtrays and toilets. Then I went home and cleaned up my act so well that I leaped at the chance to follow Trahearne on his reckless binge.

If not forgiveness, at least I had found work again. I had even found Trahearne, though I knew I didn't have a chance of finding Betty Sue Flowers. Not in a million years. So I drank my beer and pushed my El Camino down the road. That's my act. And has been for years.

Trahearne's act, however, was turning up like a bad penny or an insistent insurance salesman. When I walked into my motel room, his hulk was beached on the other double bed. A half-gallon of vodka, tonic, and ice sat on the nightstand between the beds, and a scrawled note sat on my pillow. *Stop me before I kill again.* In the corner of the room, a motley heap of unopened magazines and paperbacks sat in a silent pile.

I shook his shoulder and asked him what the hell he was doing in my room, but he just smiled like an obscene cherub between snores. I cleaned up, changed into my good Levis, and left him sleeping there without a comic note. My day hadn't lent itself to comic notes at all.

Bea had been raised in Sacramento, had never heard of Betty Sue Flowers, and didn't find out I was a fraud until much too late in the evening to make any difference. We did the town, such as it was, entertained the nightlife with laughter, lies, some of her home-grown grass, and some of my whiskey. Then we went stumbling back to the motel for the grandest lie of all. We also carried a stack of Trahearne's books up to the room, but the great man couldn't autograph them in his sleep.

"We could wait until tomorrow morning," I suggested, leaning toward my bed.

"Oh, I couldn't do that," Bea giggled. "I've got to drive to Sacramento before one tomorrow afternoon, and besides, I couldn't do it with him sleeping right in the next bed."

"Want me to wake him up?"

"No, silly," she said. "That's what I'm afraid of."

"Don't worry about that, love," I whispered into a suddenly accessible ear. "The old boy sleeps like a stone. And there's one other thing . . ."

"What?"

"Well, I don't know if I should tell you."

"Do."

"Well, the old man can't get it up anymore," I said seriously. "Whiskey and war wounds, you understand. But he really likes to sleep right next to it while it's happening."

"You're kidding."

"Not a bit," I said. "He claims that the force of the sexual emanations gives him absolutely wonderful dreams. He says that's just about the only pleasure left for him in life."

"No," she said, shaking her head but still leaning into me.

"Yes," I said into the soft little ear. "You never know, he might have a great dream tonight and write a poem about it tomorrow. I'll make him dedicate it to you." Then I had to fake a coughing fit to cover Trahearne's badly stifled giggles.

"You think he might do that?" she asked shyly.

"I think I can arrange it."

She stepped back and smiled. "Do you do this sort of chore for him very often?"

"Not nearly often enough."

"Okay," she murmured, then stepped into my arms again, "but you have to turn out the lights."

"I won't be able to see your freckles," I said.

"You can taste them, silly."

The next morning as the three of us breakfasted in our beds—hot-house strawberries and real cream, turkey crepes, and three bottles of California champagne—Trahearne sighed deeply and finished signing the last of Bea's books, then said to her, "My dear, I'm certain that my faithful Indian companion there was terribly indiscreet last night, that he spoke to you of matters most private, matters too private to discuss in the light of day, matters I would consider it a personal favor if you mentioned to no living soul. If word got around, it might be embarrassing, you understand."

"Oh I'd die before I'd say a word, Mr. Trahearne," Bea cooed, then popped a berry into her wonderful mouth.

"Please call me Abraham," Trahearne said formally. "I consider myself in your debt."

"Call me Isaac," I muttered around a mouthful of turkey.

"And what shall we call me?" Bea asked prettily.

"The Rose of Sharon, the lily of the valley, not black but nonetheless comely," Trahearne said gravely.

"How about the whore of Babylon?" I suggested.

"Don't be mean," Bea said sweetly, then set a sharp elbow loose against my ribs as she glanced at her watch. "Whoever I am," she said, "if I'm not at my mother's house in Sacramento by one o'clock, my name will be mud." Then, as if it were the most natural gesture in the world, she slipped from beneath the covers, buck-naked, gathered up her neatly folded clothes, and strolled slowly and unself-consciously into the bathroom, the morning sunlight glimmering off her untanned breasts as they bobbed, off her switching hips.

"Absolutely beautiful," Trahearne muttered as she closed the door. "And that routine of yours, Sughrue. I thought I'd heard them all—but sexual emanations and erotic dreams for the poor impotent old man! Where did you come up with that?"

"Drugs," I said. "You don't think she bought that crap, do you?"

"Women love that sort of lie," he said, "they love the role of helpmate. That's where they get their power over us, my boy, their victory in defeat, their ascendancy in submission."

"Should I write that down?"

"You never stop playing the jaded detective, do

you?" he said. "How do you like my sadly wise old man act?"

"If a pig's ass is pork, old man, how come they call it ham?"

"Envy, my young friend, is such a mean, small emotion," he said. "Did you hear me envy your lady friend's inspired thrashing last night?"

"I heard you breathing hard," I said, "Does that count?"

Trahearne laughed and I poured the champagne. When Bea stepped out of the bathroom, Trahearne said, "Let me thank you, my dear, for that beautiful display. It warmed, as they say, the cockles of my heart—"

"Is that anything like warming over your cliché?" I interrupted.

"—and restored my faith in human nature. You're simply too kind to an old, sick man."

"You're more than welcome, Mr. Trahearne," she answered, then leaned over to kiss his plump cheek. His great hand slipped up her thigh to fondly stroke her rump. "Also, you're a terrible old fraud," she added, and her firm nurse's hand shot under the covers and give his unit a ferocious honk. "Gotcha," she giggled. Trahearne actually blushed, then sputtered around trying to regain his dignity. She came over to my bed and presented me with a kiss that was supposed to make me long for home and hearth, to give up my wandering ways—for a few days at least—then she said, "And you, C.W., you're the most terrible liar in the whole world—sexual emanations, my ass—but you're sweet, too. Give me a call anytime." Then she swept out of the room, her books under her arm, scattering bright laughter like coins, leaving a faint trace of woman scent lush in the air.

"By god, that's an exceptional young lady," Trahearne harrumped.

"You old guys are too easily impressed."

"Ah ha! Do I hear the strains of true love hidden behind the bite of tired cynicism?"

"True love, my ass," I mocked. "It's the sexual revolution, the open marriage, the growing-together-apart relationship. She's meeting her boyfriend, the doctor, at her mother's house. He spent last night pranging his second ex-wife, her sister, her sister's boyfriend, and a bisexual Airedale."

"If that's true, that's sad."

"It's fairly accurate," I said.

"That's sad, then," he said. "I remember true love."

"You mean the old days when you had to get engaged before you could show your girl's ass to your buddies?"

"Cynicism doesn't become you," he said blithely.

"I'm sorry; it's the champagne, I guess."

"That's odd," he said. "It always fills me with romance."

"No shit."

"Where in the world did Catherine find you, boy?" he asked "Surely not in the Yellow Pages or something as mundane as that."

"I'm listed," I said, "but she found out about me in a bar."

"Of course," he said, raising an eyebrow built like a woolly worm. "Where?"

"The Sportsman in Cauldron Springs," I said. "The guy who owns it is an old Army buddy of mine."

"Bob Dawson?"

"Right. She went in to see if anybody had seen you, and he told her he had a friend who found lost things, like ex-husbands, and one thing led to another."

"I'll just bet it did." he said, oddly bitter, then I understood.

"She's your *ex*-wife, isn't she?" I said. "So what the hell do you care?"

"For myself, I don't," he said. "It's just that it embarrasses my mother."

"Your mother?"

"Catherine lives with my mother. In her house," he said, "and it upsets her when Catherine whores her way across the state."

"You live with your mother?"

"My house is within a stone's throw of hers."

"You don't sound very happy about it," I said.

"Sometimes I'm not."

"Move."

"It isn't that simple," he said. "She's an old woman now, crippled with arthritis, and I promised her I'd live on the ranch until she died. I certainly owe her that, you understand, at least that. And besides, every place is the same," he said.

"The people are different," I said, but he ignored me as he took a long drink from the champagne bottle, drank until he choked, then he smiled at me with wet eyes.

"If I had known how much fun we were going to have, Sughrue," he said, "I would have let you catch up with me sooner."

"Pretty expensive fun," I said.

"Worth every penny," he said as he tossed the empty bottle on the carpet. "I would have spent it all just to see that lady walk across the room." He eased himself upright, propped on his good buttock. "Wonderful naked ladies, by god, I love them," he said. "I've seen a horde of them in my time, boy, but I just can't get used to it." He shook his head and grinned. "Pop the cork on that other bottle," he said, "and let's drink to naked ladies."

When I did, the cork bounced off the ceiling and skittered across the carpet like a small rabid animal. Then I filled our glasses, and Trahearne held his up into a soft beam of sunlight that had filtered through the eucalyptus trees, watching the bubbles rise like floating jewels.

"That's funny," he said.

"What?"

Then he told me about naked women and sunlight. And that he was a bastard.

His mother had been an unmarried schoolteacher in Cauldron Springs when she was impregnated by a local rancher, who was married, and the school board had run her out of town. She had moved to Seattle to have the baby and stayed there after he was born, working at menial jobs to provide for them. By the time he started school, his mother had begun to publish stories in the Western pulps and free-lance articles in newspaper supplements and magazines, so they moved uptown into a tenement neighborhood on the edge of Capitol Hill. After school Trahearne walked home through the alleys to talk to the people his mother wrote about, the unemployed seamen and loggers, the old men who knew about violent times and romantic faraway places.

Sometimes, though, on these aimless walks, he saw a woman standing naked in front of her second-story back window. Only when it rained, though, as if the gray rain streaked on her dark window made her invisible. But the child could see her, dim but clearly visible beyond the reflections of the windows and stairways across the alley. In the rain, at the window, sometimes lightly touching her dark nipples, sometimes holding the full weight of her large, pale breasts in her white hands, always staring into the cold rain. Never in sunlight, always in rain. Sometimes she tilted her face slowly downward, then she smiled, her gray eyes locked on his through the pane, and hefted her breasts as if they were stones she meant to hurl at him. And sometimes she laughed, and he felt the rain like cold tears on his hot face. At nights he dreamed of sunlight

75

in the alley, and woke to the insistent quiet rush of the gentle rain.

Even after high school, through the first years of college at the University of Washington, when he still lived at home, he saw the woman. And even later, after he had moved closer to the campus, he came back to the neighborhood on rainy days to once again stride the bricks of that littered alley, red bricks glistening in the rain. Only when he graduated and could find no work in Seattle, after he moved to Idaho to work in the woods setting chokers, only then did he stop haunting the alley behind her house, watching, waiting.

There were girls, of course, during those days, but it was never the same in cheap tourist cabins or upon starlit blankets beneath the pines. There was one, almost, once. A plump Indian girl who went skinny-dipping with him at dawn in a lake, which had flooded an old marshy forest and filled with tiny dark particles of wood fiber held in pelucid suspension, the naked girl near but distant too, like a skater twirling in a paper-weight snowstorm. One, once, almost.

Then the war came. Trahearne enlisted in January of 1942, in the Marines, and after officer's training, his gold bars brightly gleaming, he took his leave in San Francisco instead of going back to Seattle to see his mother before he shipped out to the Pacific war. In the center of the Golden Gate Bridge, he met a young widow, still in her teens, whose husband had been an ensign on the *Arizona* at Pearl Harbor. At first, seeing her black dress and pale young face ruined with tears, he thought she might be preparing to jump, but when he spoke to her he found out she wasn't. She had only come there to throw her wedding ring into the bay. One thing, as he said ruefully, led to many others, and they fell in love, the young lieutenant anxious to be away to the war, to glory, the teenaged widow who had already lost one man to the war with a sudden violence that was as shocking as that first blot of blood that had marked the end of her girlhood only a few years before. Their love, he said, was sweet with the stink of death from the beginning, and each time they coupled, it was as if it were the last time for both of them.

On his final day of leave, they went back out on the bridge, and there on a blustery spring afternoon, the wind full of sunlight, booming through the girders like the echoes of distant artillery, cold off the green sea, fragrant as a jungle, there he told his new love about the naked woman and the rain. Before he could finish, though, she began to unbutton her blouse, and oblivious to the people around them, she bared her small breasts to the afternoon sunlight, then nestled his face between them, sending him off to die.

"Of course," he said to me, "it was the most exciting thing that had ever happened to me. And maybe still is. I don't know." Then he paused, and in his rumbling voice, added, "I'd never been so touched. Such a lovely gesture."

"What happened to her?"

"Always with the questions, huh," he said, and gave me a long, hard stare. "What happened to everybody then? The war happened, that's what. But I don't suppose you remember much about that."

"I remember my daddy went away, then he came back, and went away for good," I said.

"Killed?"

"No," I said. "After seeing North Africa, Italy, and Southern France, he said South Texas didn't look like much. He came out West, and my mother and I stayed home. She said the war just gave him an excuse to be as worthless and shiftless as he always wanted to be."

"Women are like that, boy," he philosophized.

"They don't understand moving on. Give them a warm cave and a steady supply of antelope tripe, and they're home for good."

"Maybe so, maybe not," I said. "But what happened to the woman?"

"What woman?" he asked, seeming confused and angry.

"The one with the tits."

"For a man with at least a touch of imagination, my young friend, you have a callous soul and a smart mouth."

"I told you I was a nosy son of a bitch."

"I'll buy that," he said. "What's the C.W. stand for?"

"Nothing," I lied. "What happened to the woman?"

"Hell, boy, I don't know," he grumbled. "She married a 4-F or a dollar-a-year man or another officer with a longer leave than mine. What difference does it make? It's the story that counts."

"Not until I know how it ends," I said.

"Stories are like snapshots, son, pictures snatched out of time," he said, "with clean, hard edges. But this was life, and life always begins and ends in a bloody muddle, womb to tomb, just one big mess, a can of worms left to rot in the sun."

"Right."

"And speaking of messes," he said, smiling, "what are you going to do now?"

"Take you home, I guess."

"What about Rosie's missing daughter?"

"It's a waste of time," I said. "If I had a year with nothing else to do, I might be able to find her, or find out what happened to her. But not in a couple of days. I'll just tell Rosie that you got out of the hospital sooner than I expected." But that wasn't what I wanted to say.

"Listen, boy, I don't have a damned thing to do at home," he said as I poured the last of the champagne into our glasses, "and I feel that I've earned a few days of entertainment—what the hell, I've been shot again and survived—so why don't you give it a couple more days."

"Well, sure, if you don't mind . . ."

"Mind, boy? Hell, I insist," he said grandly.

"Great."

"But I've got one little favor to ask," he said as he sat up gingerly on the side of the bed.

"What?"

"Take me along," he said shyly, mumbling and scuffing his feet on the carpet.

"What?"

"Let me go with you," he said. I laughed, and he jerked his head up. "I won't get in your way. I promise."

"Promise to stay relatively sober," I said, "and you're welcome to come along for the ride."

"How sober?"

"At least as sober as me."

"That's no problem," he crowed. "You sure you don't mind?"

"It's your ass, old man," I said.

"Please don't remind me," he muttered, grinning as he stood up stiffly. "It's a lovely day, boy. Let's stop by and pick up my barge, let the top down, and have some fresh air and sunshine, let the four winds blow the hospital stench and the, ah, ineffable odor of lust out of our noses. By god, I'll even buy the gas and the whiskey."

"What will I do for expenses?" I asked as he hobbled toward the bathroom, but he waved his hand at me as if to say *The devil take the expenses*.

While I replaced the rotor and moved our gear into his convertible, Trahearne tried to lure Fireball, dour with a hangover, out of the back seat, but the bulldog obviously intended to defend his position to the death. Or at least until Trahearne poured a cold beer into a rusty Hudson hubcap. Muzzle-deep in his morning beer, Fireball ignored us as we climbed in and lowered the top, but when we drove away, he glanced at the locked doors of Rosie's, then followed us down the road with a damned and determined trotting waddle, as if he knew we had the only cold Sunday-morning hangover beers in Northern California, as if he intended to fetch the Caddy by a rear tire and shake them loose. I slowed down to keep an eye on him.

"Dumb bastard's bound to quit," Trahearne said after we had driven nearly half a mile.

Maybe that's the definition of dumb bastards: they never quit. After another two hundred yards, I stopped the car to wait for the dog. He showed up petulant and thirsty. Trahearne opened his door, let him in, and gave him a beer. Fireball turned up his nose at it and scrambled into the back seat, where he sat with a great deal of dignity, waiting like a stuffy millionaire for the help to drive on. I did. His jowls quivered in the slipstream, and he seemed to enjoy the sunlight and the Sunday drive.

"All he needs is a cigar," Trahearne grumbled. I handed him the ones I had lifted from poor Albert, but he kept them for himself. "What a lark!" he shouted as he fired up a fog and settled back to enjoy the ride. "What a fucking lark!"

Outside of San Rafael, I had to brake hard to avoid a gaudy van as it cut across three lanes of traffic toward an exit. Trahearne flinched, then propped his haunch higher on the pillow we had stolen from the motel.

"By god," he said, "if I were a younger man—or hell if I were just whole—we'd run those punks down and see if they couldn't learn some manners."

"You sure this is what you want to do, old man?" I asked.

"Son, this is all I've ever wanted to do," he said, still grinning through his pain. "Hit the road, right? Move it on. And here I am wandering around America with an alcoholic bulldog, a seedy private dick, and a working quart of Wild Turkey." He reached into the glove box, took a nip, and passed the quart to me. "But don't call me *old man*. That's all I ask."

"Don't call me a seedy dick."

"It's too lovely a day to be crude," he said. "And if you'll pass the painkiller instead of holding it, I'll see about easing the pain." He hit the bottle hard when I handed it to him.

"No thanks," I said when he offered it to me again. "Do you mind if I ask you a personal question?"

"We're in this together, aren't we?"

"What were you doing on the road?" I asked. "Looking for your runaway wife?"

"She hadn't run away," he said. "Like most artists, Melinda needs a change of scene occasionally—fresh vistas and all that—a chance to be alone, to be anonymous, to see the world with an eye uncluttered by companionship. My god, I understand. If I can't understand that, who can? I need the same things myself. Luckily, in this marriage there's plenty of room for that sort of freedom, in this marriage, unlike my first, my wife and I aren't completely dependent upon each other." Then he paused. "Goddamned Catherine. I divorced her, but I can't seem to get her off my back. I think she had some insane idea that Melinda *had* run away, which I'm sure delighted her no end, and that I was searching for her with murder on my mind. Or something equally melodramatic. She thought she could save me by sending you to find me. Or something like that. I don't know. Damn it, I was married to the woman—saddled by the woman—for more than twenty years, and I still don't have any idea what goes on in her mind. I wouldn't be surprised to discover that she had hired you to have me shot in the ass."

"Pretty slick, the way I handled it, right?"

"Don't make jokes about Catherine," he said, grinning, "she's great at arranging things. She arranged my life for years." He was telling me something more than I had asked, but I had no idea what. "You're not married, are you?"

"Never have been."

"I thought not," he said. "You're not complex enough to survive it."

"That's what I always said."

After a long pause as he watched the frail monuments of apartment complexes soar past the moving freeway, he asked, "Do you mind if I ask you a question?"

"Nope."

"Where the hell are we going?" he asked, then laughed wildly.

When he stopped, I told him what I had found out about Betty Sue Flowers, what I planned to do, and where I meant to look, shouting above the road noise until we kicked off into the windy, blue space of the Golden Gate. As I talked, Trahearne drank, and as we crossed the bridge, he stopped listening, thinking, I suppose, of the young widow. He stared at the bottle, clutched in his hand like a grenade, then frowned, the feathers on his lark already saddly ruffled.

In the back seat, the bulldog hunkered like a heathen idol, some magical toad with a ruby as large as a clenched fist in his head, glowing through his stoic eyes, an inscrutable snicker mystic upon his face.

7 ●●●●

THEY SAY THE GODS WATCH OVER FOOLS AND DRUNKS— surely Trahearne and I qualified—and whoever *they* are, they're right too often for comfort.

Once we were downtown, we stopped at a quiet bar, and I called every dope dealer, police officer, and old girl friend I knew. They gave me some names and numbers, all of them absolutely useless. How was I supposed to know that every porno kingpin and czar in the city spent Sunday afternoons in religious retreats, consciousness-raising sessions, or *est* seminars? Out of boredom and hoping to stay sober, I hit the bars and theatres around Broadway and found a bored college student taking tickets. He knew a sociology professor who knew more about pornographic movies than either the Legion of Decency or the Mafia.

The professor was home on Sunday afternoon like any good citizen, watching an old silent porno flick about a young fellow who is fooled by two young girls at the beach into fucking a goat through a knothole in a fence. Several months later, the girls con him out of his walking-around money when one of them slips a pillow under her old-fashioned bathing suit and accuses him of having fathered it.

"I'll be damned," Trahearne whispered as he wriggled on the hard metal folding chair. "That's almost funny."

"Almost?" Professor Richter said, glancing down his sharp nose. "Almost?" he repeated with the proprietary air of someone who had written, directed, and starred in the movie. He did resemble the young protagonist. "It's hilarious!" he screeched. "And that is the major problem of modern pornography: it's too serious. With minor exceptions, of course. Usually, when it attempts humor the modern pornographic film tries for the lowest level, and when it succeeds, however slightly, as in the case of *Deep Throat*, they have a national hit on their hands," he said gravely. "It's the same in all the arts: as technology advances, humor declines. The limits and definitions of art disappear, then the art is forced to satirize itself too earnestly, and the visual arts become literary, and that, my friends, is the very first sign of cultural degeneracy." Then he slapped his slender, dusty hands together lightly, lifted the corners of his mouth, and added, "Don't you agree?"

He had the glittering eyes and pained smile of a fanatic, the long face unmarked by emotion, so Trahearne and I nodded quickly. His face wasn't unpleasant, just blandly, hysterically objective. Maybe a steady diet of porno flicks had softened his features, but I couldn't begin to guess what had happened to his clothes. Perhaps he had slept in his shiny black suit. Several times. Badly. Certainly he had dined in it. Or off it. A blossom of tomato sauce with a dried mushroom bud served as a boutonniere, and his thin black tie, tugged into a knot the size of an English pea, as a napkin.

"What can I do for you gentlemen?" he asked as it became apparent that we hadn't come to discuss the state of the art.

I showed him my license and explained my business.

Before I could finish, he scampered to a 5×8 file, rifled it, and came up with both hands full of cards, waving them at the walls of his small apartment, which were banked with file cabinets and shelves and stacks of film cans.

"*Animal Passion*," he said, holding out his right hand. "*Animal Lust*," he added with his left. "Take your choice, gentlemen. Not a particularly imaginative title, either of them, but damned popular." He simpered at his own joke.

"Low, low budget," I said, "with a group grope for a finale."

"Aren't they all," he said with his frail laugh. "Could you give me an approximate date?"

"Late sixties maybe."

"Major actress blonde or brunette?"

"Blonde."

"Right," he said, then replaced the cards into their file, shuffled them again. "Perhaps this is it," he said as he read a card, his narrow bloodless lips mouthing a long number. He dashed over to a stack of film cans and jerked one out of the middle so quickly that the ones above it fell down with a neat solid thunk. "If I remember this one correctly, it's simply trash," he said, "without a single redeeming feature. Would you like to see it?"

"You mind?" I asked Trahearne.

"Why should I mind?" he said, looking very confused.

"Your romantic illusions," I said, then laughed.

"Oh," he said, "oh yeah. Those." His confusion seemed to clear itself up. For him, though, not for me. "Roll it," he said crisply, and Richter threaded the film.

It was basic, all right, perhaps even pitiful. It was Betty Sue Flowers, too. No matter how often I looked away, when I looked back she was there. She had gained enough weight to make her figure more than Reubenesque, and if she hadn't been able to move it with some grace, she would have seemed grotesque and comic as a chubby young housewife clad only in a frilly apron, her thick blond hair gathered into two unbraided pigtails that framed her fat face.

At least the plot was thin. First, a little minor-league action with a pair of bewildered toy poodles, then some major-league work with the neighborhood help: a postman, a milkman, two meter readers, and a grocery boy with pancake over his wrinkles. Among the five men, they had enough beer guts, knobby knees, blurred tattoos, dirty feet, and crooked dicks to outfit a freak show. In the finale, as they gathered in a carefully arranged pile about the kitchen table, they looked even more distraught than the poodles had, and their faces contorted with pain as they all tried to come at once as Betty Sue worked at all of them together. Everybody was stoned blind, and the crew kept stumbling on camera or into the lights or jerking the camera in and out of focus. You could almost hear the sigh of relief when they ran out of film. The whole thing seemed about as exciting as jerking off into an old dirty sock.

But Betty Sue, in spite of the fat and her eyes, which were as blank as two wet stones, had something that had nothing to do with the way she looked. She seemed to step into the degradation freely, without joy but with a stolid determination to do a good job. In spite of myself, I was excited by her, which made the whiskey curdle in my stomach. I worked on righteous anger but only came up with quiet sadness and a sick sexual excitement. I saw why Gleeson hadn't wanted to talk about the film; I didn't either. No more than I wanted to look at a large, ugly scar that split the center of her pudgy abdomen.

"That wasn't funny at all," Trahearne growled as the film unthreaded itself and flapped like a broken shade.

"Don't blame me," Richter said as he began to rewind it.

"Think I'll hobble outside for a breath of fresh air and about a gallon of whiskey." Trahearne said as he heaved his bulk out of the chair.

After he left, I asked Richter if he knew any of the actors' names.

"Surely you jest," he said. "In this business, only the *crème de la crème* have names, and usually they are assumed. However, I did recognize the chap who played the milkman—in another context, of course."

"What context?"

"He once ran a pornographic bookstore downtown," he said, "and I think his name was Randall something . . . Randall Jackson."

"Is he still in town?"

"No, he left after this film," he said, "which was his single effort. I seem to remember someone telling me that he was some sort of paperback distribution agent. In Denver, I think."

I asked if he knew anybody else or anything else about the film, but he had never seen the girl again, which meant that she had dropped out of the business. I thanked him, then stood up to leave.

"Do you mind if I ask you a question?" I said.

"Of course not," he answered pleasantly.

"What are you doing with all these films?"

"Catalogue, classification, and cross-indexing. Preparing for a scholarly study of the decline of American pornographic film."

"Isn't all this expensive?"

"I have a grant," Richter said blithely. I didn't ask from whom. I didn't want to know. As I left, he was humming as he reloaded his projector.

Outside, Trahearne and Fireball were sitting back, drinking and watching the Sunday traffic on Folsom

Street—two cabs, a babbling speed freak, and an Oriental wino. I climbed into the car, wishing I had a greater variety of drugs with me. Or less blind luck.

"Was that the girl you were looking for?" Trahearne asked.

"No," I lied. "It looked something like her but it's some chick named Wilhelmina Fairchild."

"Could be a stage name," Trahearne suggested.

"No," I said. "Richter knows the lady personally. She's working in a massage parlor over in Richmond. So unless she's developed a German accent since she left home, it wasn't Rosie's daughter." I wasn't sure why I lied to Trahearne. Maybe because I was embarrassed for Rosie. Or for myself. Whatever, I didn't want him to know that it had been Betty Sue on the screen, flickering among so many hands.

"For Rosie's sake, I'm glad," Trahearne said. "I stopped in her place by accident and drank there a couple of days because I liked the place and her bulldog. I didn't talk to her much, but I liked the way she poured the beer and handled the bar, so I'm glad her daughter didn't end up like that. Or worse."

"Me too," I said.

"What now?"

"Palo Alto."

"Why?"

"To talk to Betty Sue's best girl friend from high school," I said.

"Maybe she's out," he said. "Maybe you should call first. Maybe we should hang around the city tonight. Have a few drinks, you know, relax and rest a bit."

"No rest for the wicked," I said, then tucked the Caddy between a taxi cab and a semi-truck, ripping off two dollars' worth of Trahearne's tires. "It's a nice day and a pretty drive," I added as soon as the truck driver stopped blowing his horn.

"If we survive it," he said.

"You want to drive this fucking barge?" I asked angrily, mad about my lie and the movie.

"You just drive it however you want to, son," Trahearne said, holding up his hands. "But don't get mad at me. I'm not in charge of the world."

"Sometimes I can't tell if I'm crazy or the world's a cesspool," I said.

"Both things are true," he said, "but your major problem is that you're a moralist. Don't worry, though."

"Why?"

"It'll pass with age," he said. "But talking about crazy—what was that fellow doing with all those films?"

"You wouldn't believe me if I told you."

I was partially right. It was a nice drive. Except for a scuffle Fireball had with a large gray poodle who wanted to sniff his ass at a rest area, and except for the rich lady in the Mercedes who belonged to the poodle and who slapped Trahearne when he suggested she do something impossible and obscene with her lousy damned play-pretty mutt, it was a lovely drive. But Trahearne was right about calling Peggy Bain first.

The girl who lived in the apartment address Albert had given me didn't know where Peggy Bain lived, but she did know somebody who might. We spent the afternoon kicking around from apartments to bars and back again, talking to a long series of people who knew where she might be. Finally, as we tried the last possible place, a backyard barbeque all the way up in La Honda, the sun headed behind the coastal hills and Trahearne began to whine like a drunken child. He had forgotten his promise to stay at least as sober as me. Trahearne and Fireball were as drunk as dancing pigs.

At least the bulldog had the decency to pass out in the back seat. As we parked in the string of cars beside Skyline Drive, Trahearne sniffed the air, muttered *party*, and stopped whining.

"Maybe you should stay in the car," I suggested.

"Nonsense," he said as he tugged a fresh quart of Turkey from under his seat. "If my famous writer act doesn't work, lad, I'll show them my invitation," he added, waving the whiskey. "I'm always welcome at parties," he said as he lurched out of the car.

Of course the old bastard was right. The bearded young man who answered the doorbell had met Trahearne some years before at a poetry reading in Seattle, though Trahearne didn't remember him, and he welcomed us into his house, introducing Trahearne to his guests as if he had been the guest of honor all along. Within minutes, he had arranged glasses and ice and Peggy Bain sitting across a picnic table. Trahearne shooed the host and his fans away, sat down beside Peggy Bain, and flopped a heavy arm over her shoulder as he called her *honey*. She was a genial lady with a face as round as a full moon looming above her thick wool poncho. When Trahearne explained what we wanted, she glanced at him, then me, then broke out in a fit of stoned laughter so fierce that she had to remove her rimless glasses and set them among the dirty plates on the table.

"You've got to be kidding," she said over and over again, only stopping to giggle. Then she lowered the pitch of her glee, rubbed the tears out of her eyes, and said, "Man, I haven't seen her since high school." She paused long enough to shake a hash pipe out of her sleeve and light it, then offered it to Trahearne. He took a greedy hit, then held his breath and muttered *dynamite dope!* like some kid. When she offered it to me, I shook my head, trying to stay straight for a few minutes longer. "I ran into her father down in Bakersfield a few years ago, and he said Betty Sue had been living in a commune up in Oregon, but she had left."

"Remember the name of it?" I said.

"Man, who can remember those names," she said. "Sunflower or Sunshine Starbright Dreaming or Sunfun or Sun-kinda-pretentious-hippie-shit." After she stopped chuckling at her own joke, she added. "Whatever its name was, it was somewhere outside of Grants Pass, I think."

"When did you talk to her father?" I asked, and Trahearne muttered *yeah* as he fondled her square shoulder through the rough wool.

Peggy's face stiffened and she slipped her glasses back on, sighed and lifted her hands. I thought I was about to get a long question about who the hell I was to ask about Betty Sue, but she turned to Trahearne, saying, "Hey, man, I ain't into starfucking, okay? See that lady over by the back door? The one with the scarf around her head and all that heavy metal hanging off her neck? That's where your action is, man, okay?" Then she lifted his large hand off her shoulder by the fingers, dangling it as if it were a dead crab, and dropped it in his lap.

"Excuse me," he muttered without a trace of sincerity, looking at his lap and peeking toward the back door at the same time.

"Don't be bummed out, man," Peggy said.

"No sweat," he said, then slid off the bench and limped toward the house.

"What's wrong with him?" she asked.

"Artistic temperament," I said. "He thinks famous writers are supposed to get fucked a lot."

"Not that, dummy," she said. "What's wrong with his leg?"

"Old war wound," I said.

"Which one?"

"Pick one," I said, "they're all the same." I had been

trained in the right radical responses by a crew-cut first lieutenant with a text on radical responses.

"Right on, man," she answered on cue.

"But back to Betty Sue," I said. "How long ago did you talk to her father?"

"At least six years ago," she said. "I know because I was still married to that redneck asshole from Santa Rosa. We were down in Bakersfield on some kind of United Farmworkers blast, and I saw Betty Sue's daddy's name in the paper. He was playing at a place called the Kicker, which I assumed was short for Shitkicker, so a bunch of us got high and went out to test the rednecks. Of course, we took two of the biggest hippies in the world, two logger kids from up around Weed. We wanted to look back to see how the other half lives."

"How were they doing?"

"Just like you'd expect, man, living high, wide, and handsome in Bakersfield," she answered, grinning. "But old man Flowers, he was one cool dude."

"How's that?"

"Singing in the band, running the bar, and dealing nose candy like a bandit," she said.

"Cocaine?"

"Nothing else makes you feel so good," she said. "At first we thought he was bragging to impress the hippies—you know how straight people do—talking about selling coke to all the big names playing around Bakersfield, but after the second set, he took us back to his office, and we did a ton and bought five grams. Good stuff and fairly cheap."

"And you talked about Betty Sue," I said, trying to bring her back from her cocaine memories. And mine too.

"Right. I asked if he'd heard from her, and he said she'd called once, a year, maybe two years before, asking for money to split from the commune scene.

Probably one of your typical fascist hippie scenes, you know, man."

"But you don't remember the name?"

"Like I said, man, Sun-something," she said, then paused to glance up at me. "You looking for her because she's in trouble?"

"No, not that," I said, then realized that after the film I didn't know why I was looking for Betty Sue anymore. "I stumbled into her mother, and she hired me to look around for a few days," I said.

"Sorry, but I can't help."

"That's okay," I said, "she's been gone too long anyway."

"Just barely long enough," Peggy whispered, looking down, all the stoned laughter gone now.

Behind her, the clouds surrendered their last crimson streaks to a soft, foggy gray. A single tall evergreen tilted against the falling sky. Behind me, the party began to rumble like thunder. Peggy relit the hash pipe, and this time I accepted it from her. We shared the smoke as the evening winds rose off the cold sea, rose up the wooded ridges, and herded the party inside, people muttering thin complaints like little children called from play to the fuzzy dreams of their early beds. The plate-glass windows along the back of the house reflected the last vestiges of the sunset, and beyond, like a double exposure, the party trundled silently onward, mouths opening, wounds without sound, gestures without meaning. Beside a doorway against the opposite wall, Trahearne stared sadly at the sunset.

"What else can I tell you, man?" Peggy asked when the pipe had gone out.

"I don't know," I said, then moved around the table to sit beside her, close but not too close, my fingers locked behind my head as I leaned against the littered table. "I just don't know," I said as I tried to see the ocean swells and the evening fog below the wide and empty sky being overcome by a nascent darkness. "Maybe you could just tell me about her," I said. "All about her."

"That's too much," she said.

"Just barely enough."

"Like what?"

"Oh, I don't know," I said. "Tell me what she looked like in the sixth grade with pigtails and elbows and knees, or tell me—"

"I'll be damned," she interrupted. "I'll just be damned."

"Why?"

"You've never met her, right?"

"Right. Why?"

"I can tell by the way you're talking," she said, "that you're stuck on her."

"It's a professional hazard," I said, trying to wriggle out of it. "I get stuck on everybody I hunt for. They stop being pictures and words and become people, that's all." I nipped at my drink to ease the dry bite of the hashish. "Sometimes the people I think I'm hunting for don't turn out to be the people I find," I babbled. "Or something like that."

"Cut the bullshit, man," she said. "You're stuck on her. I never met a man who wasn't. Goddammit, she could do a lot of things well, but nothing better than that."

"What?"

"Getting men stuck on her—she did that best of all. They used to come for miles around just to sit at the queen's feet, just to touch her hem—oh, hell, that's not fair."

"What?"

"She just never found anybody as good as she was," Peggy said, then picked up a wine glass in her stubby fingers. "She was the most beautiful woman in the world and she was only a girl—just like me, man, just a little high school kid from Sonoma, but she was so beautiful, a beautiful, lonely lady, lonely because nobody was good enough for her."

"Stuck up?"

"Not a bit of it, man," she said, "or why would she like me? Listen, man, I spent my school years watching pretty girls try to be my friends so they'd look good standing next to me, but Betty Sue, she didn't care about that, she was my friend, and better-looking than the whole bunch of them, and smarter and nicer—the whole bit."

"You've thought about her some?"

"Not a day goes by, man, that I don't."

"I see."

"You don't see shit, man," she said quietly. "I loved her, you see, loved her. I didn't know what it was all about until I had survived two nightmare marriages, but since then I've found out, and I loved her. When she ran away, I cried my eyes out, man, cried myself blind. Before that, I thought that was a cliché, but when she left, I wept until I couldn't see."

"I'm sorry," I said.

"I hated her too," she confessed, "but that was my fault. I lined up with the smitten swains but didn't know what I was doing for years. And hell, if she was here tonight, you and I could stand around with our tongues out." Then she tried to laugh as she socked me on the arm. "Lined up to meet the lady."

"I never stand in line for anything," I said lightly.

"This is a lady you'd kill for a chance just to stand in line," she said with a sad smile. "Or something like that. That didn't make sense, did it?"

"I know what you meant," I said. "Thanks for your trouble."

"No trouble, man," she said. "I'm like this all the time now. And when I finish law school, I'm gonna make the world pay for it."

Since it was the first happy thing I had heard her say, I wished her well and thanked her again. Then I wandered toward the far side of the yard to find a bush to water.

Betty Sue Flowers. I had talked to three people but hadn't found out anything worth knowing, except that everybody who knew her was stuck on her still. Maybe I was too. Maybe I didn't have any choice in the matter any more. But I had to make up my mind. Her daddy lived down in Bakersfield, Randall Jackson might still be in Denver, and the remains of the commune were in southern Oregon—long trips in three different directions, and none of them on the way to Montana. Rosie's eighty-seven dollars was getting a workout, and I was getting nowhere, but that's always where I knew this one was heading anyway. So I shook it off and headed back to the party.

When I walked through the kitchen, Trahearne was leaning against the wall beside the lady with the chains, offering her the slug they had removed from his hip, saying, "You charming little devil, you, I'd like you to have this as a good-luck piece." He tickled her under the chin.

"Why don't you lick her on the arm," I said, but they both ignored me. She giggled and accepted the good-luck gift, and Trahearne lifted her hand to his lips. As I tried to walk past, he grabbed my neck with a meaty hand and hugged me toward him, his huge face rubbery and flushed with the whiskey, hanging over mine like something butchered in a nightmare.

"And what did the little dyke have to say?" he asked.

"Nothing I didn't already know," I said. "Let's get the hell out of here."

"The party's just getting interesting." He leered at the chained lady, sloshed whiskey into my glass, and patted my shoulder. "Hang around," he said, gathering the lady with silken clinks beneath his arm and leading her into the twinkling night.

"Have a good time," I said. "Have a hell of a good time."

"You've got to learn to relax," he advised over his shoulder, "learn to have a good time."

Ah, yes, the good times. The parties that last forever, the whiskey bottle that never runs dry, the recreational drugs. Strange ladies draped in denim and satin, in silver and hammered gold. Ah, yes, the easy life, unencumbered by families or steady jobs or the knave responsibility. Freedom's just another word for nothin' else to lose, right, and the nightlife is the right life for me, just keep on keepin' on. Having fun is the fifth drink in a new town or washing away a hangover with a hot shower and a cold, cold beer in a motel room or the salty road-tired taste of a hitch-hiking hippie-chick's breast in the downy funk of her sleeping bag. Right on. The good times are hard times but they're the only times I know.

The next morning, I woke up with a faceful of sunshine in the back seat of Trahearne's convertible, sodden with dew, dogspit, and recriminations of high degree. When I sat up to look around, it looked like California, then a passing paperboy told me it was Cupertino, but that didn't tell me anything at all. Two houses up the street, a curly-headed guy was standing in his driveway, sucking on the remains of a half-pint as he tried to dodge a barrage of kitchen utensils that flew from an unseen hand inside the house and glittering out into the morning light. He ducked a large spoon and a heavy ladle, chortled and dancing, but a potato masher caught him on the lower lip with a sudden burst of bright blood. As he started weeping, a blond woman in a housecoat rushed outside and led him back inside.

I shook my head, shared the last cold beer with Fireball, then let him out to water somebody's lawn. As soon as he was finished, I leaned on Trahearne's horn until he stumbled out of the house across the street, his shirt in one hand, his shoes in the other, his tail tucked between his legs.

"Damned crazy woman," he complained as I drove away. "How was I supposed to know she wanted to wear all that goddamned junk jewelry to bed. Jesus Christ, it was like fucking in a car wreck."

"Beats sleeping in the car," I muttered.

"Wasn't my fault," he grunted as he tied his shoe. "You refused to come in the house."

"At least you could have put the top up."

"I did," he said. "Twice. But you insisted on having it down, and you gave the world a forty-minute speech about sleeping under the stars to clean out your system, so I left you alone."

"Good idea," I said.

"You're a surly drunk, Sughrue."

"Surly sober, too."

"What happened to the woman?" he asked.

"What woman?"

"The one with you."

"Whatever happened," I said, "I'm sure I enjoyed it. What did she look like?"

"Soft and furry," he said. "She's not dead in the trunk or something awful, is she?"

"I don't have any idea," I said, "and I'm not about to look before I have a drink."

"Let's not even act like we're going to have breakfast," he said, grinning. "Let's just find the nearest bar."

"Then it's off to Bakersfield," I said.

"Oh my god," Trahearne groaned.

8 ••••

BETWEEN DRUNKS AND HANGOVERS, IT TOOK TRAHEARNE and me two days to drive to Bakersfield, but as we drove from the motel to Betty Sue's father's place, we were both sober and not in any great pain, which was good because his place looked like the sort of dance hall and bar where a man wanted his wits about him when he went inside. The marquee promised dancing nightly to the strains of Jimmy Joe Flowers and the Pickers, and the bar, a cinder-block square building in the middle of a parking lot, promised all the trouble you could handle. Since it was early, though, we went inside with the lunch rush—two welders and a traveling salesman who wanted beers and Slim Jims. The day-time bartender told me that Mr. Flowers usually came in about one-thirty, and sure enough at two o'clock sharp, his ostrich-skin boots thumped through the doorway. Ostrich skin makes a lovely boot leather—if you like leather that looks as if the animal had died of terminal acne—and it went well with Flowers' wine Western-cut double-knit leisure suit, just as his suit matched the woman who followed him.

Flowers was all happy handshakes and smiles until I showed him my license and told him what I wanted. Then he frowned and led his secretary into the closet he called his office. When I didn't follow on his heels, he stepped back out and waved me hastily inside. He said he had something he wanted to say to me. At some length.

"Ungrateful little bitch," he said, then slapped his flimsy desk. "I never thought a child of mine would turn out to be a hippie, you know, never thought it for a minute. I mean, what the hell, I like to see kids have a good time, but they got to work for it, and you know, I lost a boy over there in Vietnam, and might have lost the other one, but he had a bum knee, and here I turn around and find this damned hippie for a daughter. I mean, you know, first I hear she's run off without finishing school—and you know how important an education is nowadays—and here I am her own loving father, you know, and I don't hear a single solitary word from her for four, maybe five years, then one night she calls, collect, mind you, and wakes me out of a dead sleep." He paused to look up at his secretary. "You remember that, don't you, honey?" he said to her, and she reached down to pat his freshly shaven and powdered cheek as if the effort of waking up had been just more than he could bear.

"And you know what she wants?" he asked me suddenly. He didn't give me time to answer. "Money, by god, she wants money so she can leave that damned dirty commune where's she been shacked up like some animal." He paused to shake his head. "And you know what I told her?" I didn't make a move. "I told her that I hadn't sent her a single thin dime to get herself into trouble, and I wasn't going to send a damned cent to get her out. Not by a damned sight I wasn't, you know what I mean."

Even if he knew anything else, Betty Sue's father wasn't going to tell me, so I didn't have to be nice for effect. "You mean those dirty hippies were probably stuffing drugs up their noses, too," I said.

"You got a smart mouth, fella," he said, his eyes as

flat as yesterday's beer. Then he smiled with just his mouth. "But that's okay, because you must have a smart head on your shoulders to come into town and tell me that."

"Peggy Bain told me," I said, not wanting him to think I was too smart.

Flowers sighed heavily, as if the conversation had been the hardest work he had done in years. His secretary patted his shoulder again. "Remember your heart, honey," she murmured. She had dressed for the occasion too, but her idea of a sex kitten looked like something the cat had dragged in.

"Most drugs make you stupid," he lectured me, "but cocaine is a smart man's high. You have to be smart to enjoy it and rich to afford it."

"A man in my business needs his wits," I said, "so I don't know anything about drugs."

"I can see that," he said scornfully. "How much is Rosie paying you for this wild goose chase?"

"Not nearly enough," I said, meaning to insult him.

"She was always tight with a dollar bill," he said ignoring my tone. "Goddamned old woman."

"Well, her place isn't doing as well as yours," I said. "You must have done well in the aluminum cookware business."

"How would you like that smart mouth on the other side of your head, fella?" he said quietly. "Or maybe one of your legs busted at the kneecap."

"You'd need help," I said stupidly.

"All I have to do is snap my fingers," he said as he held up his hand. "You know what I mean?"

"You have the right connections, right?"

"You could say that."

"What's a good ol' boy like you doing with connections like that?" I asked pleasantly.

"Making a living," he said.

"Okay," I said, "I'm sorry."

101

"Don't let the door hit you in the butt on the way out," he said.

"Give my best to the family," I said, then left. He could have been bluffing, but I didn't want to find out. I made a quick exit, which made Trahearne happy.

"This place gives me the creeps," he said as we left.

"Me too," I said, and on the way to the car I told him why.

Since I needed some time to think about Betty Sue Flowers, and since Trahearne demanded a few days of luxurious recuperation, we drove straight through to San Francisco, and he checked us into a suite at the St. Francis.

Some time for reflection and recuperation. Cigarettes and whiskey and wild, wild women. One commercial type spent the whole time babbling in my ear about her shrink, so I faked an orgasm for her and hid in the shower until she went about her business. Then there was a lady poet, an old friend of Trahearne's, who was so mean that she scared me into hurrying. Hiding in the shower didn't help a bit. She came in and gave me an endless lecture on my responsibility to women in general and herself in particular. Somewhere in the drunken blur, Trahearne walked off the balcony bar in the lobby and fell headfirst into a rubber tree, much to the consternation of the management. Somehow, I drove his convertible into the rear of a cable car. Nobody was hurt, but I had to endure a monsoon of abuse about trying to destroy a national monument. The conductor and his passengers acted as if I had run over a nun. The worst thing that happened, though, was that Fireball took to wearing a rhinestone collar and drinking Japanese beer.

One afternoon, it finally came to an end. Fireball was drinking water out of the toilet bowl, a naked blond woman wearing red boots slept on the couch in an extremely revealing position, and the suite smelled like a Tenderloin flophouse.

"This is no way for a grown man to live," Trahearne announced as he woke me up. "Let's go home," he said.

"Home's where you hang your hangover," I said.

"Let's have more movement, jack, and less piss-ant redneck homilies," he grumbled, holding his head very carefully.

When he decided he wanted to go home, Trahearne wasn't about to wait for anything. Not even to wake up the blond lady. He griped about the length of time it took me to pack, then he whined all the way to Sonoma as I detoured by Rosie's to drop off her dog and pick up a tow bar and my El Camino. But there was a strange woman behind the bar. She told me Rosie was asleep in her trailer house, and not to bother her, but I had to.

Rosie came to the door after Fireball and I had spent several minutes standing on the steps. She was hastily wrapped in a faded purple chenille bathrobe, her hair tangled with sleep and sweat. Fireball elbowed past me and trotted toward the rear of the trailer, where the sounds of masculine snoring rumbled.

"What the hell's that thing around his neck?" she asked, not sounding all that happy to see me. "You shoulda called, gimme a chance to clean up," she added.

"Sorry," I said, "but I didn't know we were coming until a few minutes ago."

"Been on a toot, huh?"

"Had about as much fun as a man can stand," I said.

"You find my baby girl?" she asked.

I shook my head and looked down. Rosie tried to hide her long, crooked yellow toenails, first with one foot, then the other. I looked back up.

"You come up with any leads?" she asked.

"One rumor," I said, "that she was living up in Oregon six or seven years ago."

"Where'd you hear that?" Rosie looked puzzled.

"From her daddy."

"You talk to that worthless bastard?" she asked.

"Just about as long as I could," I said.

"How's he doing?"

"Got his own band," I said, "and a place to play it in."

"Somebody must be running it for him," she said.

"He's got himself a secretary," I said.

"Naw, it wouldn't be that," Rosie said. "Jimmy Joe's scared sideways by a smart woman. He might've loved Betty Sue if she hadn't been so smart."

"Maybe so," I said. "Listen, since I didn't come up with anything definite, why don't you take your money back?" I tried to hand her a sheaf of folded bills.

"Get away with that," she said.

"Take it."

"You earned it."

"Okay," I said, "I'll stop in Oregon on the way through and ask around some more." Which was exactly what I didn't want to do. I didn't want to look anymore, didn't want to find any more scraps of Betty Sue Flowers. "If I find anything, I'll give you a call."

"I'd appreciate that," she said, "but you've already done more work than I paid for." Down the hallway behind the living room, the squeak of springs and a series of muffled curses filled the close air. Fireball had joined the gentleman in bed, and the gentleman hadn't enjoyed it. Rosie looked embarrassed and turned to quiet the man. When she did, she exposed a life-sized poster of Johnny Cash on the wall behind her. Then she glanced back at me. "You did more work than I paid for, didn't you?"

"I told you it was wasted money," I said.

"It's mine to waste," she said, "and I thank you for

trying. Give me a call, collect, you hear, whatever you find in Oregon, and if you're ever down this way, you got a place to drink where your money's no good."

"Sounds like heaven," I said, and Rosie smiled.

"You taking the big fella's car home?" She nodded over my shoulder. I had already hooked Trahearne's Caddy to the tow bar and my El Camino.

"The big fella too," I said.

"What's the matter? Can't he drive?"

"He can't even walk yet," I said.

"Must be nice," Rosie murmured.

"What's that?"

"To have enough money to hire somebody to tow you around," she said.

"I don't know," I admitted, then as Rosie and I exchanged goodbyes, a bald, hairy man, his beer belly drooping over his sagging boxer shorts, wandered into the picture, demanding cold beer, scrambled eggs, and true love. Rosie asked me in for lunch, her eyes pleading for me to leave, so I did. I had to drive Trahearne home anyway.

Trahearne had made his literary reputation with six highly praised volumes of poetry, two of which had been nominated for national prizes, but he had made his fortune with three novels, the first published in 1950, the second in 1959, and the third in 1971. I had read all three, and although they were set in different places with different characters, I couldn't keep them separate in my mind. The first one, *The Last Patrol*, had been set on a nameless island in the Pacific during the final week of World War II. A Marine squad had been sent on a mission behind Japanese lines to blow up a crucial bridge. Before they can make the march, though, they receive a radio signal telling them that the war is over, but the young lieutenant who is leading the patrol keeps the information to himself. At the bridge, the Japanese soldiers, sick and hungry, rush out to surrender, and the Marines slaughter them. During the one-sided fire-fight, the young lieutenant takes a round through the chest, and as he is dying, he tells his men the truth, and he laughs, happy that he is dying before the fighting ends. The war is over, he says, and the peace is going to be hell.

In the second novel, *Seadrift*, the survivors of a yachting accident, cast adrift on a small raft, work hard to elude their rescuers. One of the survivors, a Hollywood screenwriter, convinces the others that surviving on their own in more important than living. By the end of the novel, I expected them to be eaten by a whale, but only the screenwriter dies, leaping into the jaws of a shark, his sole regret that he doesn't have time for a dying speech.

In the third one, *Up the River,* an alcoholic playwright and his pacifist son team up to wreak a terrible vengeance on a party of elk hunters who have accidentally killed the wife and mother. Even as the last of the hunters dies in a bear trap, the father and son still don't know which hunter actually did the shooting, and they don't even care, trapped as they are by their love of this wild justice. The son joins the Army to go to Vietnam and the father sobers up to write a great play about love.

All three novels were best sellers, all made into successful movies, and perhaps because of his reputation as a poet, well reviewed. But as far as I could tell, the books were fair hack work cluttered with literary allusions and symbols. Fancy dreck, one unimpressed reviewer called them. The male characters, even the villians and cowards, cling to a macho code so blatant that even an illiterate punk in an east L.A. *pachuco* gang could understand it immediately. The female characters serve as stage props, scenery, and victims. And the stories were always incredible. But Trahearne had found his niche and mined it as if it were the mother lode instead of a side vein, and he made a great deal of money, back in the days when money was still real.

But maybe that was the only choice he had. When he came back from the war, he found that his mother had become a rich and successful writer with two novels about the tender, touching, and comic adventures of a young widow with an infant son as she makes her way in the world as a teacher in a one-room schoolhouse in western Montana. As Trahearne said, she made a million dollars, then never wrote another word, and she made it up out of whole cloth, since she only taught one year in Cauldron Springs before she became pregnant and lost her job. And he told me also that she didn't bother to write the best novel of all, she lived it. When the money came flooding in, she left Seattle and moved back to Cauldron Springs, where she bought the hot springs and the hotel and most of the town, and she kept the town running through the lean years when hot baths were no longer in vogue, when the cattle market fluctuations ruined the ranchers. She never said an unkind word to a soul, never mentioned the fact that the small town had run her off, she just lived in her house on the hill and looked down, smiling kindly, watching the town look up.

With his first money, Trahearne had built a house across the creek from hers, and except for occasional trips to Europe and a few visiting-writer jobs at colleges, he had never lived anyplace else, but had never written a poem set within fifty miles of Cauldron Springs. He wrote about the things he saw on his binges, about the road, about small towns whose future had become hostage to freeways, about truck-stop waitresses whose best hope is moving to Omaha or Cheyenne, about pasts that hung around like unwelcome ghosts, about bars where the odd survivors of some misunderstood disaster gathered to stare at dusty brown photographs of themselves, to stare at their drinks sepia in their glasses. But he never wrote about home. As I drove him there, I had too much time to think about all the runaways.

My El Camino was a bastard rig—half sedan, half pickup, a half-crazy idea out of Detroit for lazy drugstore cowboys who want to drive a pickup without driving a pickup—and I loved it. The Indian kid up in Ronan who had ordered it out had it set up so he could hit the rodeo circuit as a calf-roper, which means plenty of high-speed travel towing a heavy load. The kid got tired of the circuit and bored with making payments, and when I repossessed it, I bought it from the dealer cheap. It was a beauty, fire-engine red with a black vinyl roof and a fancy topper for the pickup bed, all chrome and conception, but it had a heavy-duty racing suspension, a four-speed box, and a tricked up 454-cubic-inch engine stuffed under the hood. It was a real beast, it could dust a Corvette on the straight, outcorner a Porsche Carrera, and I carried an honest ticket from a South Dakota radar trap for 137 mph. Of course it got six miles to the gallon, if I was lucky, and not even Lloyd's of London would sell me insurance, but with a CB radio, a radar detector, and a stack of 15-grain Desoxyn speed tabs, even a child could make time towing Trahearne's barge, and I burned up the highway.

We were in Lovelock, Nevada, before Trahearne woke up from his nap, and when I stopped for gas there, he moved up to ride with me. He was quiet, except for the occasional gurgle of Wild Turkey, until we reached Elko.

"I'm tired," he said, "and my ass hurts, so let's stop and sleep."

"Why don't you go back to your car and sleep there?" I said. "I've got so much speed in my system that I couldn't sleep if you knocked me out."

"That's not my fault," he said. "Let's stop."

"I thought you were in a hurry to get home."

"Listen, son, I'm paying the ticket here, and when I say stop, we stop, you understand," he said.

"Right," I said. "One minute I'm your best drinking buddy and the next I'm your nigger for the day." I pulled into a darkened service station and got out.

"What are you doing?" he asked. Then he followed me to the rear of my rig to repeat the question.

"I'm taking this son of a bitch off," I grunted as I heaved on the tow-bar nuts. "You can drive yourself home, old man—you can go when you're ready, stop when you want to. I quit."

It took him a bit, but he finally said it. "Hey, I'm sorry. And hell, I'm not even sleepy anymore."

"You sure?"

"Yeah."

"You ain't going to change your mind?"

"No," he said. "And I am sorry. Money makes a man stupid sometimes, you know."

"I don't know yet," I said, "but when your ex-wife pays me, I'll have a better idea."

Trahearne laughed and got me a beer out of the cooler. "You have to learn to relax," he said, "to take it easy."

"I didn't want to stop," I reminded him, and he laughed again as we drove on.

South of Arco as I watched the headlights flash across the sagebrush and desert scrub, Trahearne woke up again and wanted to know what Betty Sue's father had had to say.

"I tried to tell you on the way back to San Francisco," I said, "but you wanted to talk about this lady poet I was going to love."

"She's mean, son, but she's full of life," he said, then he laughed. "She gave you a hard time, huh?"

"You could say that."

"You don't like them mean, huh?" he said.

"Do you?"

"Sometimes," he murmured, "sometimes it helps."

"Helps what?"

"Helps me forget that I'm performing a mindless act that I've performed too many times already," he said quietly, "with too many different women in too many shabby places."

"That's a different tune," I said.

"Right," he said without further explanation. "Did her father know where she had been in Oregon?"

"No. And if he had, he wouldn't have told me anyway."

"I sort of thought you might drive back that way," he said.

"I thought about it," I admitted. "Then I decided to take you home first. I'll drive down next week."

"You're going to a lot of trouble over that girl," he said.

"Storing up my treasures in heaven," I said. "Rosie promised me free beer for a month the next time I'm down in Sonoma."

"Don't kid me," he said. "You're obsessed with the girl."

"Maybe," I said. Then we passed a sign telling us how far it was to the Craters of the Moon National Monument. "Hey," I said, changing the subject. "We banged the same whore at the Cottontail, you know."

"Why did you do that?" he asked.

"Thought it might give me a clue."

"Jesus Christ," he said, "no wonder you're such a cynic, you're a goddamned mystic in disguise." Then he paused. "Did she tell you anything?" he asked nervously.

"She expressed some doubts about man having conquered the moon," I said, "but that's all she said."

"That's the way women are, son—either too easy to fool or too hard," he said, then sighed. I didn't ask him what that meant. I just drove on toward the dark heaps of the mountains beyond the desert, trying to push Betty Sue Flowers to the back of my mind with the gentle shove of Trahearne's whiskey.

In spite of a minor drunk, I got Trahearne home around midnight the next evening. His house was a long, low expanse of log and stone set over a daylight basement that jutted into the side of a shallow hill. As we parked in front, I saw a woman leaning in the open doorway, silhouetted against the light, her arms and ankles crossed patiently as if she had been waiting for us, had stood for days like a woman on a widow's walk staring into a dark and stormy sea.

"Home again," Trahearne said. "Every time I get home, I'm surprised that I made it back alive. I keep thinking I'm bound to die on the road. But I guess I'm doomed to die in my own bed."

"I know what you mean," I said.

"You'll stay the night, of course," he said.

"If there's going to be a big domestic strife scene," I said, "I'd just as soon drive back to Meriwether."

Trahearne laughed loudly, breaking the quiet in the cab, and said, "Don't worry. Melinda's a saint. She forgives me even before I transgress. So come in and let's have a homecoming drink." Then he slapped me on the shoulder and climbed out, shouting, "Whiskey, woman!" His great voice echoed across the shallow valley. Across the creek, a light appeared in an upstairs window of his mother's house, and the dark blot of a woman's head came to the window.

"In which order?" the woman in the doorway asked, her soft, unaccented voice unhoned by even a hint of rancor.

"Order be damned," Trahearne shouted back. "Celebrate, love, the sailor, home from the sea, the hunter home from the hill."

"On his cliché or bearing it?" she answered happily.

As the big man limped up the redwood steps to the deck, I followed with his suitcases and my duffle like some faithful native bearer.

"Who's that behind you?" his wife asked. "Gunga Din?"

"Come, Gunga Din, you swine, sahib needs water for the whiskey," he said as he came back to help me with the bags.

"Thanks," I said, then paused on the steps to ease the amphetamine trembles in my legs. Trahearne and his wife embraced in the doorway as she fondly murmured *you maniac,* and she chuckled as she led him through the doorway. In the silence, the creek whispered in its rocky bed, and the face at the far window seemed to be staring at me. I crept up the stairs in silent guilt, away from the face.

By the time I reached the doorway, which opened directly into a living room as big as a house, Trahearne had fallen into a huge leather lounge chair and propped up his feet. His wife was behind a small bar, rattling ice cubes. Across the room, in a fireplace large enough to roast a Volkswagen, three four-foot logs crackled merrily against the mountain chill. From where I stood, it looked like a cozy little fire.

"A drink, Mr. Sughrue?" Trahearne's wife asked.

"A beer, please," I said, and she opened a bottle and poured it into an earthenware mug, then brought the drinks around, Trahearne's first, then mine.

As she handed the mug to me, she said, "I'm afraid

Trahearne has the social grace of a stone. I'm Melinda Trahearne." She held out a rough hand, which I shook as I introduced myself. "Make yourself at home," she said, then smiled. "Walk around until your butt wakes up, then have a chair."

"Thanks," I said as she walked back to Trahearne.

So I stood around like a knot on a log while she sat on the arm of his chair and fiddled with his sparse hair. She was so obviously pleased to see him home that I did my best not to watch them, not to overhear her whispered greetings.

I had been so wound up with Betty Sue Flowers that I hadn't thought about what Trahearne's second wife might look like, and even as I tried not to look at her, she seemed a rather plain woman of about thirty, not at all what I would have expected if I had thought about it.

She wasn't ugly, just plain, and she looked as if she had just come in from a hard day's work in the fields. Her hair was a dull shade of brown, neither dark nor light, and she wore it in a closely cropped tangle that made her nose seem too long, her mouth too wide, and her eyes set too far apart. Except for a streak of pinkish-gray clay across her forehead, her face was unpainted, and even in the soft light, her tan seemed sallow, the skin color of a convict or a barmaid. She wore a pair of baggy jeans and a loose velour sweat-shirt, so I couldn't tell about her body; she didn't seem fat or skinny but she moved with the sort of controlled grace rich girls seem to learn as soon as they take their first steps. Her bare feet, too, were slender and elegant, well-manicured, although her hands were as rough and hard as a brick mason's, and her eyes were an odd shade of blue-green, which might have made them striking, but they didn't seem to match her hair or coloring.

113

She glanced at me, caught me watching her, and her smile was generous, her teeth as straight and even as money could buy. If her voice hadn't been completely without accent, I might have thought that she was one of those rich East Coast girls who majored in English Lit and field hockey at one of the seven sisters. As I watched, she slipped off the arm of the chair to stand behind Trahearne, her strong hands kneading the thick muscles of his shoulders. It looked like it felt good, but he groaned.

"Enough, woman," he said, "the cure surpasseth the disease." Then he patted her hands to hold them still.

"Sissy," she said, laughing as she walked over to pick up his bags. When she lifted them, heavy as they were, her shoulders didn't dip, and she carried them toward a dark hallway as if they were empty. I knew they weren't. As she walked away from me, the firm outlines of her hips swayed with a force of their own beneath the baggy jeans. As I turned back, I caught Trahearne watching me watch his wife.

"How long have you two been married?" I asked, then applied my mouth to a worthier project, my beer.

"Nearly three years," Trahearne answered without interest.

"Seems like a nice lady,"

"Yeah," he answered. "A nice lady." His voice seemed to drift away with fatigue.

"Maybe I should unhook the cars and hit the road," I said.

"Nonsense," Melinda said from the hallway. "You've been on the road too long, and I insist that you at least stay the night."

"Thank you, ma'am," I said, "but I don't want to impose."

"No imposition at all," she said graciously. "The basement is filled with guest rooms—it's private, quiet, and you can come and go without bothering us at all.

114

There's a wet bar, an icebox full of beer, a small kitchen, and two color televisions. You must stay."

"Well . . ." I said.

"Oh to hell with him," Trahearne growled. "He's some kind of ultimate redneck country boy, and he can't sleep except under the stars. Besides, he's never been married and he's scared shitless of domestic strife."

"Don't be silly," Melinda said, then laughed. "The only strife in this household is the sound of Trahearne's snores." She walked over and picked up my duffle bag. "Come on, I'll show you your room."

"And I'll show myself to bed," Trahearne said as he stood up. "Good night, C.W., and all that social grace crap," he added, then lumbered toward the hallway like a wounded bear.

"In the morning," I said, then followed his wife through the large, open kitchen to the stairway.

Downstairs, a large room with full-length glass walls on the daylight side filled most of the basement, and the bedrooms lay down a hallway that followed the track of the upstairs hall. Melinda carried my bag to a small bedroom beside the bathroom, then led me back to the game room to show me the bar and the small kitchen.

"Please make yourself at home here," she said. "You'll find everything you need for breakfast in the icebox. For lunch too. I'm sorry, but because Trahearne and I work at different hours, we only eat one formal meal at dinner. Usually around seven. Until then, I'm afraid you'll have to fend for yourself."

"I'll be fine," I said.

"I'm sure you will, Mr. Sughrue," she said. "Bachelors always make the best houseguests. They're more capable of fending for themselves than most married men, it seems." She smiled slightly. "You never married?"

"No, ma'am."

"Do you mind if I ask why not?"

"I don't mind," I said, "but the truth is that I don't rightly know why not. I've never jumped out of an airplane on purpose. Even in jump school they had to kick me out. I guess nobody ever kicked me into marriage."

"I've done some skydiving," she said softly, "and found marriage to be just as exciting."

"You seem to be happy," I said.

"Yes, I am," she said. "And as I'm sure you noticed, I'm very fond of my husband."

"Yes, ma'am."

"And he seems fond of you," she said. "I'm pleased about that. I don't begrudge my husband's friends. I only hope we can be friends too." Then she held out her hand again.

"Yes, ma'am," I said as I shook her hand.

"Of course, if you call me 'ma'am' again, I'll have to knock the shit out of you," she said calmly, then burst out in a fit of giggles.

"I guess I could break down and call you Miz Melinda," I said, and we both smiled.

"That's an improvement," she said, then wished me pleasant dreams.

As she left me, her voice echoed in my head, words and phrases that seemed to have no meaning—"my husband" and "icebox"—but I didn't pay any attention to myself.

The drive and the Desoxyn had left me too rattled to sleep, so I sat down in front of the television to drink beer and catch the late movies by cable from Spokane. Although they were quiet for twenty or thirty minutes, after that the Trahearnes made a great deal of commotion for a couple not engaged in domestic strife. Since I began in the business, I always did the whole number, so I had done more divorce work than I should have, more than my share back in the days when I still had a partner. I didn't want to hear it unless I got paid for it, so I turned up the volume on the television, but I could still hear the heavy rumble of Trahearne's voice through the thick floors. Whatever he was angry about, he told her about it all the way through the second half of *Johnny Guitar* and through the first half of *The Beast with a Thousand Eyes*. I switched to whiskey, found a pack of cigarettes behind the bar, then stepped outside through the sliding glass doors. Even there, the sound of his complaints, of her lilting compliance still echoed. I went back to the movie and turned up the sound again.

Finally, it was over, and the noises changed to the groan of bedslats, the slap of flesh. That made me even sadder than the fight. I left the basement again and walked all the way out to the cars and leaned against the dew-damp fender of the El Camino. In the pasture, cattle shifted their hooves and breathed in soft, snuffling grunts, and their flat teeth ground gently against the grass. Across the creek, the other house was dark now, but I still felt the watching face, hidden behind the frail glimmer of a nightlight that glowed like a spectre beyond the black windows.

Once more, I took Betty Sue Flowers' picture out of my pocket. I had been carrying it for over a week and hadn't shown it to anybody but myself. In the sudden flare of a match, she looked somehow familiar, as if she were a girl I had grown up with, but as the flame died, the flickering image of the film filled my blindness. I didn't even know why I cared about it, didn't know what to think. I was like the rest of them now, I suspected, I wanted her to fit my image of her, wanted her back like she might have been, but I feared the truth of it was that she wanted to stay hidden, to live her own life beyond all those clutching desires. Unless she was dead, and if she was, she had already lived the life she made, as best she could. I stared at the picture in my hand, the one I couldn't see, and saw the pictures I couldn't look at without flinching, the pale, doughy flesh that moved with an undeniable grace, both fragile and determined, endlessly vulnerable but unharmed. Ashamed that I had been aroused, ashamed that I was ashamed, and aroused again thinking about it, I went back to the now-silent house, back to my empty bed.

Not to sleep, though, or even unpleasant dreams. I drank and smoked and watched the ceiling. When the ashtray beside the bed filled, I took it to the bathroom to empty it, and out of habit I wiped it clean. It was a lump of glazed clay, as formless as any rock, with a smooth, shallow depression in the center. As I wiped away the caked ashes, a woman's profile came into view, a high, proud face molded into the clay, a tangle of long hair streaming away from the face, as if the woman stood in a cosmic wind. When I looked more closely, I saw what seemed to be a ring of watchers, lightly impressed eyes around the rim of the depression, staring at the woman's face with a lust akin to hatred. Then I noticed a slim ceramic vase on the bathroom counter, which held a small bundle of straw flowers, and on the vase a series of women's faces, their hands over their eyes, their long, tangled hair bleeding over their shoulders. The pieces must be Melinda's, I thought, a plain woman understanding the curse of beauty, and I was impressed. The ashtray was as heavy as a stone, the vase as light as if it had been moulded from air, and the women's faces too fragile for words.

Usually, on those sleepless nighttime trips to the bathroom, I had to take a long look at my own battered, whiskey-worn face, searching it for a glimpse of the face it might have been but for the wasted years, the bars, the long nights. But this night, I rubbed my thumb over the faces locked beneath the brown translucent glaze, all the weeping women, and I had no pity left for myself.

I had made my own bed and went to it to sleep, then to rise and do what I knew I had to do, to pay what I owed the women.

9 ●●●●

AN OLD DRINKING BUDDY OF MINE HAD COME HOME FROM a two-week binge with a rose tattooed on his arm. Around the blossom was written *Fuck 'em all/and sleep till noon.* His wife made him have it surgically removed, but she hated the scar even more. Every time he touched it, he grinned. Some years later she tried to remove the grin with a wine bottle, but she only knocked out a couple of teeth, which made the grin even more like a sneer. The part that I don't understand, though, is that they are still married. He is still grinning and she is still hating it.

I didn't have any tattoos or any marriages, but the morning after I brought Trahearne home I slept until noon anyway. When I woke, I knew that I had to roll out of the sack and shuffle into my sweat suit and jogging shoes. I had been on the road too long, and I could hear various invaluable parts of my body whine for exercise. Maybe it would clear my mind. Maybe I would break my leg and have to forget about driving to Oregon.

Eventually, I did just that, dressed in tired athletic gear and strolled outside into the noon sunlight. I sat down in a deck chair to survey the landscape.

Trahearne's mother owned a half section of land northwest of the small town of Cauldron Springs. Her land lay in a shallow valley between two low ridges. At their highest elevations, the ridges were timbered, but on the lower slopes they were covered with sagebrush scrub. Between the houses and the highway, she kept a few head of cattle in a small pasture. Cold Spring Creek ambled between the ridges to the pasture, where it broke into a series of long smooth willow-choked bends, then it flowed alongside the highway until it joined the warm mineral waters of Cauldron Springs Creek east of the small town. Trahearne's house sat on the east side of the creek, his mother's on the west. Her house looked like something off the Great Plains, a square and sturdy farmhouse, its only decoration a porch across the front, and it seemed to stare down upon the small town with the austere gaze of a wheat farmer driven mad by the whims of the weather.

The town had grown up around a hot spring that bubbled up in a limestone cup the size and shape of a washtub. An old man who had made his fortune in silver and tin mines had built the hotel and the bathhouse, claiming great curative properties for the spring waters. He had sunk his fortune into the project, built a huge wedding cake of a spa around the spring, then settled back to enjoy his declining years, but he had built his spa too far from the people, and the flow from the spring didn't have enough volume to keep his pools and baths hot enough to please those few who came. When he died, he was the only guest in his hotel, the only bather.

Trahearne's mother had reopened the bathhouse and one floor of the hotel, but only as a courtesy to the town, like the tennis courts she built behind the bathhouse, a reminder of her money. She wouldn't have the buildings repainted, though. She let them fade and weather from white to an ashen gray as dull as raw silver.

As I jogged slowly down the gravel road toward the highway, Melinda ran past me like a deer. Six seasons of Army football and four at various junior colleges had left me with legs that only remembered running swiftly, and I envied Melinda's easy, quick pace. She ran as nicely as she walked but she still kept her body bundled, hidden now beneath a loose sweat suit. She reached the highway and turned west up the long rise toward the end of the pavement. When I got to the highway, I followed her briefly, then slowed to a walk as she topped the rise and turned back. I waited where I stood, and when she came back, I swung alongside her, and we jogged back to the gravel road.

"You'll never get in shape that way," she said, breathing slow and easy.

"This is penance," I puffed, "not physical therapy."

She laughed, then ran away from me, dust spurting from beneath her tennis shoes with each powerful stroke of her legs, her short hair bouncing ragged in the sunlight.

When I finally reached the house, she was standing up on the deck watching me, her fists on her hips, her legs spread in a wide, strong stance. I limped up the steps and fell into a redwood lounger.

"I wish I could get Trahearne to exercise," she said.

"I wish you could get me to stop," I huffed.

"Don't you just love to run?" she asked.

"It's not as bad as getting poked in the eye with a sharp stick," I said, "but at least that's a quick pain."

"Exactly," Trahearne boomed as he stepped out the front door. "How about a Bloody Mary?" he asked as he rattled a pitcher at me as if it were magic charm.

"Only because it's before breakfast," I said as he poured me a drink.

"Around here, this is breakfast most days," Melinda said.

I turned around to study her face for some evidence of wifely irony, but she was smiling, almost prettily, and patting Trahearne on his plump cheek. Whatever the shouting had been about during the night, they both seemed to have forgotten it, or had chosen to act as if they had. Melinda kissed him lightly on the corner of his mouth, then stepped inside. Trahearne settled into a lounge chair beside me.

"That's an exceptional woman," I said, "for a wife."

"You don't know the half of it," he said, then blushed. I grinned at his blush, but he didn't smile back. He just filled up my glass again, saying, "Drink this, my boy, and then I'll show you what real people do with their hangovers."

"So this is what taking the waters is all about?" I said as Trahearne and I lowered ourselves into the warm waters of the hotel's main pool. He just grunted and sank to his shoulders. His white T-shirt, which he had insisted upon wearing, billowed briefly with trapped air, then burped under his neck. After we had finished the Bloody Marys, Trahearne had forced me to drive him to town to take the waters. He had a key to the back door and to a private dressing room, where we changed, and we had the pool to ourselves except for an old couple from Oklahoma. They had left as we climbed in, on their way to a hot mud bath for their feet, behind a door appropriately labeled The Corn Hole.

"How do you like it?" Trahearne sighed.

"It's okay," I said, lying to be polite. The water, which stank faintly of sulphur and other minerals my nose refused to identify, was tepid rather than hot and it seemed slimy like a fever sweat.

"It beats the hell out of running around," he said, "and I guess it works. My mother swears by it—she's down here every morning at six—and Melinda comes down late at night to swim laps after she's been working."

"And what do you do?" I asked.

"I come down for hangovers," he said, "and sit around until I break a sweat." Then he ducked his head under the water and stood up. "Am I sweating?" he asked, then smiled. "I feel like I'm sweating."

"You're certainly all wet," I said, trying not to look at the maze of purple scars glowing across his chest through the wet T-shirt. He lowered himself into the water again.

"Anytime you're ready to go, let me know," he said.

"This wasn't my idea," I said.

"Let's get out of here," he said, "this place always stinks like a hospital." Then he stood up and lumbered toward the steps. He had even more scars on his back. They looked like the deep painful gouges of shrapnel wounds, reminders etched into his flesh of a long-forgotten war. I followed him out of the waters to the dressing room.

As we changed clothes, he said, "Okay, so I'm bashful about my scars."

"They're not that bad," I said.

"Bad enough," he answered. "Hurry up," he added, "I think I may be sober enough to try to write this afternoon."

"I know I'm sober enough to drive back to Meriwether," I said.

"Tomorrow," Trahearne commanded. "Melinda's got a steak thawing for you."

"Yes, sir," I said, then walked with him out to the car, which was parked between the back of the pool house and the tennis courts. An elderly man was bouncing balls off a backboard, and two teenaged girls were engaged in a furiously contested point.

"Don't watch," Trahearne said as he climbed into the passenger seat. "All that nubile flesh will drive you mad."

"It already has," I said as I drove us away.

Later that afternoon, after a short nap in the sun, a shower, and a light lunch, I called Trahearne's mother's house to let Catherine Trahearne know that I hadn't forgotten who had hired me. She said that she was on her way to town to play tennis, but she told me to come over for a drink before dinner, and I accepted. Trahearne was ensconced in a large study off the living room, rattling papers and ice cubes and cursing loudly, and Melinda had gone up the hill to her studio, so I fixed a drink and wandered along the graveled footpath toward the creek and a narrow wooden bridge across it. The creek was small and choked with rocks and brush, but it picked its way energetically through the clutter, pausing occasionally in a shallow pool. Creek-watching is a patient art, and I leaned on the bridge rail and practiced, sniffing the cool riffles of breeze over the creek, watching the pan-sized trout shimmer in the crystal water, their gills fanning like vestigial wings as they waited for dusk and whatever fly hatch the day demanded.

"You must be the detective," a gruff woman's voice said from the shadowy willows beside the pool, and I nearly jumped into the creek. "Sorry," she said. "I didn't mean to startle you but I was having an unplanned nap when you got here."

"That's all right," I said as she stepped out of the shade.

She was a tall, angular woman with short gray hair, wearing a worn red flannel shirt, Malone pants, and a pair of battered Bean's hunting boots. She carried a knotty cane and leaned on it heavily as she limped along the creek side to the path.

"I'm Edna Trahearne," she said as she offered me a gnarled hand to shake. She had to be in her late seventies, but her eyes were clear, her handshake firm in spite of the twisted fingers. Deep wrinkles had eroded the strong features of her face, and her heavy but withered breasts hung loose beneath the flannel shirt like useless flaps of flesh. "And you're that Sughrue fella."

"Yes, ma'am."

"How's my son?" she asked.

"A little tired," I said, "but he's got the constitution of an ox."

"He comes by it naturally," she said, "but someday he's going to tie one on and there won't be anybody around to untie the knot. I told Catherine not to send anybody after him this time—a waste of money and effort—but of course she refused to listen to me. I don't know what that slut he lives with does to him— I haven't spoken to him since she arrived—but his binges come on the heels of each other now, and he hasn't written in over two years. If he doesn't rid himself of her, he'll be in his grave before me." Then she paused to stare at me with a look that almost seemed coy. "You don't agree?"

"I don't know," I said. "She seems to love him," I added lamely.

"He doesn't need love, young man, it confuses him," she said. "He needs tending like a child. From what I can tell, my son's young wife makes the mistake of thinking he's a man. He's an artist, and all artists are children."

It's true, I thought, some men do need tending, but it's degrading to talk about it to strangers. I decided to

126

see if the old woman was as tough as she acted. "I understand that you once wrote," I said.

"It was the only way for a woman alone to work at anything besides serving men, and as soon as I had the money to afford this place, I stopped."

"You weren't dedicated to the art?" I said.

"If you've read my two novels, then you know what sort of fairy tales they are," she said, "and if you've talked to my son, you know the truth of my life here. I took money from fools, boy, and I earned it, but don't give me any bullshit about art."

"All right," I said. She was as tough as she seemed to be, so I went back to watching the little creek.

"Are you a fisherman?" she asked suddenly. "Or just another dude with a fancy fly rod?"

"I'm not much of a fisherman, no, but I have caught a few trout."

"If I were to loan you my fly rod, do you think you could catch half a dozen of those little trout?" she said. "I can't see well enough to tie a leader anymore," she added, "even if I had the hands for it, and I would dearly love a mess of pan-fried trout tonight."

"I've got my fly rod in the pickup," I said, then sat my drink down and trotted toward it as obedient as a son.

The creek hadn't been fished in some time, and the trout rose to whatever fly I offered them, but I caught more willow branches and wind-tangles than trout, and it took me an hour to get a stringer of small cutthroat trout. The old woman watched me like a fish hawk, but she didn't offer any snide suggestions or sage advice about my back-casting. I cleaned the fish in the creek, then followed her to the back door of her house and into the kitchen. While I washed my hands, she got me a beer and asked me to join her on the front porch.

We walked through the living room slowly, as if through a museum. A war museum. The walls and tables were covered with mementos of Trahearne's war: framed pictures of young, freshly commissioned Marine officers, a thinner Trahearne standing tall among his contemporaries; the same faces during the jungle campaigns, hollowed-eyed and worn among the gray rain-forest debris after the fire storm of battle; Japanese battle flags, a .25 Nambu automatic pistol, and an officer's Samurai sword hanging crossed with Trahearne's Marine officer dress sword; and embroidered pillows and shell necklaces and bone earrings— all the random junk they brought back from the islands. One of the photographs was a wedding picture, Trahearne in dress blues beneath wind-twisted Monterey pine with white beaches and a phony blue ocean tinted into the background, but the attractive woman holding the white bouquet beside him was dressed in black. It was odd, as if he had been killed in the war. Nothing of his life after the war was in the living room, and I half expected to see a faded gold star hanging in the front window. When I looked, though, the old woman was waiting at the front door, looking irritated. I shook off the chill the room filled me with and followed her outside, where I took a deep breath, the air in the living room too old and bloody to breathe.

"Were you in the war?" she asked politely.

"Not that one," I said. She shook her head and smiled as if I had given the wrong answer. I stepped around her, careful not to touch her, to introduce myself to the handsome woman sitting in a rocker on the front porch.

She was dressed in white today instead of black, a short tennis dress, with a racket and ball bag set beside her chair. Beads of sweat sparkled across her forehead and up into the hairline of her tied-back copper hair. The years hadn't hurt her at all. If anything, she was even more lovely now, her complexion smooth and tanned, her flesh firm and elastic.

"I'm Catherine Trahearne," she said unnecessarily as she stood up. "I've been playing tennis in town, and I haven't had a chance to clean up, so you will have to excuse me."

"That's okay," I said. "I've been fishing."

"Any luck?" she asked.

"Enough for our dinner," the old woman said, "but just barely." It sounded like both a rebuke and a command, but for what and to do what escaped me.

"Every one I catch is luck," I said.

"You found Trahearne," Catherine said, "so I choose to believe that you fish with skill rather than luck."

"Ha," the old woman snorted. "A complete waste." I didn't know if she meant my fishing or my hunting.

"Whatever, thanks for bringing him home in one piece," Catherine said. "I'm certain that it was no easy task."

"It wasn't all that hard," I said.

"Ha," the old lady added.

"Mother Trahearne, may I get your glass of wine?" Catherine asked.

"I think I'll wait until I go to bed," the old woman said "Maybe I'll sleep tonight if I wait."

"Of course," Catherine said, then to me she added, "I would ask you to stay for dinner but I'm sure that you have other plans. You must excuse me now, though. I must shower before dinner." I had the uneasy impression that she had told me she was going to shower not out of politeness but rather so I would think of her tanned and naked body standing under the rush of hot sudsy water. "If you will send my your bill, Mr. Sughrue, I'll see that it is taken care of immediately. And let me thank you once again. It has been a pleasure meeting you." She shook my hand and went inside the house, the flat, smooth muscles of her thighs rippling in the afternoon sunlight.

"How my son could give up a woman like that, I'll never understand," Edna Trahearne said.

"I wouldn't know about that," I mumbled.

"Don't be such a twit," the old woman chided me. "I appreciate the trout, son, but not enough to allow you to be a twit on my front porch."

"I'm sorry," I said.

"Don't appologize, either," she said.

I picked up my rod and said goodbye. As I walked back to Trahearne's house, I was convinced that I had been manipulated in ways I didn't even begin to understand, for reasons way beyond me. Maybe I was just a convenient target. Or maybe I had wandered into a loony bin. They all had to be slightly crazy to live so close to one another, but I didn't know what was going on. My job was over anyway. All I had to know was that Melinda had promised steaks for dinner. I wanted red meat, two drinks of good whiskey, a sober night's sleep, and then I wanted to get the hell away from all of them.

Dinner was ready when I got back to the house, but Trahearne was too hammered to eat. He sat in his sutdy, looking at his desk, which was covered with scraps of yellow paper off a legal pad, idly twirling an old .45 service automatic while Melinda tried to hold the steaks at medium rare.

"Now you know," he mumbled as I stepped into the study with a drink for the two of us.

"I know dinner's ready," I said.

"You've met the crone and the dragon lady and seen the hall of lost dreams," he said, "so what else is there to know?"

"Let's eat," I suggested.

"Eat, eat," he said, then broke into his poetic

brogue. "Matched with an aged wife, I mete and dole unequal laws unto a savage race who eat and sleep and breed and know not me—"

"It little profits that an idle king," I added, moving back a line, "fucks up the dinner."

"How the hell do you know that line?" he asked, drunken puzzlement twisting his face.

"When I was a domestic spy at the University of Colorado for the United States Army," I said, "I took an M.A. in English Literature."

"You're shittin' me," he said, rearing back in his chair.

"Not at all."

"By god, boy, let's have a drink," he said, "an' you can tell all 'bout your life as a spy."

"Over dinner," I suggested.

"All right, goddammit," he grunted as he heaved his hulk out of the chair. "All right, you bastards and your goddamned dinner," he complained, but he followed me to the table.

If I had known how he was going to act, I would have left him in his study quoting bad Tennyson. His steak was overdone, his baked potato cold, his salad too vinegary—or so he claimed in a loud, drunken voice. He ate a few bites, moved his food about his plate as if he were playing some sort of victual chess, then he slumped in his captain's chair at the head of the table, sleeping, thankfully, with only a few light snores. Melinda smiled at me and shook her head. But not in reproach.

"Poor dear," she whispered. "His work never goes well when he first gets home. If you don't mind, we'll just let him sleep there while we eat."

"I don't mind," I said. "I'm so hungry I could even eat with him awake."

"Don't be mean," she said lightly, then smiled again and brushed her hand through her short hair, the clay dust in it fluffing out in a soft cloud. She went back to her steak, eating like a farm hand at the end of the harvest season. When she finished it, she sliced off a portion of Trahearne's, then ate that too with equal relish. When she finished that, she suggested coffee on the deck, and we left the big man sleeping in his chair.

It was past eight o'clock but the northern sun still settled slowly toward the low mountains in the west. The grass of the pasture grew darkly lush in the limpid air, and the forested hills shifted from green to a darkness as black as dead coals. Over the flats, nighthawks flitted with throbbing cries through the willows, and small trout leapt into the floating haze above the creek. In the near distance, the lights of Cauldron Springs flickered like signal fires.

"It's a shame," Melinda said softly, "that he can't write . . . about this place. My work has never gone better, his never worse, and yet he says it isn't my fault. Sometimes I wonder, though . . ." She paused to sip her coffee and stare at me over the cup.

I had had all the confidences I could stand for one day, so I turned to idle conversation.

"Were you raised around here?"

"What?" she said. The fading light was kind to her features, and I thought that if she worked at it—maybe fixed her face and let her hair grow and wore something besides baggy clothes—she might be an attractive woman. As I studied her, she blushed, and I wondered what she felt when she saw the polished beauty of Catherine, wondered what her fingers felt as she molded the lovely profiles on her clay.

"Were you raised in Montana?" I asked.

"Oh no," she answered quickly, almost as if she felt guilty because she hadn't been. "Marin County," she said, "across the Bay from San Francisco, and Sun Valley, and the south of France." It sounded like a line

132

she had said so many times it had begun to bore her. She noticed it too. "I'm sorry," she added, "I love this part of the country, and I'm afraid that I sounded a bit supercilious. Poor little rich girl, you know, and all that. I wish I had been raised on a little ranch just like this, but my parents were both well-off—not wealthy, mind you, but well-off—incomes from estates and trusts—and they dabbled at things, you see, the cello and violin, abstract painting, scuba diving, and skiing. The worst sort of dilettantes, I'm afraid," she said with a gentle laugh, "but very good and kind people."

"Are they still traveling about?" I said, still making conversation with the poor little well-off girl to whom Trahearne, for all his faults, must have seemed as real and exciting as a storm in the North Atlantic.

"My parents?"

"Yes."

"No, I'm afraid they're dead."

"I'm sorry," I said.

"My mother died in a skiing accident in the Alps," she said, "and my father died of grief. Or so I told myself. He ran his Alfa off a curve on the Costa Brava."

"I'm sorry," I repeated.

"Thank you, but there's no need," she said. "It seems so long ago now, so far away." Then she sat up and brightened. "I'm certainly glad that you two weren't hurt in the accident."

"Just a fender bender," I said, wondering what Trahearne had told her.

"Oh, it must have been more than that," she said, "for Trahearne to be in the hospital for three days."

"Observation," I said, glad that I had my wits about me. If Trahearne didn't want his young wife to know that he had been shot, then I certainly wasn't going to tell her.

"He must have taken quite a spill when he was thrown out," she said. "Those scars on his ham look as if it might have been serious."

"Minor stuff," I said.

"How did it happen?" she asked, but I didn't have the impression that she was pumping me.

"Frankly, I was too drunk to know exactly what happened," I said.

"Well, thank you for taking care of him," she said.

"We had a pretty good time," I said, "and I'm not sure who was taking care of whom."

"It sounds like . . . sounds like a wild trip." She paused. "You know, we got to know each other on just the same sort of trip. I was teaching in a summer workshop in Sun Valley and having a drink with some of my students in the lodge, and Trahearne came in off the terrace, this huge, beautiful, alive man, and he sat down at the bar beside me, bought me a drink, then another, and somehow we ran away with each other. I didn't realize who he was until we had driven all the way to Mexico—we wouldn't tell each other our names, it was like that, you know—and then I heard him spell his name for the Mexican border people, for that form—visitor's card, you know—and I just couldn't believe it. Here he was, the most *alive* man I had ever met, and he turned out to be Abraham Trahearne. Life is so strange. Who would have thought all this could come of a simple thing like buying me a drink."

"Speaking of the great man," I said, trying not to be ironic, "would you like me to help you get him to bed?"

"Not at all," she said. "He'll wake up in a couple of hours shouting for whiskey and wild, wild women." The grin on her face suggested that she could handle the wild woman part perfectly well. For an instant I believed her, then she turned her face, and I thought that if she was wild, she kept it well hidden behind plain. "I've bored you, haven't I, with my little love story?"

"It's not that," I said. "I thought I'd hook it up and leave while I'm still sober."

"Trahearne will be so disappointed," she said as if she meant it.

"Yeah, but I've got this other case I'm working on," I said, "and I need to be in Oregon yesterday."

"Tomorrow's never soon enough, is it?"

"No."

"And that's such an exciting phrase."

"What's that?"

"'Working on a case,'" she said. "It suggests dark intrigue, tangled mysteries, the sort of romance denied to mere mortals."

"I'm afraid the reality is usually repossessing cars and combing bars for runaway husbands," I said.

"Or runaway children."

"Sometimes."

"That should be exciting," she said. "A prince stolen by gypsies or something like that."

"I don't know any gypsies or princes," I confessed.

"That's no reason to quit looking," she said, a plaintive note creeping into her voice, soft like the cry of a lost and dying animal. "I do wish you wouldn't leave."

"I have to go," I said.

"I understand," she said. "I'm sure that Trahearne would want me to tell you that you're always welcome in our house. I feel the same way. Please come back whenever the mood suits you."

"Sure," I said, "thanks." But I couldn't think of any moods that would bring me back to this crazy place. We said our goodbyes, and as I drove away, in contrast, my search for Betty Sue Flowers seemed almost sane.

Driving hard, I made it to Grants Pass in one straight shot, nineteen calm hours behind the wheel, then checked into a motel and slept like a child until ten the next morning.

At the Josephine County Sheriff's Department, when I stopped by to let them know I was in the county and I wasn't planning to break any laws, they seemed bored by the prospect but they told me where to go. They didn't tell me what to look for, though, and a couple of hours later I was driving up into the Siskiyous, following a washboard gravel road along a small creek that ran into the Applegate River. About ten miles up the road, the land opened up into a nice little valley, and I understood the smile on the deputy's face.

A prefab A-frame cabin sat beside the road surrounded by multicolored plastic flags flying from loose guy wires. A large sign in front announced SUNDOWN SUMMER ESTATES. When I parked, a tall young man bounded out of the cabin, his hiking boots rattling the cheap pine porch.

"Yes, sir," he said brightly, "what can we do for you today?"

"I think I'm looking for a place to retire," I said, and it sounded suddenly true. A quiet place where I could settle back and think about all the wild goose chases of my life.

"I've got just the place for you," he said quickly, "a ten-acre plot with creek frontage, a spring, and a great building site. Unimproved, of course, but cheap."

"Actually, I was looking for a hippie commune," I said.

"You're in the wrong place," he said, his spiel over, his voice hard now.

"This place belong to you?"

"That's right," he said.

"No hippies, huh?"

"Not now."

"Where did they go?" I asked.

"Wherever hippies go when they find out that living on the land in the old way is hard work."

"How did you get the place?" I asked.

"If it's any of your business, I inherited it from my grandmother," he said, then looked away and shuffled his feet. "You're some kind of law, right?"

"Private," I said, then showed him my license.

"Wouldn't you know," he grumbled. "I've had three prospective buyers today—a Fresno chicken farmer, two kids driving a brand-new Continental, and a rent-a-cop."

"Didn't mean to raise your hopes," I said.

"That's what they're for, aren't they?" he said sadly.

"It was your commune, right?"

"Everybody makes mistakes." He grinned. "What the hell, man, I turned twenty-one in Nam and came into this place and a little bread, and when I came back, all I could think of was peace and dope and hairy-legged hippie chicks. Sounded like heaven on earth."

"What happened?"

"Times changed," he said simply, "and my money ran out. I thought we could make a living up here, but nobody wanted to be on the duty roster. The lazy bastards wouldn't work, so I got a little freaked on acid and conducted a search and destroy mission of my own, burned their hooches and relocated the fuckers. Man, you should've seen them run."

"So now you're selling out?"

"Everything but the back quarter section," he said. "It's either that or another six months up on the pipeline, and Alaska is great, man, if you don't have to work out in the cold—but it's always cold."

"How long ago did everybody leave?"

"Four or five years ago," he said. "Who're you looking for?"

137

"Betty Sue Flowers," I said, then showed him the picture.

"You've got to be kidding," he said as he looked at it.

"No, I'm really looking for her."

"Not that, man, I mean you got to be kidding that this is her," he said. "When she was here, man, she was a cow. A sweet fuck but as big as a barn."

"You remember her, huh?"

"Nobody ever forgets a fuck like that," he said, then sighed darkly, as if he remembered too many other things, too. "Say, you wouldn't have another one of those beers, would you?" I nodded and got two fresh ones out of the cooler. We strolled over to sit on the steps of the A-frame porch. "She was wild, man, too much. How come you're looking for her, anyway?"

"She hasn't been in touch with her family for a long time, and they'd like to find her, see her again."

"Probably not."

"Why?"

"Man, I've known some crazy ladies—in Nam and up on the pipeline—and I've done some numbers I don't like to remember during the daylight hours, but this one, she was something else."

"Was she your lady?"

"Everybody was everybody's," he said. "You know, trying to destroy the concept of private property and personal ownership. What the hell, man, you do enough drugs, it sounds okay."

"At least you hung on to the land."

"Just barely," he said. "They were pushing me to put the title in all our names, you know, telling me that I was on some sort of power trip because I owned the land, and that's when I finally freaked."

"Was that when she left?"

"No, she was gone by then," he said. "She didn't stay around too long before she split with this older dude. She may have even come with him, you know, but I just can't remember."

"Remember his name?"

"Jack. Something like that. We weren't too heavy on last names, you know, shedding another vestige of the middle-class fascist life or some such crap."

"Randall Jackson."

"Sounds good to me, man, but I don't remember."

"Potbellied, bandylegged, balding?"

"That's the creep," he said.

"Creep?"

"He wanted me to finance a skin flick dressed up as a sociological study of sexual freedom in the communes. He said he had all sorts of distribution connections and claimed we'd make a bundle. You know him?"

"We haven't exactly met," I said, "but I know him."

"Whatever happened to him?"

"I heard a rumor that he was in Denver dealing dirty books," I said.

"Figures," he said, then we sat for a bit listening to the flutter of the plastic flags. "Looks like a fucking used car lot, doesn't it?" I nodded. "I guess when I decided to sell out, I wanted it to look as sleazy as possible," he said. "Hey, if you've got another beer, maybe I'll trade you a lot for it."

"You can have a beer," I said, "but I've already got five acres up in Montana on the North Fork of the Flathead. Sorry."

"Don't be sorry," he said as he came back with two fresh beers.

"How are the plots selling?"

"Like cold hot cakes," he said. "Two five-acre plots in the last month, and I had to carry the paper on those. Money's too tight. But I've got a standing offer from a land syndicate—you know, one of those outfits that sell acre lots on television and in the Sunday supplements. Only thing is, they want the whole place, you know, they say that if I keep my quarter-section, it ruins the development potential or some such shit, but if I don't sell some more plots soon, I'll have to take their offer."

"Better than nothing, I guess."

"Just like nothing," he said, "just money, and damn it my great-grandfather was born on the Oregon Trail in Applegate's second train, and my grandmother was born in a log cabin that is still standing five miles up the creek, so here I am sitting under a raft of plastic flags."

"Like you said, times change."

"Yeah," he murmured, "but you know what I hate most of all?"

"What's that?"

"One of these nights, man, I'm gonna be sitting down in Santa Cruz stoned out of my mind watching the late movie, and some washed-up TV cowboy is gonna come on the tube offering my land in piss-ant lots, and man that's gonna be a bummer."

"Maybe you could run a few cattle or something."

"Hell, have you seen the market quotations lately?" he said. "You've got to have a wad of capital just to get into the cattle-raising business and lose your ass," he said. "Besides, I've been lazy too long to quit now," he said, then paused. "Say, man, you look like you might have been high once or twice, and I've got this dynamite number in my pocket. If you've got a couple more beers, we can sit here and get high and wait for the customers who ain't about to come here anyway."

We smoked his dope and drank my beer, watched the sun ride the wide open spaces of high blue sky, talked about wagon trains and trails, about what it might have been like, talked about the motorcycle shop he might open down in Santa Cruz, but we didn't talk about Betty Sue Flowers and we didn't get very high.

10 ••••

Two afternoons later, I knocked on Randall Jackson's office door. He worked out of a cubicle in the corner of a large warehouse filled with cartons of books and magazines. He hadn't been hard to find. The clerk in the first porno bookstore I had hit on Colfax told me where to look. But I guess I arrived at a bad time. After my knock, the voices inside the office stopped suddenly. The cheap door opened quickly, nearly jerked off its hinges, and a very large, very ugly man with a dark face and a three-hundred-dollar suit stepped outside and asked me what I wanted. I should have known, I suppose. Where there's money, there's dirt, and when you work my side of the street, you have to expect to deal with those people. They're everywhere. Not as well organized as they would like you to think, but organized well enough.

"Can I help you?" he asked politely, a soft trace of a Mexican accent in his voice. His twenty-dollar haircut looked as if it belonged on somebody else's face.

"I'd like to talk to Mr. Jackson," I said, even more polite than he had been.

"I'm sorry but he's busy right now," the big man said.

"Who is it, Torres?" a voice from inside asked.

"Nobody," he answered, not meaning to insult me.

"Tell him to wait," the voice inside said.

"It's a nice day," Torres said. "Why don't you wait outside?"

"I'll be on the loading dock," I said.

He nodded, and we went our separate ways. I was just as glad. The hairy pie of pornography is a big business with a small capital investment and a great cash flow, and freedom of the press is a fine theory, but none of it is any of my business. I waited outside, watching two black dudes hand-truck cartons into the rear of an unmarked blue van. It wasn't a nice day at all, but I didn't complain. Denver had a dose of smog as thick as L.A.'s, but I stared through the gray, dirty haze toward the Rocky Mountains as if I could see the peaks, standing like ruined cathedrals against a crystalline cobalt sky.

Randall Jackson wasn't the man with the voice inside the office. He had a wheedling whine, as unctuous as old bacon grease as he ushered the man with the voice into the back seat of a black Continental with blank silvered windows. The large dark gentleman drove it away. Then Jackson turned to me, his whine gone.

"You wanted to see me, bud?" he said. Time hadn't been kind to him. His gut had grown rounder, his hair thinner, and his legs more bowed. His wardrobe didn't help, either—a maroon blazer with electric blue slacks that sported a bright chrome stitch in the weave. His fancy loafers had a new shine and dandy tassles, but they were run-over at the heels. His name might be on the business license, but he didn't even flush the toilet without permission. "Well, what was it?" he demanded.

"I'm looking for Betty Sue Flowers," I said. I didn't think he was going to tell me anything anyway, and I knew I didn't want him to know my name, so I didn't explain anything or show him my license.

"Never heard of her," he said quickly.

"Maybe she was using another name," I said. "I've got information that you were with this girl in Oregon several years ago."

"You got shit for information, bud, I ain't never been to Oregon," he said, his tiny black eyes glittering like zircons.

"Must be the wrong Randall Jackson," I said. "Sorry to have bothered you, Mr. Jackson." Then I climbed back into the El Camino and drove away.

That was that. For now. I couldn't muscle him with a warehouseful of help watching. But he had lied to me, probably out of habit, and I intended to find out why. It had to be the hard way, though. His telephone would be unlisted, his home address in the city directory faked, and he had seen my El Camino, so I couldn't tail him in it. I had to have another car.

One of the reasons that I spend so much time driving back and forth across the country, aside from the fact that airplanes scare me spitless, is that I can't rent a car when I arrive in a strange city. I can't rent a car because I don't have any credit cards. I don't have any credit cards because I can't get one without stealing one. It's easier to steal cars. I have more experience in that line of work.

Nobody likes to talk about it because it's such a shoddy business, but private detectives spend a lot of time repossessing cars. That's how I got in the business, in fact. After my third hitch in the Army, a friend of mine got me a job on the sports desk of the Wichita *Eagle-Beacon*, which is what I did in the Army when I wasn't playing football, and since I was short of money and bored, I started moonlighting for a finance company skip-tracing and repossessing cars and stereos and furniture and televisions. When I got fired from the paper for being a lousy reporter, I headed out to San Francisco, where I hustled runaways for a year, then up to Montana, where my father had died, and took up skip-tracing and repo's as a full-time job. I had stolen lots of cars legally with court orders in my pocket, and without, and I thought I could at least borrow one in Denver without too much trouble.

I drove out to Stapleton Airport and parked in the lot farthest from the terminal, then waited for the right car, something inconspicuous in a company car preferably, driven by a tired salesman with his flight luggage in his hand. I didn't have to wait very long for the right one, and as soon as the salesman was out of sight, I lifted a brown LTD that belonged to the Hardy Industrial Towel Company. With the right tools, it only takes a minute. I was out of the lot before the salesman hiked to the terminal.

I had a supply of blank titles and a set of Alabama plates in my toolbox, plus a batch of blank repossession papers, but I didn't have time to fill any of them out, so when Jackson pulled his plum-colored Cougar into the afternoon rush-hour traffic on Santa Fe, I had to stay close but drive carefully. He made it easy, and I stayed behind him all the way back downtown to a topless place on East Colfax. Two hours later, when he stepped out of the bar into the dusk, his face inflamed with whiskey and visions of naked, dancing flesh, I stuck a revolver in his ribs, and he drove us to a cheap motel out in Aurora. We didn't even have to get out of the car.

"Okay," he admitted, "I knew her, all right. We came down here together, and I was flat busted, so I put her on the street, and she took a soliciting fall the first night. I couldn't make the fine, so she did thirty days down on the county farm."

"And then?" I said.

Jackson lit a cigarette and glanced up at the motel rooms. "After that she wouldn't have anything to do with me."

"Can't blame her, can you?"

"Guess not," he said.

"Where'd she go after that?"

"Up around Fort Collins, I heard," he said. "There's some rich lady who lives up in Poudre Canyon, and she does rehab work, you know, pulls girls out of the slam and takes them home. A real do-gooder, you know, and I heard that Betty Sue had stayed there for a while. Then I didn't hear any more."

"Nothing?"

"Nothing at all," he said.

"How come you lied to me?" I asked.

"I thought you might be some of her family," he said, "the accent and all, you know, come to get even or something."

"Even for what?" I asked.

"You know," he said, "she was just a kid." As if that explained everything.

"You shouldn't have lied," I said.

"I see that now," he said as he glanced at the .38 in my hand. "What did you have in mind up in that motel room, man?"

"Taking you apart," I said.

"That's what I figured," he said. "Hell, I thought you were going to blow me away on the street, man. You should've seen the look in your eyes. You were crazy, man."

"I'm tired," I said.

"What the hell are you looking for Betty Sue for?"

"I don't even remember," I said, then Jackson drove us back to his car. "No hard feelings," I said as he got out.

"None at all," he said, then hitched his pants and walked away.

As I drove back to the airport, it crossed my mind that it had been too easy, and I thought about going back, but I had enough trouble as it was. I parked the

145

salesman's company car near the spot where I had taken it, then picked up my own and headed north toward Fort Collins up I-25. Halfway there, my hands began to shake so badly that I had to pull into the nearest exit and off the road. I didn't think it was nerves, though. Mostly anger working its way to the surface. Jackson had been right. When I shoved the piece in his back on the street in front of the topless place, I had wanted to pull the trigger as badly as I had ever wanted anything, pull it and pull it until I had blown him all over the sidewalk. I thought about what Peggy Bain had said about me being willing to kill just to stand in line for Betty Sue. I thought about it, but the line just seemed too damned long. I crawled under the topper and locked my .38 in the toolbox, then drove on north, the mountains to the west, the vast empty stretch of the Great Plains to the east.

One summer when I was a child, after my parents separated, I had lived with my father out on the plains east of Fort Collins, north and east of a little town called Ault, during that summer, stayed with him and a short widow woman and her three little kids. He was trying to dry-farm her wheat land, and we all lived in a basement out on the plains, a basement with no house over it, where we lived in the ground like moles, looking up through the skylight, waiting for the rain that never came.

When I turned off the freeway at the Fort Collins exit, I thought about driving east to try to find the basement. I had found it once in the daylight when I was living in Boulder but I knew I would never find it in the dark. So I checked into another motel, went into another bar, had another goddamned drink.

The next day I had some luck. First, a little good luck that turned bad, then a little bad luck that turned worse.

The second probation officer I called told me where to find the right rich lady. The first one I talked to could have told me but she just didn't want to.

Selma Hinds lived in a large octagonal cabin of log and glass set on the spine of a ridge south of the Cache la Poudre River. As I drove up the canyon, I could see it sitting up there like a medieval fortress. I parked by her mailbox at the base of the ridge and changed into hiking boots, throwing longing glances at the old mine cable hoist at the side of the road, but it was for groceries and firewood. I had to trudge up the steep, winding trail for three quarters of a mile, wondering if Selma Hinds had many casual visitors or door-to-door salesmen. She didn't have a telephone, so I also wondered if she was home. If she wasn't at home, I would just have to wait, unless I wanted to walk the trail twice in one day.

Finally, sweating and sucking for air, I broke out of the scrub pine into a large clearing on the saddle of the ridge just as half a dozen dogs discovered my presence. They greeted me happily, though, especially a large three-legged black lab who stabbed me in the groin with her single front leg. The others, mostly medium-sized mutts, were content with a gale of barking.

The octagonal cabin sat on the highest point of the saddle with a large garden in the swale between it and five smaller cabins and a bank of wire cages set in the edge of the trees on the other side of the clearing. Two young girls and a boy were working in the garden among the spring planting, which was protected by sawdust and plastic sheeting, and the dry, rocky soil of the ridge had been mixed with compost until it was as black as river-bottom land. In the wire cages, small animals and birds seemed to gaze at me with the dazed eyes of hospital patients. The young people looked up from the garden but then went about their work.

A tall, smooth-faced, motherly woman with brown

hair streaked with gray stood in the doorway of the large cabin holding a big yellow cat in her arms. Her hair was tucked neatly into a bun, and she wore a long, plain dress. Even from twenty yards away, her gray eyes stared at me with a calm kindness, the sort you might expect to see in the face of a pioneer woman standing outside a soddy on the plains, a woman who had seen all the cruelty the world had to offer, had seen it and found forgiveness beyond reason or measure.

She was nothing like my mother, who was a short, pert Southern woman, bouncy and mildly desperate, somewhat giddy, slightly sad because rogue circumstance in the guise of my father had left her working below herself as an Avon lady in Moody County, Texas, but as I walked toward Selma Hinds, I felt light-headed and joyous, as if I were coming home after a long and arduous war. She smiled, and I broke into a childish grin, nearly ran to throw my arms around her, but as I stopped in front of her, something in her gaze, perhaps a slight lack of focus in her eyes, lessened the impression.

We exchanged introductions, and she invited me into her home. Inside, among the plain wooden furniture in the open cabin, a number of cats lay sleeping or walking about, switching their tails as they kept a weather eye on the dogs standing with drooping tongues and wistful faces just outside the door. As soon as Selma Hinds sat down on the couch and waved me to the opposite chair, the dogs sat too, their dark eyes watching us calmly, their frantic barking stilled.

"You have the look of a man searching for something," she said quietly, "or someone."

"A girl," I said. "Betty Sue Flowers."

"I see," she said, "and as you can see, I take in strays—the halt, the lame, the sore of foot." She paused to smooth the fur of the calico that had replaced the large yellow cat in her lap. "And the spiritually damaged too, I take them in, do what I can to restore them—rebuild the body, replenish the spirit. Those who have homes they want to return to, I provide for their trip, and those who don't I help to find a place to go, and sometimes, those who aren't able to leave, I keep by my side."

"Yes, ma'am," I said, thinking that she must be mad or way too good for this world.

"Mostly it works out that the human animals go on, and the others stay . . ." She paused again, just long enough for me to think that Betty Sue might still be here. "These are trying times for the young, and I provide a place away from the world, the violence and the drugs, a haven with a sexual king's-ex," she said.

"And Betty Sue came here?"

"Yes, for a time."

"Then she left?" I asked, confused now.

"She left her spirit among us, it walks among us even now," she said, "and her ashes are mixed with the garden soil."

"I beg your pardon?"

"She's dead, Mr. Sughrue," she said. When I didn't say anything, she added, "You seem shocked. We all must die many times."

"I don't know if I can explain that to her mother," I said.

"Tell her then that while Betty Sue was among us, she regained her innocence, restored her youth," she said. "She was happy here, she grew young again."

"I've heard it's possible," I said, still stunned, "but I've never seen it happen."

"That's a pity, sir, since it is one of life's delights to watch the young grow young again."

"What happened?" I asked, wanting to know how she died.

"She blossomed like a flower here," Selma said, misunderstanding, "she came to value herself again. If you have been searching for her for some time surely you know something about her life after she ran away from home. She came here from jail, beaten and whipped by life, fat and ugly, but once she fasted and cleansed her system of animal mucus, the compulsive eating stopped, and she grew lovely again, whole. She stayed longer than any of my charges, before or since, even though her stay was more difficult than most."

"Do you mind if I ask why?" I said.

"This isn't just a job to you, is it?"

"No, ma'am."

"You're not a member of the family, are you?"

"No, ma'am."

"I sensed both those things immediately," she said, "which made it possible to talk to you. You understand that I do not judge or criticize my charges or their life before, but when they come here, they must follow my rules or leave. No meat, no drugs, no sex. What they do when they leave is their business, and if they come back up the mountain in emotional rags, I take them in gladly, but while they are here, they must obey the rules or leave."

"And Betty Sue had trouble?"

"The boys followed her like a bitch in heat," she answered flatly, "as well they should. Betty Sue had a great capacity for love. She fended the boys off, but it was so hard for her. She seemed to need that sort of male affection—I suppose her father never gave her the sort of love she needed—but she fought it to a standstill." Then Selma paused to laugh. "She also admitted to an intense longing for red meat, but she never gave in to that desire either." The bit of light laughter seemed to bring back memories, and her gray eyes turned cloudy. "Then one afternoon in late summer," she continued, whispering so softly that I had to lean forward to hear her, "just after she had decided to leave in the fall to return to school, she drove my pickup down into town for supplies, and as she drove back, a stray dog ran in front of the truck, and she swerved to miss it, off the pavement and into the river . . ." She rose and walked to the window, the cat limp over her arm, and pointed down toward the sparkling flow. "It happened on that corner right down there."

I followed the finger's direction down the ridge to a narrow bend, a sharp curve ending in a swift green pool.

"She survived the crash but drowned," Selma said. "I am so very sorry."

"You had no way to notify her mother?" I said.

"Her mother? No. I did what I could, placed advertisements in the San Francisco papers, but Betty Sue never talked about her childhood," she said. "Never. Not a word the whole time she was here. In that, too, she was different from others who have stayed with me for a time."

"I understand," I said.

"Why do you think she wouldn't talk about her childhood?" Selma asked, her eyes damp and serious.

"I don't know," I said. "Maybe she felt like a princess stolen by peasants. I don't know."

"Children feel that way too often," she said, "it's so sad."

"I guess the trick is to take what you get for parents and try to live with it," I said lightly.

"That's very easy to say," she said, "and often very difficult to do." I understood that I had been rebuked for a lack of gravity. "Parents must make their children feel loved and wanted. If they do nothing else, they must do that, they owe at least that to their children," she said with such a brittle tone to her voice that I thought she must have been either an unwanted child or a failure as a parent. But I didn't ask.

"You had the body cremated?" I said.

151

"Graves are too sad, don't you think?" she said.

"Yeah," I said, "it's just that her mother might not like the idea—country people are sometimes funny about cremation."

"It's done," she said sharply, "and there's little to like or dislike about it now."

"Of course," I said. "You wouldn't have a snapshot of Betty Sue?" I asked, nodding toward a corkboard covered with photos. "Her mother might like a picture."

"Those are photographs of those who have found other lives after leaving," she said. "They send them back. We take no photographs here, no reminders of how they looked here to remind them of how they came to be here."

"I guess I can understand that," I said. "Do you mind if I ask why you do all this?"

"I would mind very much," she answered. "My motives are my own."

"Then I won't ask," I said, and she smiled at me. "I'm sure Mrs. Flowers would want me to thank you for your kindness and love, and I want to thank you for talking to me."

"I'm sorry to be the bearer of sad tidings," she said, then shook my offered hand. "Once, years ago, I believed that after death we moved on into some universal consciousness, some far better life than this flawed world upon which we must somehow survive, but now I know, I understand that terrible knowledge that the dead do not rise again to walk the earth, and I take no false joy in the knowledge, I simply endure it, so I am immensely sad to tell you of Betty Sue's death."

"I guess we should be glad she had some happy times here," I said, "since she was so unhappy everywhere else. You have a lovely place here."

"Thank you."

"Thank you," I said. "I'm a little old to give up

strong drink, red meat, and women all at once, but some morning you might find me curled up on your front steps," I added. "If I can make the hill."

"I'll take that as a compliment," she said as she patted my hand. "My door is always open."

"Thanks," I said. "I guess I should know the date of her death, too. Her mother will want to know."

She told me without hesitation, and I left.

Down the switchbacks of the dusty path, I walked without looking to either side, and as I drove down the sweeping curves of the canyon highway, I didn't watch the sunlight dancing on the riffles, didn't see the towers and battlements of pink rock rising above the river. I didn't stop or think or look until I reached the Larimer County Courthouse and checked the death certificates. It was there. I cursed myself for a suspicious bastard, cursed the emptiness of my success, the long drive to California before the long drive home. Then I thought about getting drunk, a black ceremonial wake, a sodden purge.

Thus did the good luck turn bad.

The bad luck turning worse came later when I stumbled back to my motel room more tired than drunk, tired of trying to get drunk without success. As I reached with my key for the lock, somebody sapped me just hard enough to drop me to my knees, to bring bright flashes of darkness, stunned me long enough to hustle me soundlessly into the room, pat me down, and shove me into a corner. When I could see, I saw the man who had been inside Jackson's office sitting relaxed in the motel chair, his large ugly associate, and another hired hand with his back against the wall as he covered me with a small silenced automatic.

"No trouble," I muttered.

"You're in no position to cause any trouble at all," the man in the chair said mildly.

"That's what I meant," I said.

"Mr. Sughrue, you have to understand that I can't allow you to treat my friends badly," he said.

"Hired help," I said.

"What?"

"Jackson's hired help," I said, "not your friend."

"Whatever, I can't have you shoving a gun down his throat and making empty threats," he said.

"Okay, I'll give it up for Lent."

"I'm afraid that won't do," he said.

"Listen," I said, "if you wanted me dead, you wouldn't be here—"

"Don't be so sure," he interrupted.

"—wouldn't be within thirty miles of here, but if you've got some misguided sense of vengeance for whatever it was I was supposed to have done to Jackson, I'm willing to take my medicine," I said as I eased up the wall, "and I'll be as quiet as I can."

"How nice," the man in the chair said.

"Nothing personal," Torres said softly as he eased a glove on his right hand.

"Nothing personal," I agreed, then took it as best I could.

They didn't seem to have their hearts in it, and I didn't resist a bit, didn't give them the slightest reason for any emotional involvement. Maybe it worked or maybe they didn't plan to hurt me too badly from the beginning. Whatever, they didn't do any permanent damage. No broken bones, no missing teeth, no ruptured spleen. I had forgotten, though, how much a professional beating hurts, and I was very glad when they stripped me, strapped me with tape, and sat me in the bathtub. I didn't know why they did it, I was just glad the hard part was over. Maybe they knew what I had planned for Jackson in the motel room in Aurora.

Before they gagged me and turned on the cold shower, the one in charge said, "Hey, buddy, you've got discipline, and I like a man with discipline. You ought to come to work for me."

"Leave your name with the desk clerk," I muttered.

"Your only problem is that you think you're both tough and smart," he said as he patted me on the cheek, "and the truth is that you're only tough because you're dumb."

"What the hell," I grunted. "I don't take orders worth a damn, either."

"Maybe you should take up another line of work," he crooned, as he held up the photostat of my license.

"Is that an order?"

"You never quit, do you?" he said laughing. "I hope this was worth it, you know, hope you found the chick you were hassling Jackson about."

"She's dead," I said. "She's been dead for nearly five years. It was a waste of time."

"Too bad," he said, then laughed again. "Just be thankful that you didn't hurt my friend and be thankful that I'm in a good mood."

"I am," I said.

Then his associates gagged me with a sock. I was thankful that it was clean, thankful that after they left I was able to shove the water control off with my foot, and thankful too that when the maid came in the next morning, she jerked the sock out of my mouth instead of screaming. I had no idea how I might begin to explain my condition to the police. I tipped the maid and told her to tell the desk that I would be staying over another day. I needed the rest.

11 ••••

"It's just not true," Rosie said for the fifth time.

"I'm sorry," I repeated, "but I saw the death certificate and talked to the woman she was living with who saw the body. I'm sorry, but that's the way it is."

"No," she said, and struck herself between the breasts, a hard, hollow blow that brought tears to her eyes. "Don't you think I'd know in here if my baby girl had been dead all these years?"

It was an early afternoon again in Rosie's, soft, dusty shadows cool inside, and outside a balmy spring day of gentle winds and sunshine. Even the distant buzz of the traffic seemed pleasant, like the hum of bees working a field of newly blossomed clover. After a quick visit to the emergency room for an X-ray and some painkiller, I had left Fort Collins and driven straight through on a diet of speed, codeine, beer, and Big Macs, and had arrived at Rosie's dirty, unshaved, and drunk. My nerves felt as if their sheaths had been lined with grit and my guts with broken glass. Even bearing good news, I wouldn't have looked like a messenger from the gods, and with bad tidings, I was clearly an aged delivery boy from Hell's Western Union. I looked so bad that Oney hadn't even asked me to sign the cast on his foot, and Lester expressed real concern. He even offered to buy me a beer. Fireball woke up long enough to slobber all over my pants, but when I didn't give him any beer, he slunk over behind the door. Rosie wouldn't look at me, though, not when I came in, not even when I told her the news.

"I'm sorry," I said again, "but she's dead."

"Don't say that anymore," she said, not pausing as she furiously wiped off the bar one more time.

"She is," I said, "and you'll have to accept it."

Finally, she stopped cleaning and looked at me. "Get out. Just get out."

"What?"

"Out of here," she said softly. "Get out."

"Aw now, Rosie . . ." Lester began, but she turned on him.

"You just shut your damned mouth, you worthless bastard. And get out. All of you get out. Especially you." She pointed an angry finger at my face.

"I'll get out, all right," I said, then threw her eighty-seven dollars on the bar, "but you take your damned money back."

"You keep it," she said, her voice as flat and hard as a stove lid. "You earned it, you keep it."

"You damned right I earned it," I said as I picked it back up. "I've been lied to, run around, and beat up, by god, and I've driven four thousand goddamned miles and I'm still twelve hundred from home, and you're damned right I earned it."

"Nobody asked nothin' extra of you, so don't come whinin' to me," she said. She couldn't look at me, though. Her eyes faded to a brittle, metallic gray, like chips of slate. "Just get the hell away from me."

"I'm going," I said.

"And take that damned worthless dog with you too," she added. "He ain't been worth killin' since you brought him back."

I snapped my fingers and Fireball woke up and followed me out the door. Lester and Oney had beat us outside, and they were walking in aimless circles like children during a school fire drill.

"Woman's got a temper on her," Lester said, shaking his head.

"She's got some grieving to do," I said as I walked toward my pickup.

"Where're you headed?" he asked.

"Home," I answered, as if I knew where that was.

Home? Home is Moody County down in South Texas, where the blackland plain washes up against the caliche hills and the lightning cuts of the arroyos in the Brasada, the brush country. But I never go there anymore. Home is my apartment on the east side of Hell-Roaring Creek, three rooms where I have to open the closets and drawers to be sure I'm in the right place. Home? Try a motel bar at eleven o'clock on a Sunday night, my silence shared by a pretty barmaid who thinks I'm a creep and some asshole in a plastic jacket who thinks I'm his buddy. Like I told Trahearne, home is where you hang your hangover. For folks like me, anyway. Sometimes. Other times home is my five acres up beyond Polebridge on the North Fork, thirty-nine dirtroad miles north of Columbia Falls and the nearest bar, ten miles south of the Canadian border. There's an unfinished cabin there, a foundation and subflooring and a rock fireplace, and wherever home might be, I had been up on the North Fork for a week or so when Trahearne found me.

I was working. On my tan and my late afternoon buzz. It had been a dry spring, and I saw the plume of dust rising like a column of smoke ten minutes before I saw the VW beetle convertible that had caused it as it charged through the chugholes like a midget tank. It skidded into my road and braked to a stop about six inches from a stack of stripped logs. Through the beige fog of dust, Trahearne looked like a man wearing a bathtub that was too small for his butt.

"What the hell is that?" I asked as he pried himself from behind the wheel.

"Melinda's idea of transportation," he grumbled. "My car's in the body shop."

"Well, listen, old man, the next time you come up the road raising a cloud of dust like that," I said, "one of the natives is liable to shoot holes in the poor beast until it's dead."

"Spare me your country witticisms, Sughrue," he said as he pounded dust from his khakies like a cowhand after a long drive. "Where the hell have you been?" he demanded.

"Here and there," I said.

"You're the devil to find," he said.

"I wasn't hiding," I said. "You just don't know how to look."

"Cut that crap," he said. He hadn't shaved or changed clothes in several days, and he still limped, but he seemed reasonably sober.

"What's happening?"

"Not a thing," he growled as he sat down on my steps and struck a kitchen match on the subflooring, "not a damned thing, and since you do nothing as well as anybody I know, I thought we could do it together. It's not as dangerous or boring as when I do it alone."

"Is that a compliment or an insult?"

"Just give me a beer and shut up," he said, and I pitched him a can from the cooler I had been using as a footstool. "So what are you doing?" he asked out of a billow of beer foam and cigar smoke.

"Working on my retirement home."

"Nice place you've got here," he said, looking around.

"Thanks," I said. "I like it better than cheap irony."

Actually, I liked it far better than that—enough so

159

that finishing it seemed redundant. I had built the foundation and subflooring three summers before, and had helped with the fireplace and the chimney base the summer after that. Instead of walls and a roof, though, I had erected a wooden-framed surplus officer's tent that faced the fireplace. Beyond the missing front wall, a small pine grove caught some of the road dust, and beyond the North Fork road, a range of soft, low mountains partially blocked the western sky. To the north, Red Meadows Creek scattered across a grassy flat, then gathered itself to plunge through a large culvert and on into the spring-thaw swollen waters of the North Fork. Across the river to the east, the towering spires of the peaks in Glacier Park rose into a sky as pristinely blue as an angel's eye. To the south, however, the view, mundane on the best of days, was sullied by the dirty haze that still roiled and billowed in the road thermals.

"I guess it's all right," Trahearne allowed, "but there's no place to hang the Mondrian." Then he chuckled and finished his beer.

"Abstract painting gives me—"

"Goddamn it," he interrupted, "can I hole up here for a few days?"

"Be my guest," I said.

"That's what I had in mind," he said. "Thanks." He sat, waiting for me to ask him why, but when I didn't he told me anyway. Trahearne was dependable that way. "Nothing was happening at home. I couldn't work. Not a lick. Goddamn it, sometimes I wonder if I haven't topped the last good woman, had the last good drink out of the bottle, and written the last good line, you know, and I can't seem to remember when it happened, can't remember at all." He glanced up at me, tears brimming his bleary eyes. "I can't remember when it happened, where it went."

"Try to relax," I said.

"Don't give me my own lines."

"You shouldn't have given it to me in the first place," I said, as I pitched him another beer.

"You can be a real bastard, can't you?" he muttered, his trembling fingers struggling with the pull tab.

"Want me to open that for you, old man?"

"I guess that's why I came," he said, smiling suddenly and brushing at his tears with fingers as thick as sausages, "for the quality of the sympathy. It's got a sharp edge on it here, Sughrue, and I can deal with that." He sounded like a man who got more sympathy than he wanted at home, but I wasn't about to say that. He did it for me anyway. "I just can't stand all that damned solicitude. It's as if she was an intensive-care nurse and I was about to croak." Then he paused. "I always go back to work eventually," he said. "I just haven't found the right moment yet."

Since I didn't have anything to say, he finally shut up, and we sat around enjoying the silence. A light wind rustled the lodgepole pines, clearing the road dust, and behind us the river roared mightily in its stony course. The afternoon drifted slowly toward dusk, lingering like wisps of feather ash in the air, and Fireball returned from his afternoon explorations, trotting down the road like a man returning from a serious mission. He nosed Trahearne's ankle, and the big man leapt up.

"What the hell's he doing here?"

"Rosie said we had ruined him for polite company," I answered.

"You've been back to California?"

"There and other places," I said. "I've been on the road so much I think I've worn out my ass."

"Looks like you've done considerable damage to some other parts, too," he said, nodding toward the yellowed bruises on my abdomen. I hadn't been working on my tan hard enough to hide them.

"I took second-best in a political discussion in Pinedale, Wyoming," I lied. I still didn't know what to think about the beating, and even if I had known, I didn't want to talk about it.

"Did you find Rosie's daughter?" he asked as he rummaged through the ice for another beer.

"Found out that she died some years ago," I said.

"How?"

"Drowned after a car wreck."

"That's too bad," he said. "How'd Rosie take it?"

"She ran me off her place," I said.

"Why?"

"She didn't believe me," I said.

"Why not?"

"Said she knew in her heart that her daughter was still alive," I said. "But I checked the death certificate and talked to a woman who identified the body."

"That's too bad," he said again.

"Runaways get killed all the time," I said. "For every three or four I find, one will be toes-up on a slab. Running away is not a good life. At least Rosie's daughter had six good months before she died." I stood up and struck a match and dropped it into the logs laid in the fireplace. The kerosene-soaked sawdust caught swiftly, and the logs began to crackle. Instead of a cheery fire, though, it seemed too much like a funeral pyre. "Six good months," I repeated.

"Sometimes I think I'd give up the rest of my life for six good months," he said softly.

"It doesn't work that way."

The flames rose without smoke, sparks flaring up the stubby chimney and into the velvet night waiting to the east.

Trahearne stayed sober that night, easing by on slow beers, and the next day he stayed dry. The third morning he limped the five miles down and back to the

Polebridge store to buy of box of pencils and a Big Chief school tablet. The fourth morning he went to work at the picnic table beside the tent. After that, for more than a week, our days and nights became as orderly and measured as the rising and falling of the sun, the gentle waxing and waning of the fickle moon.

In the mornings, I jogged up the North Fork road, heading for the border and dodging logging trucks. I never made it, of course, but the walk back was always nice. Until I stopped at the creek for a heart-stopping plunge into the shallow pool below the culvert. When I got back to the cabin, Trahearne would close his tablet, boil another pot of cowboy coffee and fix breakfast on a Coleman stove while I sat on the steps with a cup of coffee and my first cigarette of the day, coughing and spitting up phlegm and what felt like scraps of lung tissue.

One morning as he stroked a fluffy pile of scrambled eggs in the skillet, he asked, "What's all that running about?"

"It makes me feel so good." I choked, then coughed and spit again.

"Boy, I guess I'm the lucky one," he said, grinning.

"Why's that?"

"I can feel like shit without doing all that work," he said, then laughed like a man full of himself and empty of cares.

In the afternoons and evenings, we talked about things—our wars, our runaway fathers, the nature of things—then we crawled into sleeping bags to wait for the next day, wait for it to begin all over again.

Then one morning I came back to find a note nailed to the steps. *Sorry,* it read. *Back in a few days.* I thought about the bars myself but went fishing instead.

Two nights later, about three A.M., he roared back, crunched the right front fender of the VW on the pile of logs, then stumbled into bed, muttering about his life and hard times. I acted like a dead man until he finally went to sleep. He stayed in bed the next day, rising only to piss, guzzle water, and gobble aspirins and Rolaids. The next day he wasted bitching about the weather: it was too nice to suit him. Then he went back to work.

This time he only lasted four days. On the fifth morning, when I showed up dripping cold water, he had the whiskey bottle sitting on the tablet like a child's dare. In the fireplace wads of crumpled paper huddled like the scat of some odd nocturnal beast.

"How long do you think you can stand this goddamned solitude?" he asked peevishly as he splashed Wild Turkey into his cup.

"What solitude is that?"

"Goddamn it, Sughrue, has anybody ever talked to you about your hospitality?"

"Never twice," I said.

As I dried on a dirty sweat shirt, he grunted to his feet and huffed over to the VW convertible, then raced away on a cloud of dust. Perhaps the same one he had ridden in upon.

That evening, as I used the scraps of poetic paper to start a fire, I found one that seemed longer than the others, and I smoothed it out on the table.

It read:

Once you flew sleeping in sunshine, amber limbs
locked in flight. Now you lie there rocky
still beyond the black chop, your chains
blue light. Dark water holds you
down. Whales sound deep into the glacier's
trace, tender flukes tease your hair,
your eyes dream silver scales.

                        Lie still,
wait. This long summer must break before

endless winter returns with tombstone glaciers
singing ice.

> I will not mourn.

When next the world rises warm, men will chip
arrowheads from your heart . . .

His large, childish scrawl raced across the page,
breaking at times into an almost indecipherable frenzy.
I didn't know what he meant by the poem, but the
handwriting was that of an insane child. For a moment,
I felt sorry for him. I folded the poem and slipped it
into my wallet. It seemed mannered and stilted to me,
but for reasons I wouldn't think about, I wanted to
keep it.

Later that evening, I took a tin cup full of his whiskey
down by the river. A new moon burnished the rough
waters. The river was rotten with the stink of old snow,
cold and brackish green, roaring like a runaway freight,
an avalanche of molten snow.

Once, when I summered with my father in that
basement on the Colorado plains, he had come home
drunk and awakened me to take me to see my first
snow. He lashed me behind him on his motorcycle, an
old surplus Harley with a suicide shift, and drove across
the midnight plains toward the mountains, flying as if
he were being pursued by fiends, the rear wheel spitting
gravel on the twisting curves. He found snow, finally,
on the northern face of a cut bank, and he stopped and
we took off our clothes under a slice of moon to bath in
the snow. He meant something mystic, I think, but like
me, he was a flatlander who had grown up without
knowing snow, and within minutes the two of us were
engaged in a furious snowball fight, laughing and
screaming at the stars, wrestling in the shallow skim of
frozen snow. On the way home, tied once more to his
back with baling twine, I slept, my cold skin like fire,
and dreamed of blizzards and frozen lakes, a landscape

sheathed in ice, but I was warm somehow, wrapped in the furs of bears and beaver and lynx, dreaming of ice as the motorcycle split the night.

As I thought of that and sipped the smoky whiskey, I heard Trahearne return, more slowly than he had departed. He parked by the cabin and left the engine running, grinding like teeth in the darkness, as he gathered his gear, stumbling about like a drunken bear. I waited by the river until I heard his car door slam, then I walked back to the cabin. He drove away slowly, jammed into the tiny car, slow and almost stately, like a funeral barge loosed on a black, deep-flowing, silent river. The embers of his taillights grew pale in the dust.

It wasn't until the next morning that I missed the bulldog.

12 ●●●●

I DROVE BACK DOWN TO MERIWETHER THE NEXT DAY, AND for lack of anything better to do, I went back to work. One midnight repossession up on the reservation, some lackadaisical collection work, and a divorce case so sordid that I checked my bank account and found it still fat with Catherine Trahearne's money. I shut down the operation, closed my office, and told the answering service that I was unavailable, out of town on a big case, then I spent a few easy days and nights playing two-dollar poker and staring at the remains of my face in barroom mirrors. In the right light, I could pass for forty, though I was a couple of years younger than that. I stayed fairly sober and faintly sane, and although the highway called to me several times, I stayed in town. Then a bartender out at the Red Baron had to take off for his mother's funeral over in Billings, so I filled in for him.

When I first moved to Meriwether, and for years before, the Red Baron had been a fine working and drinking man's bar called the Elbow Room, the sort of place where the bartender comes out into the parking lot at seven A.M. to wake up the drunks sleeping in their cars, then helps them inside, and buys the first drink. The Elbow Room didn't have a jukebox or a pool table or a pinball machine. Just a television set for the games and an honest shot of whiskey for the watchers. Then one summer old man Unbehagen died in his sleep a few weeks after I had come into the possession of a bundle of very hot cash, so hot nobody would claim it. So I went in with the Schaffer twins as a silent partner, and we bought the license and premises. Unfortunately, the Schaffer boys were as loud and ambitious as I was silent and outvoted. They took my favorite bar and turned it into a business, a topless-dancer, pool, and pinball success. Since I was tied to the hot money, I couldn't even raise my voice in silent protest. I took my cut and kept my mouth shut.

On Monday nights the Baron was the scene of amateur topless dancing, feckless young ladies exposing their mediocre bodies with enthusiasm in place of talent to a horde of young men driven quite mad by the mere idea of amateurism. The middle of the week was devoted to straight semi-pro tits and ass, and the maniacs usually settled into a dull roar, broken by the occasional drunken fistfight. Friday and Saturday nights were given over to heavy metal rock or bluegrass and free-form boogie, but Sundays were, thankfully, a day of rest from the reckless abandon of entertainment. On Sunday night, the drinkers had to have their own fun, and the place was usually as quiet as a graveyard.

Catherine Trahearne could have come in on a Sunday night, but she didn't. It had to be Monday. When she came in the vinyl-padded door that night, she looked as out of place as a chicken in church, but she walked directly to the bar and stood behind a group of flushed and shame-faced young men until they cleared a space for her. Dressed in wool and leather—soft beige slacks, a dark cashmere pullover, and a deerskin vest—she looked even better than she had in a tennis dress. The dark umber tones of her clear skin hinted at sultry, mysterious nights, and her slim, athletic body promised to fulfill the hints. Whatever women were supposed to lose in their early fifties, she hadn't lost it yet. Not a bit of it. A hunk of polished but uncut turquoise as large and roughly the same shape as a shark's tooth dangled from a heavy silver chain between her breasts.

When she sat down at the bar, she took out a cigarette, and I leaped to light it for her. She stared over my shoulder toward the stage, where Boom-Boom, our resident amateur heavy-weight, lifted her shift to reveal breasts as large and round as a bald man's head with a screaming giggle that should have shattered glassware. As always, the crowd exploded into hoots and cheers, table-thumping fists and whistles. In her real life, Boom-Boom was an improbably demure barmaid, but on Monday nights she came out and killed them. Catherine smiled at the furor, seemingly with honest amusement. I ignored the shrill pleas of the topless dancers doubling as cocktail waitresses, ignored the bar customers, and asked her if she wanted a drink.

"What an odd way to make a living," she said, then blew out the match before it burnt my fingers.

"She's an amateur," I said.

"But joyously enthusiastic, don't you think?" she said, staring into my eyes with a steady gaze that reminded me of how I had felt when she told me she had to take a shower the first time I met her. To get away from the gaze, I glanced over my shoulder. Boom-Boom was having a hell of a time, and I felt like a cretin for not having noticed before. "Actually, though, I was talking about your new line of endeavor, Mr. Sughrue."

"Just filling in for a sick friend, Mrs. Trahearne."

"Catherine," she commanded softly.

"C.W.," I said.

169

"What do the initials stand for?" she asked, smiling.

"Chauncey Wayne," I confessed.

"C.W. will do fine," she said, then laughed.

"Would you like a drink?"

"Actually, I'm here on business," she said. "But it could be conducted over a drink. Later, perhaps? Someplace more conducive to conversation?"

"Where are you staying?"

"The Thunderbird."

"They've got a quiet piano bar," I said, "and I could meet you around midnight. If that isn't too late?"

"Not at all," she said, "it's a date." Then she extended her slim hand. Her nails were painted a dark, dusky red that matched her lips and picked up the tones of her skin and hair. When I shook it, she held my hand and focused her bright green eyes on mine until I nearly blushed. "Trahearne is quite fond of you," she said, "and I hope we can be friends." I had heard that before; all Trahearne's women wanted to be friends of mine. Catherine gave me an expensive smile and left. As she walked out, even the dumbest, drunkest of the kids turned away from Boom-Boom's mighty breasts to watch Catherine's delicately switching hips.

In the rosy, diffuse light of the piano bar, she looked even better. She could have passed for thirty. A great thirty. And she damn well knew it. After we had settled into a plush booth with our drinks, she went to work on me with the wise eyes, the slightly amused smile, and more random body contact than the law allows in public places.

"Thank you for coming," she whispered.

"You said something about business," I said nervously as I finished my drink before the cocktail waitress walked back to the bar. As much as I had enjoyed the first trip, I didn't feel up to chasing Trahearne around

Western America just yet, and I certainly didn't want to mess around with his ex-wife.

"Yes, I have a small complaint about how you handled the recovery of my ex-husband," she said with mock seriousness.

"What's that?"

"When you called from the hospital," she said, "you told me a little white lie about Trahearne's accident which we won't even bother to discuss, but now I want a full report into all the lurid details of his latest odyssey."

"Right," I said. It seemed odd that Trahearne's ex-wife seemed to know more about what had happened than his present wife did. I assumed that he didn't care if I told Catherine. "What do you want to know?"

"Everything," she answered sweetly. "Where he went, how you found him, how he came to be wounded in the butt. All the sordid details." She sipped her vermouth. "I've always wanted to know exactly what transpired on one of his trips," she continued, "but his versions were already literature by the time he returned, and none of the other gentlemen I hired were able to either find him or provide me with the details. They seemed to lack both intelligence and imagination. Are most of the members of your profession as pedestrian as those I've done business with in the past?"

"This may sound strange," I said, "but the only other private investigator I know is my ex-partner here in town, and he's an even worse drunk than I am. I know PI's have conventions, but I've never been to one. They're all about electronics and industrial security and crap like that. I just repossess cars and chase runaways and follow cheating husbands, stuff like that."

"You don't sound very ambitious," she said.

"I'm not," I said, "not about anything. I spent nine years in the Army in three separate hitches, mostly playing football or sitting in a gym or writing sports stories for post newspapers, and I spent four years playing football for three different junior colleges under two different names, and I got in this business strictly by accident, so I'm not Johnny Quest or the moral arbiter of the Western world. More like a second-rate hired gun or a first-rate saddle tramp."

"A classic underachiever?" she said.

"Classic bindle-stiff, apple-knocker, pea-pickin' bum," I said.

"But still you found Trahearne," she said, "and you must tell me about it."

As I told her what I thought she wanted to hear, she moved closer, occasionally smiled and touched my hand with her fingers, then our hips and thighs were nudging each other, and her nails drifting across my wrist. When I finished, she told me to tell the rest of it now, and she laughed and held my hand as I filled in the gaps. When I finished the second time, she hugged my arm against her breast.

"How simply delightful," she said.

"Hey," I said, trying to make a joke of it, "you're going to have to turn it down a few notches."

She didn't play coy at all, just laughed openly, the tones ringing crystal through the cozy bar like vesper bells chiming in a pastoral dusk.

"Don't be so serious," she said. "I won't attack you."

"Damn it," somebody using my voice complained. I knew better than to fool around with the ex-wives of friends, and for all our troubles, Trahearne had become a friend. But I said it again anyway, "Damn it." And Catherine lifted my hand to touch a flattened knuckle with her lips. Damned if I wasn't as spooky as a sixteen-year-old kid as I followed her out of the lounge.

Afterward, as we lay on her motel bed, my hand resting on the taut muscles of her thigh, I asked her, "Is this what you drove down for?"

"Flew," she said, and laughed. "I flew down by way of Seattle. I'm supposed to be visiting friends there. This is what I came for, yes, and I would have walked."

"Why?"

"Please don't be shocked when I tell you this," she said, pausing to light two cigarettes, "and please remember that I might have chosen you anyway. I work like the very devil keeping this aged body intact, and I endure yearly humiliations at the hands of expensive plastic surgeons so I can enjoy my declining years. You see, I sleep with whomever pleases me" —she paused again and her voice grew hard—"especially Trahearne's friends. Do you mind?"

"Well, it makes me feel a little like I've been rutting in the old man's track," I said, thinking about the skinny whore in the desert, "but it's a damn fine track. So I guess I don't mind."

"Thank you," she said. "I've only a few more years before I become withered and old—don't interrupt me—and I have a great many lonely years to recover."

She stopped to look at me. I watched the cigarette smoke drift across the shadowed ceiling in mare's tails.

"You're not curious about my motives?" she asked, her fingernails lightly plucking at the hair on my chest.

"Nope."

"I thought detectives were endlessly curious," she said.

"Only in the movies."

After another long silence, she said, "It's odd, you know."

"What?"

"I almost never explain my actions to anyone," she murmured, "but since you didn't ask, I feel somehow obligated to tell you."

"Old Chinese interrogation tactic," I said, and she chuckled and slapped me on the belly.

"Be serious," she said, still chuckling. "I'm about to tell you the story of my life."

"Okay."

"We met during the war, you see," she said as she leaned over to stub her cigarette out. "I was still a child, only eighteen, but already widowed. My first husband was one of those smart young men from Carmel who stabled his polo ponies and dashed off to join the RCAF, visions of the Lafayette Escadrille dancing in his head. In the excitement of his departure, he took my virginity, then with a burst of daylight remorse he drove us up to Reno, where he made an honest woman of me. Six months later, his Spitfire went down into the Channel during Dunkirk. It was like something out of a novel at the time, and I suppose it still seems that way to me.

"Then I met Trahearne, and it seemed like the next scene," she continued. "To the horror of everyone concerned, I married him still wearing widow's weeds, then sent him too off to the war."

"You're the woman on the bridge," I whispered.

"Oh, he told you that absurd story too," she said. "I didn't know what it all meant to him, but something inside me knew what to do."

"I wonder who the woman in the window was," I said absently.

"His mother, of course," Catherine answered softly.

"Jesus Christ," I said, then sat up and fumbled for another cigarette. "That's why I'm not curious," I said. "I find out too many things I don't want to know as it is. Jesus Christ."

"I don't suppose it was that terrible," she chided me. "And it was such a long time ago. Trahearne only acts as if it was so important because he's never been able to write about it."

"Let's get back to the war," I said, "something I can understand."

"Four long years of wretched fidelity," she said, "then another fifteen years while he worked out his guilt because I could be faithful and he simply couldn't. I don't think I minded his whoring, you know, not nearly so much as I minded his guilty rages of which I was the object of hatred. It wasn't an easy life at all." She took my cigarette from me. "One day two years ago he called from Sun Valley to tell me that he was divorcing me. I wasn't surprised; he had done that sort of thing before. This time, though, he went through with it, and let me tell you, he paid dearly for it. I stripped him, as he said, like a grizzly strips a salmon, left him wearing fish eyes and bones. That might have been enough to bring him back, but he had already remarried before he realized just how badly I had taken him. Now he has a wife who is as recklessly unfaithful as he is, so he doesn't have to feel guilty anymore, and he hasn't written a word worth keeping in two years. It's driving him quite mad, I suspect."

"And you're living with his mother," I said in amazement.

"Edna was quite kind to me during all those years," Catherine said, "and it was the least I could do. She was more like a mother than my own had been, and living with her, I can keep an eye on Trahearne. I have my freedom now, more money than I can possibly spend before I die, and I also have my revenge." She paused and rolled over to hold me, saying, "Don't let them tell you that revenge isn't sweet, either."

"You still love the old fart," I said.

"Of course," she said as she straddled my hips, "but I love this, too. You don't mind, do you?"

The complications and confusion worried me a bit, but Catherine was a sweet and loving woman, her passion fired by the years when she had kept it banked, and during the night I didn't seem to mind at all. The next morning, though, when she checked out of her motel and moved her bags into my apartment, I had a few doubts. We laid those to rest, though, for the next three days. She cooked a better breakfast than Trahearne and she was easier to get along with, but I had to admit that I was relieved when she announced that she had to fly back to Seattle, then home. It wasn't until we were standing in the airport terminal that I realized how much I was going to miss her.

"Somehow, this stopped being a weekend fling," I said as we watched the passengers disembark from her flight.

"I know, I know," she said, squeezing my hand angrily. "It sounds so terribly trite, but I wish I had met you twenty years ago. It's not only trite, it's a lie. Thirty years ago would be closer to the mark, and you didn't have your first pair of long pants yet."

"I was born an old man," I said, but she ignored me.

"You or somebody like you might have saved me from this damned emotional martyrdom I seem to have chosen," she said bitterly. Then it was time to go, and she presented me with a tilted cheek for a matronly goodbye kiss. "We'll pretend you were some anonymous lover I picked up in a cocktail lounge," she said.

"Whatever you say."

"This is goodbye," she said, then tilted her cheek toward me again.

"To hell with that," I said as I grabbed her shoulders and kissed her on the mouth so hard that it blurred the careful lines of her lips, mussed her hair, and made her drop her carry-on bag.

"You bastard," she muttered when she caught her breath and picked up her bag. A blush rose up her slender neck like a flame, touching her cheeks with umber sweetly burnt. She reached up to wipe my mouth, repeating, "You bastard. That was the last one." Then she walked through the security check and boarded the airplane without glancing back.

As she climbed the steps, I swallowed some dumb pain and walked away too.

Nobody lives forever, nobody stays young long enough. My past seemed like so much excess baggage, my future a series of long goodbyes, my present an empty flask, the last good drink already bitter on my tongue. She still loved Trahearne, still maintained her secret fidelity as if it were a miniature Japanese pine, as tiny and perfect as a porcelain cup, lost in the dark and tangled corner of a once-formal garden gone finally to seed.

After she left, I wandered around in a dull haze for days, telling myself what an idiot I was, trying to swallow with measured amounts of whiskey the stone in my chest. It was June in Montana, high enough up the steps of the northern latitudes to pass for cruel April. Blue skies ruled stupidly, green mountains shimmered like mirages, and the sun rose each morning to stare into my face with the blank but touching gaze of a lovely retarded child. I drove down to Elko to try to find a landscape to suit my mood, but the desert had bloomed with a spring rain and the nights were cool and ringing with stars. I put Rosie's eighty-seven dollars in a dollar slot machine and hit a five-hundred-dollar jackpot. Then I fled to the most depressing place in the West, the Salt Lake City bus terminal, where I drank Four Roses from a pint bottle wrapped in a paper bag. I couldn't even get arrested, so I headed up to Pocatello to guzzle Coors like a pig at a trough with a gang of jack Mormons, thinking I could pick a fight, but I didn't have the heart for it. Eventually, none the worse for wear, I drifted north toward Meriwether like a saddle tramp looking for a spring roundup.

13 ••••

ONE OF THE ADVANTAGES OF MY BUSINESS WAS THAT IT didn't leave me much inclined to mourn lost loves too long. Back in town, I worked a couple of divorces and repossessed a few televisions from households where domestic strife was the commodity of exchange. It worked like a charm. My cynicism restored itself, and my bank account remained flush. Then Trahearne called one afternoon.

"Hey, I'm sorry I left the cabin in such a snit," he said.

"Looked more like a funky blue huff," I said.

"Always with the jokes, Sughrue," he complained. "When are you coming up to get your damned dog?"

"My dog?" I said. "You stole him, old man, you bring him back."

"Not a chance. I'm at home for as long as I can manage it," he said.

"How's Fireball?"

"Last time I saw him, he was the bull of the woods around here."

"The last time?"

"Yeah, he took to Melinda like a long lost brother," he said, "and they're off on a little trip. You know how Fireball likes to travel."

"In style," I said. "If she's down this way, maybe she could drop him off."

"Be too far out of her way," he said too quickly.

"You don't know where she is, do you?"

"Not exactly, no," he said, "but it's okay."

"Want me to go looking for her?"

"She's not lost."

"Neither were you," I said, "but I found you anyway."

"Yeah, thanks," he said. Over the telephone, his sneer sounded like the snort of a wounded cape buffalo. "What's the matter? Are you getting bored down there?"

"I was born bored."

"Well, hell, drive up and help me stay dry," he said. He almost sounded serious.

"Isn't that like the halt leading the lame or something like that?"

"I'm doing pretty good on my own," he said. "I'm just about ready to go back to work."

"Your public's waiting with bated breath," I said. "Hey, you're a literary type—what the hell's that mean?"

"How should I know? Maybe it just sounds good."

"Great," I said. "Give me a call when she comes back with my dog, and I'll drive up for a weekend."

"All right," he said cheerfully.

Then we chatted aimlessly about the weather and the fishing we intended to do—all the assorted foolishness that keeps Ma Bell whistling a happy tune. It wasn't until we had hung up that I thought of Catherine, which I assumed meant that I was cured. As they say, I heaved a sigh of relief. When I tell folks that I've never been married, I neglect to mention the fact that I've been engaged about forty times.

Once I decided that I had stopped moping about,

though, my foot started itching so badly that I had to take my boot off. I scratched it furiously, but the itch went deeper than I could reach with anything but five hundred road miles. I got back on the horn and called every bailbondsman I knew, but nobody had any jumpers to chase. Then I tried all the usual things—walking around my tiny office, three steps one way, four the other. I got a glass and tried to listen to the marriage counselor next door, but the aluminum walls didn't do much for vocal reproduction. My office is in a double-wide trailer house that I share with the marriage counselor, who gives me a lot of business, and two shady real-estate salesmen. None of my neighbors were known for their conversational versatility, so I moved the plastic drapes to look at my view. How long can you stare across an alley at a battered Demster Dumpster behind a discount store, though. I thought about going out to talk to the current inept secretary I shared with my neighbors, but she buzzed me before I could leave.

"You have a call," she said.

"Who is it?"

"Long distance," she crooned.

"Ol' long calls a lot," I said.

"Sir?"

"Nothing," I said. "If it's not collect, put them on."

"Oops," she muttered. "I'm sorry, sir, but we seem to have been disconnected." Which meant she had forgotten how to use the hold button again. "Maybe the party will call back."

"Hope so."

The party did. It was Rosie. Before I could say hello, she said, "I tol' you she wasn't dead."

"You told me," I answered. The itch raced up my leg and burrowed under the skin between my shoulder blades. "What happened?"

"Jimmy Joe called me and said he got a picture

180

postcard from her this morning," she said, "mailed from Denver."

"Was he sure it was her handwriting?"

"It had to be," Rosie said. "Who'd be playing a mean trick like that?"

"I don't know," I said.

"He read it to me and it sounded like Betty Sue," she added.

"You haven't heard from her in ten years," I said. "How would you know what she sounds like?"

"I just know," she said.

"I'll be damned."

"Don't be down on yourself, C.W., anybody can make a mistake," she said. "How much would you charge to go down to talk to that lady who said my baby girl was dead and in her grave?"

"Not a cent," I said.

"Now, don't be that way," she said.

"Okay, I'll send you a bill. If I find anything," I said. "You can do me a favor, though."

"What's that?"

"Call your ex-husband back and ask him to send me the postcard general delivery in Fort Collins, Colorado, okay?"

"Good as done."

"I'll call you in a couple of days," I said.

"If you should just happen to find her, just tell her she don't have to come home or nothing," Rosie pleaded. "Just ask her to call me collect. That's all. Just hearing her voice would be more than enough."

"Okay."

"Say," she said, "how's that worthless bulldog doing?"

"He's doing fine," I said, "but he's homesick. I thought I might tote him back down that way sometime. If you'd like me to."

"I guess I would at that," she said. "And, say, I'm terrible sorry for the way I talked to you before . . . when . . ."

"Don't worry about it," I said. "Take care."

"You too, son."

Within the hour, I had the El Camino packed and headed out for Colorado.

During the fourteen-hour trip, I had plenty of time to think about things, this all-too-convenient postcard and the beating I had suffered on my last trip to Colorado, but nothing made any sense. Even if I had had fourteen years instead of fourteen hours, I probably wouldn't have worked it out. That's not how I work. My ex-partner once found me in a bar puzzling over a contorted divorce case that had me completely baffled—I couldn't find out who was doing what to whom—and he advised me to forget about thinking and to get my ass out on the street and put my hands on somebody. He was drunk, of course, but drunk or sober, he was a hell of a divorce detective.

But I was on the road, instead of the street, and didn't have any idea who to put my hands on. Either Selma Hinds had lied, for reasons that made no sense, or somebody had lied to her, which made even less sense. If she had lied and wanted to keep on lying, my hands were tied. Unlike Jackson, Selma Hinds was a proper citizen, and if I laid a finger on her, she would scream for the laws, and I would probably end up in the slammer down in Canon City doing twenty to life. I didn't know what was going on, didn't understand a bit of it, didn't like any of it. Maybe that's why the first thing I packed was my guns. If your brain won't work, wave a gun around. Sometimes that helps.

As it turned out, though, all the worry and thought was wasted. When I pulled off the Poudre Canyon highway at Selma Hinds' trailhead, I parked behind a red Volkswagen convertible with Montana plates and a crunched right fender. At first, I wondered what the hell Melinda Trahearne was doing up at Selma's, then I wondered why I had been so blind and dumb. That crazy, goddamned Trahearne had been leading me around by the nose from the moment I had found him in Rosie's. Maybe even before that, which would explain that long insane jaunt through the bars, explain why he had been so easy to follow and so hard to find, why he waited at Rosie's. He wanted me to look for Betty Sue Flowers, wanted me to nose around in her past, like a hungry dog turning up the buried bones and ripe flesh of her life so he could have an excuse for the bitter taste in his own mouth, the stink of corruption in his nose. If I hadn't been looking so hard for Betty Sue, I would have seen her face in Melinda's the first time. Goddamned Trahearne. I had been bounced around like a foolish little rubber ball on an elastic string, and seeing it now made me so tired that I didn't even care who held the paddle—I just wanted off the string.

Selma and Melinda were on their knees weeding the garden, their soft voices and laughter echoing across the ridge like windchimes. At the edge of the garden, curled in a shallow depression, Fireball slept among dry pine needles. The rest of the dogs were sleeping too, in a wire kennel beyond the small cages.

"Excuse me," I said when I stopped at the edge of the garden.

The two women paused, then stood and turned toward me. Selma's face wore the same forgiving look, but now it seemed like a gaze painted on a stone, passive and permanent. When she recognized me, though, her face broke into a thousand fragments, wild and frightened like that of a deer poised to run. Melinda sighed and relaxed with the patience of an eternal victim flooding her eyes.

"I guess I knew that you'd come," she said. "I guess I've been waiting. How did Trahearne find out?"

"Find out what?" I said. "Your mother sent me."

"But I'm her mother," Selma whimpered.

"Didn't you tell her I was dead?" Melinda said.

"She wouldn't believe me," I said. "And then you sent your daddy a postcard."

"A postcard?" she said, looking amazed.

"I'm her mother," Selma repeated, trying to draw herself back together.

"If you didn't, somebody did," I said. "Trahearne, maybe, or some of your friends in Denver. Somebody sent a postcard so Rosie would know you're alive, so I'd come here. I just don't understand why."

"I don't either," she said. "Nobody's looking for me anymore but my mother."

"I'm your mother," Selma wailed, then sank to her knees in the soft dark soil, weeping.

"It's all right," Melinda said, holding Selma's head against her thigh.

"Tell him I'll pay . . . pay anything for his silence," Selma sobbed. "Pay anything."

"Listen," I said, "as far as I'm concerned Betty Sue Flowers is dead. I only walked up that damned hill to be sure. If you want your mother to think you're dead, that's on your conscience, and if you want to act like Trahearne doesn't know who you are, that's between the two of you. I'm out of it. I'm going home."

"I'll pay anything," Selma moaned.

"Hush," Melinda said kindly. "It had to happen sometime. It'll work out." Then she looked at me. "Wait for me, please," she said. "At the bottom of the trail. I've got to take Selma inside and calm her down. But please wait. I have to talk to you."

"You'll just tell me things I don't want to know," I said.

"I'll pay!" Selma screamed. The dogs in the kennel

woke and began to yap, which in turn woke Fireball out of his sun-dazed stupor. He yawned, sniffed the air, then trotted over to greet me. As I scratched his head, Melinda helped Selma to her feet and led her toward the cabin. When they were inside, I headed down the hill.

"Please wait for me," Melinda said from the doorway. "Please."

"All right," I said from the edge of the clearing.

Fireball followed me down the trail, plodding steadily through sunlight and shade, his nose lifted in the morning air as if he could smell a beer.

"No drugs on the mountain," I said to him, and he quickened his step.

At the bottom of the trail, I crossed the highway to wash my face in the river, to lave the miles away with cold water. Fireball gave me a dirty look, then lapped up a quick drink, shaking his head as if the water horrified him. I took him back across the road and gave him a beer. We had both earned one.

I woke up with the can warm in my hand in the middle of the afternoon. Melinda was sitting in the passenger seat, dressed now in hiking boots, shorts, and a tank top. It was as if she had shed her baggy clothes to show me what it was all about—long, shapely legs rippling with muscle, high, firm breasts, the sort of body men dream about.

"You were sleeping so hard, it seemed a shame to wake you up," she said. "Selma doesn't have any coffee, but I made you some herb tea," she added, holding up a thermos.

"I'll have a beer," I said. "I don't want to get too healthy."

As I rustled up a beer, she said, "Trahearne must know, then?"

"He led me right to your mother's place, and then after Rosie hired me to find you, he encouraged me. He must have had it in mind."

"I should have told him the truth about my . . . my life," she said as she poured herself a cup of the weak tea.

"You should have told him," I agreed. "In the course of my search, he had the wonderful chance to see your acting debut."

She sighed. "Oh, that poor, poor man. Now he'll never believe me."

"About what?"

"I have to travel a lot, have to be alone, too," she said, "and he's convinced that I . . . I sleep with other men when I'm away from him." When I didn't say anything, she added, "And it isn't true. He just wants it to be true. I know he does, and it doesn't matter to me, but I don't fool around."

"Okay."

"You don't sound convinced," she said.

"I don't care," I said, "and it's none of my business anyway what either of you do or don't do, okay?"

"You don't even care why Betty Sue had to die, do you?"

"Nope."

"They came looking for me," she said, "and I had to die to make them leave me alone."

"Randall Jackson and the Denver hoods," I said.

"You know them?" she asked, amazed all over again.

"Intimately."

"I was in jail," she said defiantly, "and I . . ."

"I know," I said. "You got busted for soliciting."

". . . I lost thirty pounds in jail, a pound a day," she continued as if she hadn't heard me. "Selma came to the jail when I was in, and I wanted to come up here, but I had to go by Jack's place to get some things, some books and things, and he saw me, you know, with all the fat gone, and he made me go to work for those awful people. It wasn't like San Francisco at all—that time we were just high and having fun and making money for bread and dope—this was a business, and they made me go to the hospital to have this scar I have . . . made me have plastic surgery on this scar, and they spent a lot of money and they wouldn't let me leave. You understand, don't you?"

"Right."

"So I stole a little money from Jack's billfold and ran up here to hide, but they came looking for me in a week or two, and I had to hide in the woods and Selma had to lie—she hates to lie, she hated lying to you before. Then later that summer her daughter drowned in the wreck, and she told the sheriff it was me, you see, and I could start over again, could act like none of it ever happened, don't you see?" She sat the plastic thermos cup very carefully on the dash, then began to weep. "But you don't care, do you?" She sobbed between her hands.

I had had a bellyful of weeping women. "Jesus fucking Christ!" I shouted as I threw my unfinished beer can out the open door and across the road. "Your mother paid me eighty-seven dollars to find you," I said, "and I chased you all over the fucking country, and I don't know if I did it for Rosie or for myself or for some idea I had of you, but I know fucking-a well that I didn't do it for eighty-seven fucking dollars, so don't tell me I don't fucking care!"

"I'm sorry." She giggled, then moved her hands and began to wipe away the tears. "I was so involved in my own problems that I forgot how hard you had worked trying to find me."

"You didn't know," I said huffily.

"I understood without knowing," she said with a smile.

"Bullshit."

"You're cute when you're mad, C.W.," she said.

I got out of the pickup and kicked a few rocks around, raising a cloud of dust that nearly choked me.

"So what now?" I said as I climbed back into my seat.

"I truly don't know," she said. "I'll have to think about it for a few days. That was always the trouble before—I did so many things without thinking about them first."

"In spite of what I said up there, I've got to tell your mother something."

"Will you wait a few days?" she asked. "Just until I've straightened this out with Trahearne?"

"I've got to call your mother tomorrow," I said.

"All right, I'll call Trahearne tonight," she said. "I'd rather not do it by telephone, but if he already knows about me, I can tell what he thinks about it. Come back tomorrow. I'll meet you down here about ten. I think it might be best if you didn't come up the hill . . . you know, for Selma's sake. She's taken this whole thing so hard. She buried her daughter with my name, and of all the things I owe her, I owe her most for that. She gave me my life back, you see, and that's the most one person can do for another. That's how I feel about Trahearne sometimes—that I can give him his life back, take it back from those two awful women who have held him captive so long. You've seen them—you understand."

"Maybe I do," I said, "and maybe I don't. It doesn't matter. I would like to know one thing, though."

"I thought you didn't want to know anything," she said with a gentle smile. I was amazed that I hadn't noticed how beautiful her smile was before. "I thought you had no curiosity at all."

"Don't be a smartass," I said. "Just tell me why you ran away in the first place."

"Well, you don't know everything, do you?"

"Nope."

"I was pregnant," she said, "and my boy friend took me to San Francisco for an abortion. On the way out of the hotel where they did it, I started hemorrhaging—it's an old story, you know, so old it's almost trite until it happens to you—and he ran off and left me bleeding to death on the emergency room steps of the Franklin Hospital. He dumped me there and ran away—"

"Albert Griffith?" I interrupted.

"You know some things, don't you?" she said. "They stopped the bleeding all right, but I came down with a raging case of septicemia, and they had to do a hysterectomy to stop the infection. Pretty, isn't it? I had left my purse in Albert's car and lied about my name and my age, so nobody knew. I was afraid for anybody to know, ashamed, too, I guess. Anyway, by the time I was released from the hospital, I had been gone too long to go home, or so I thought, so I lived on the streets in the Haight until Jack took me in, and then so many other things happened that I just couldn't face going home at all. Not even when I heard about Bubba getting killed in Viet Nam."

"Is that your brother Lonnie?"

"Yes."

"Your little brother's dead too," I said.

"I know," she whispered. "I sneak back every now and again to hang around Sonoma, and I heard about it. I nearly went home then, too."

"You should have gone home in the first place," I said. "A lot of grief could have been spared a lot of folks, including you."

"I know," she said, "god, I know, but my daddy was gone and he didn't care, I called him once and he didn't care, and my momma was a slut . . ."

189

"Hey," I said.

She looked at me. "Guess I've no right to judge, huh?"

"Not even if you had lived the life of a vestal virgin," I said.

"You're right," she sighed. "It seemed so important back then. Momma tried to act like it didn't mean anything when she divorced Daddy, but I could tell it did. She got to drinking a lot and bringing men into the trailer house, and I'd lie back there in the back bedroom and listen to them laughing and banging around and tell myself that if she'd stop that, my daddy would come home, which was silly, since he never paid any attention to me when he was there. About the nine hundredth time he looked at me like a stranger when I was a little girl, I decided I had been adopted. I guess every little kid does that, huh?"

"It's an easy way out," I said.

"And it was all so long ago," she whispered.

"Now it's all come back."

"I think I'm glad, you know," she said as she patted me on the thigh. "I really think I'm glad it's all over."

"Me too."

"You drove straight through from Montana, didn't you?"

"Right."

"You must be exhausted," she said, then moved her hand from my thigh to the back of my neck. "Go check into a motel and sleep," she said, "then come back tomorrow about ten. I'll meet you down here. Is that all right?"

I yawned. "It's fine."

"You've been so kind to me," she said, "kind to everybody—Trahearne and Selma and my momma. It's always like that, you know, for me. Every time things look bad somebody shows up in my life, and they're so

190

much kinder than I deserve—like you and Selma and Trahearne, even poor old Jack in his own twisted way."

"Maybe you deserve it," I said.

"Nobody deserves it," she said, "it just happens. I'll see you tomorrow." Then she leaned over to kiss me lightly on the corner of my mouth, a sisterly kiss, but her breath smelled of herbs and dried flowers and spring water, fresh and cool. "About ten," she whispered, and I kissed her on the mouth. Her lips parted slightly, our tongues touched for a brief electric moment, and her eyes widened, darkened to a stormy blue. "I'm sorry," she said, apologizing for something she hadn't done, something she wouldn't do, then she climbed out of the pickup, snapped her fingers at Fireball, who lumbered out from under the VW, and they pranced up the trail.

In that sudden sleepy moment, it became clear to me that, like it or not, I was standing in the lady's line and I didn't care about my position. She left me breathing like a hard-run horse. As I eased back down the sweeping curves of the canyon highway, I told myself that if I didn't watch out, Trahearne's women were either going to break my heart or change my life or be the death of me. I also told myself to drive north toward home as fast as the El Camino would go, but I didn't. I had a few drinks instead of lunch, but the taste of her mouth remained in mine like a sweet communion cracker unbroken before the bitter wine. In the middle of the afternoon, I checked into a Holiday Inn, checked out into a dreamless sleep, a wake-up call waiting like a death sentence.

14 ....

THE NEXT MORNING, THE CONDEMNED MAN, WHO HAD slept like a child and showered like a teenager preparing for a date, ate as hearty a breakfast as the Holiday Inn could provide, then stepped outside to contemplate the delicate air and the clear blue sunshine of the high plains. Interstate 25 was two hundred feet to the east, though, and the diesel stench took the edge off my enjoyment. Sixty-five miles south, the gray cloud of Denver's smog humped over the horizon like a whale's back. But the morning was finally ruined when I saw Trahearne sitting in his Cadillac barge, an obscene grin on his round face. He looked like a fat, mean child.

"What's happening?" I said, trying to stay calm.

"Hell, boy, I checked every motel in town before this one," he said. "I thought you had more taste than to stay at a Holiday Inn."

"Some of my best friends are Holiday Inns," I said. "What are you doing here?"

"Looking for you, what else?" he said. "After we talked, I decided to drive down to Meriwether, and when I got there, your secretary told me that you had driven down here, so I picked up a couple of hitchhikers, and they helped with the driving, and we drove all night and here I am . . . ." His voice ran slowly down, like one of those talking dolls whose string had been pulled too many times.

"Let's not have any more lying, okay?" I said as I opened the door of the Caddy and got in. "No more lying."

"I couldn't find her without you, son," he sighed. "I didn't know where to look."

"You were already here when you called me, weren't you?" I asked, and he nodded. "And you sent her daddy a postcard, didn't you?" His head rose and sank once, then lay heavily on his chest. "Why?"

"I've got to know who she's seeing," he muttered.

"Okay," I said, "I'll show you."

"Would you drive?" he asked.

There seemed no need to hurry, so I eased the convertible through town. Trahearne didn't say anything until we were four or five miles on the other side of town on the Laramie highway. As we topped the first hill and dropped into a little valley beyond a hogback ridge, he said something, but the wind through the convertible covered his words.

"What?" I asked.

"I'm sorry," he said.

"Not sorry enough to suit me, old man," I said, and he started to weep. "Stop your goddamned whimpering," I said. "Just stop it. You know what she said when I told her that you'd seen that movie?" He shook his head. "She said, 'That poor, poor man.' She's too good for you, you know that?"

"God do I ever know it," he said.

As we turned off 287 onto the Poudre Canyon road, I asked him, "Why? What the hell did you have in mind? How did you know where to go?"

"I didn't have anything in mind," he said, "except finding her. I was out there, driving around in circles and drinking, you know, hoping to find her but not looking for her, you know, and when I stopped at the Cottontail, I couldn't . . . Well, the little whore must have told you."

"Told me what?"

"I couldn't get it up," he said blankly.

"She didn't even remember you," I said.

"That's even worse."

"If you want them to remember you, old man, stay out of whorehouses," I said. "How did you know to go to Sonoma?"

"Once she was gone, off on a trip, and I went through her things and found a clipping from the San Francisco paper, a review of a Little Theatre group production of Anouilh's *Antigone*. When I read the description of the girl who played the lead, I knew it had to be her." Then he paused. "I've always known she wasn't who she said she was," he admitted, "knew right from the beginning. She had never been to the south of France, never been to Sun Valley before that summer. At first it seemed exciting, you know, not knowing who she really was. But it was like the promise she made me give her before she would marry me—the novelty wore off quickly and began to drive me mad."

"What promise?" I said as I parked the Caddy behind Melinda's VW. A battered gray GMC pickup was parked in front. It looked like it had been wrecked once, then towed out of the river. "What promise?" I repeated.

"That she could come and go as she pleased," Trahearne muttered. "That I wouldn't ask any questions."

"She promised you the same thing, didn't she?"

He nodded, and glanced around. "Does he live here?" he asked.

"He?"

"You know, the man . . . the man she sees."

"She's supposed to meet me down here around ten," I said. "I'll let her tell you about it."

"It's you now, isn't it," he said sadly, a statement not a question. "It's you."

"Just shut the fuck up, all right?" I said, then got out and walked across the road to watch the river.

What a case. Private detectives are supposed to find missing persons and solve crimes. So far in this one I had committed all the crimes—everything from grand theft auto to criminal stupidity—and everybody but poor old Rosie and I had known where Betty Sue Flowers was from the beginning. I had the odd feeling that if I didn't go home soon, instead of ending up with a bank account fat with Catherine Trahearne's money I would end up with holes in my boots and moths in my pocket. The more I thought about it, the angrier I became. I stood up and charged back across the highway, shouting at Trahearne.

"I'm sending you a bill, old man, and I don't care if it breaks your ass, you better come up with the scratch!"

"All right," he answered meekly.

"Oh, stop being such a damned dope," I said. "She's up on that mountain staying with a woman who saved her life once and she's not doing a number with me—she's never done a number with anybody since she made the colossal mistake of falling in love with your sorry ass."

"All right," he said, not believing a word of it.

As I thought about it, I wasn't too sure that I believed it either. Like too many men, Trahearne and I didn't know how to deal with a woman like Melinda, caught as we were between our own random lusts and a desire for faithful women so primitive and fierce that it must have been innate, atavistic, as uncontrollable as a bodily function. That was when I stopped being angry at the old man.

"What time is it?" I asked him.

"Ten-thirty," he said.

"She should be here soon," I said. "Let's have a midmorning nip."

He looked startled, then reached under the seat for the bottle. As we shared the whiskey, I wondered how long men had been forgiving each other over strong drink for being fools.

At eleven, when Melinda still hadn't shown up, I hiked up the trail toward Selma's place, Trahearne following at his own pace, ten steps and a halt for some heavy breathing.

"I'll go ahead," I told him, "and warn them of your arrival so it won't be so much of a surprise."

"It'll be a hell of a surprise if I get there," he joked as I went on ahead. Two switchbacks up the hill, I could still hear his tortured breaths.

By the time I reached the clearing, my lungs were working overtime too. As I paused to rest a bit, I noticed a black splotch in the dust of the trail and splatters of dried blood on the rocks beside it, then I wondered where the dogs were. Across the clearing, the kennel gate stood open, as did the bank of small animal cages.

I ran to the large cabin, but it was empty, so I ran outside and around it. A young boy was digging a large hole with a pick and a young girl knelt beside a pile of dead dogs and birds and small furry animals. Selma sat on the far side of the clearing, her back against a pine, a shotgun cradled on her knees.

"What the hell happened?" I said to the boy.

He started, then climbed out of the hole quickly, the pick raised like a club. An ugly mouse closed his left eye, and he spit blood between broken teeth.

"You'll have to kill me this time, you son of a bitch," he said as he came at me with the pick.

"Hey," I said, holding up my arms and backing away. He didn't stop. The girl beside the grave moaned and covered her face with her hands. "Hey, wait a minute," I said, but he kept coming. "Calm down, son," I said, still walking backward, "I didn't do anything."

"You led them here!" Selma screamed as she stood up and pointed the double-barreled shotgun in my general direction.

The boy with the pick glanced over my shoulder, and I heard the scuffle of feet on the rocky dirt. I didn't wait to find out what the sudden inhalation of breath behind me meant; I ducked and rolled away, catching a glimpse of the other young girl as she swung the ax she carried. When it hit the ground where I had been standing, the blade glanced off a rock and the ax bounced out of her hands. She didn't take her eyes off me, though, she just locked her fiercely calm gaze on my face as she picked up the ax again. There's nothing like a woman with an ax to get you moving. I chunked a handful of dirt and stones at the boy with the pick, scrambled to my feet, and ran back to the trail, stepping high and moving out. The ax looped and whistled over my head, and I picked up the pace. Just as I hit the tree line, Selma touched off the first barrel, and shot dusted a small pine to my left. I dodged, and she got a piece of me with the second barrel. The edge of the pattern stung me high on the right side but it didn't knock me down. It helped my progress, though. I abandoned the trail to leap straight downhill through the small trees.

Combat at close range is the sort of thing you have to train for until you operate by reflex. Once the ball is rolling, there usually isn't much time to think and just barely enough time to react. It had been nine years since I led a squad with the 1st Air Cav in the central highlands of Vietnam, and Trahearne's Pacific war was twenty years beyond that. When I found him on the trail midway down the hill, we were two civilians scared out of our wits, as effective a combat unit as a couple of headless chickens.

"Jesus Christ, what happened?" he asked me in a breathless whisper.

"I don't know," I said, trying to think. "Go back down the hill," I told him. "Take your car a mile up the highway and if I'm not back in an hour, go get the sheriff."

"I've got a shotgun in my trunk," he said.

"There's already too many shotguns up here," I said. "Just do what I say."

"What are you going to do?" he asked with a hurt look. When he remembered his war, he remembered being in command.

"Going back up the hill," I said, "and you get your ass down it."

"Lemme go with you," he whined.

"Move," I said, then hit him on the shoulders with the heels of my hands.

The big man went ass over teakettle, and I dodged into the trees, circling right over the lower end of the ridge and into the next drainage, then I dropped down the far side of the ridge about a hundred yards, and worked my way back up toward the clearing. If I had been in better shape, I would have gone the other way, uphill, and dropped down on the clearing. If I had had any sense, I would have gone home.

Fifteen minutes later, I bellied up to the clearing behind the large cabin. Three of them were on the far side, peering into the trees beside the trail—Selma with the shotgun, the boy with his pick, and the crazy girl with her ax—but the other young girl sat on the edge of the unfinished grave, still weeping into her hands.

Sweat poured off me so furiously that I couldn't tell if

my back was still bleeding, and I was too tired to crawl on my belly anymore. I stood and walked up behind the girl as quietly as I could, with all the cunning and grace and animal stealth of an old milk cow, but she didn't hear me until I sat down beside her.

"Don't be afraid," I said to her. "I won't hurt you."

She fainted right into my arms. I lifted her in front of me like a shield, then shouted at the others. They turned and walked back toward me.

"One more step and I break her neck!" I shouted melodramatically. She was so limp her neck might as well have been broken. The three of them stopped, then took a hesitant step. "Throw all that crap away!" The boy flung his pick to the ground in disgust and Selma sat the shotgun at her feet but the girl with the ax kept it on her shoulder. "You gotta throw it away, honey," I said.

"Don't *honey* me, motherfucker," she answered calmly, clutching the ax handle tightly.

"Please, young lady," Trahearne growled from the trail as he lumbered into view, "please put it down." His face was fiery red and his shirt completely soaked with sweat, but he walked straight up, carrying the ugliest shotgun I had ever seen—a riot gun, a 12-gauge Remington pump with an 8-shot magazine, a 20-inch barrel, a pistol grip, and a metal stock that folded over the receiver and barrel. I knew what it was because I had one just like it. "Please," he said again.

She let the ax head fall to the ground beside her tennis shoe but she kept her hand on the handle. I was willing to settle for that. Without their weapons, Selma and the boy lost their angry spirit, and their shoulders sagged like empty sacks, but the girl stood defiant and erect. She even managed to spit on the ground toward me. I couldn't have spit if my life depended on it. I lifted the unconscious girl and walked toward the cabin.

"Where the hell did you come from?" I asked Trahearne.

"I don't know," he said, "but wherever it was, it was a hell of a walk." A grin brightened his tired face.

"Let's go in the house and sit down," I told everybody as I carried the girl toward the doorway. They all followed like ducks in a row.

"They came just at dusk," Selma said as she lifted her hand to touch her swollen cheek, "came up the hill with silenced revolvers and began shooting the dogs. They shot the dogs and some of the animals and birds in the cages, then they took Melinda away." She moved her hand from her cheek, down to caress the forehead of the girl sleeping in her lap. Her voice sounded so distant and hollow that the interior of the cabin seemed to darken as she spoke. "Benjamin tried to stop them but they beat him senseless, then one of them hit me when I tried to help him."

"I should've been here," the other girl said bitterly, then banged the head of her ax against the floor.

"You'd have just been hurt too," Selma said quietly. "I'm glad you were gone." Then she stared at me. "Melinda kept screaming that she would go with them, go with them gladly, but they kept laughing and kicking poor Benjamin and shooting at the dogs."

"They shot the bulldog?" I asked, already knowing the answer.

"Gut-shot him," the girl with the ax answered, "but he and the three-legged bitch were still alive this morning when I left the vet hospital down at CSU."

"They're gonna be damned sorry for that," I said.

"What about kidnapping my wife, for god's sake," Trahearne said.

"That, too," I said. "For all of it." Then I straightened up. "How many of them were there?"

"Four," Selma answered.

"Was one of them a big dude, a Mexican with a pug's face?" I asked.

"They all seemed like giants," Selma said blankly, "and they wore ski masks."

"You didn't call the sheriff, did you?" I asked.

"They said they would kill Melinda if we did," she answered, "then come back and kill all of us. I believed them. You should have seen them shooting the dogs, the crows and hawks and the bobcat in their cages. I believed them, so I didn't call the sheriff." She raised her hand to touch her face, palpating the bruise as if the wound went deep within her. "What could we do?" she pleaded. "What can we do?"

"I can damn sure do something," Trahearne threatened, lifting the shotgun as if it were a holy ikon, the rallying banner for his private jihad.

"Try to relax," I told him. He gave me a foul look, then stood up and walked about the cabin, glaring down his puffy nose at the sleeping ranks of cats. Then I asked Selma, "Why did you jump me?"

"We thought you must have brought them," she said.

"Why?"

"You're the only one who knew who she was—where she was," she answered. "Why did you come back?"

"She wanted to talk to me," I said, "to tell me what to tell her . . . her natural mother."

"And what are you going to tell her?" Selma asked.

"I don't know," I said. "Maybe I'll tell her that I have climbed the mountain and seen the prophet, but all I know is that I'm getting too old for this sort of foolishness." I tried a wry grin, and it seemed perfectly at home on my face.

"You're hurt too," Selma said with a brief smile. "I suppose I did that."

"It's nothing," I scoffed like John Wayne.

"Stacy," Selma said to the girl with the ax, "why don't you see to Mr. Sughrue's wound." She leaned her ax against the low couch where she sat, then walked across the room with a sheepish grin. "Stacy has attended a year of vet school," Selma said.

"I guess that's good enough for me," I said. "I was delivered by a vet."

Trahearne laughed. "Goddammit, Sughrue, if you were any more country, your feet wouldn't fit shoes," he said, then laughed again.

Stacy peeled the dried bloody shirt off my back with hydrogen peroxide and professional fingers, then she cleaned off the wounds. The pattern of shot was larger than I had suspected, circling from the back of my neck to the middle of my upper arm.

"I'm glad you weren't any closer," I said to Selma.

"You haven't spit up any blood, have you?" Stacy asked.

"Not lately," I answered.

"Don't try so hard to be funny," she said. It sounded like medical advice.

"How many pellets?" I asked.

"Eleven," she answered as soon as she finished counting them.

"What size shot?" I asked.

"Seven and a half," Benjamin answered.

"Steel or lead?"

He had to go over and open a drawer to check the shell box to answer that. "Steel," he said.

"If you've got some sort of antibiotic salve," I said to Stacy, "we can leave them in for a few days."

"I've got probes and some local anesthetic that I use on the animals," she said. "I could freeze 'em and pop 'em right out, then suture up the wounds."

I looked over my shoulder at her. She had high cheekbones, dusky skin, and dark brown eyes. If I

202

hadn't seen her in action with the ax, I would have thought her a delicate type.

"What the hell," I said, and she went after her bag.

As she worked on me, Trahearne persuaded Benjamin to go down the hill for the bottle of whiskey. For himself, though, not for me. When the boy brought it back, I had a drink anyway. As soon as Trahearne took a second hit off it, I made him give me the bottle. I held it until Stacy finished working on my back. She put the last circle of tape over the sutures so they wouldn't catch in the weave of my shirt, then she patted me on the shoulder lightly.

"What now?" she asked.

"We go get the lady back," I said.

"You know where she is?" Trahearne asked anxiously.

"I know how to find out," I said.

"You need some help?" Benjamin asked.

"Right," Stacy said.

"We'll all go," Selma said, and the girl sleeping in her lap stirred.

It was a great romantic notion, a band of righteous misfits rescuing the princess, and I even thought about it for a second, but we already had enough troubles.

"You been in the service?" I asked Benjamin.

"No, sir," he answered, then hung his head.

"You stay with Selma, then," I said. "Help her take care of things here."

"I've never been in the service either," Stacy said with heavy irony, "but I'm meaner than any Marine in the world, by god, pound for pound."

"I can use you for bait," I said, "but you'll have to be nice to a creep."

"That should be easy," she said, smiling, "I've spent my life doing that."

"Are you afraid?" I asked.

"Damn right," she said, "but I'm too mad to give a shit about being afraid."

"It won't be very pretty," I said.

"I can tell you things about ugly that would make your ears curl up in self-defense, mister," she said.

"Okay," I said, "you're on."

"Take care of her," Selma said in a quiet voice.

"I'll be fine," Stacy said firmly, letting me know that she damn well meant to take care of herself.

"You all take care," Selma said.

"This is what I'm supposed to do for a living," I said, which made me laugh. I don't think I sounded full of joy with the laughter. When I glanced around the room, nobody would meet my eyes. Except Trahearne, and he looked infinitely sad.

As Stacy, Trahearne, and I walked down the trail, he paused to rest, leaning against a stone outcropping.

"What are we going to do?" he asked, and slapped me on the shoulder.

"First of all, we're going to stop slapping me on the shoulder," I said, meaning it as a joke, but he took it seriously.

"I'm sorry," he said. "Goddamn it, I haven't done anything right since the war."

"You came back up the hill with that shotgun," I said.

"It was all over by the time I got there," he said, looking up at me. "You're going to need me, aren't you?" he asked.

"Of course," I said. "Particularly your plastic money."

"And what am I supposed to provide?" Stacy asked.

"Your nubile body," I said.

"Well, you ain't gettin' no cherry," she said jauntily, then led off down the trail.

After a wildly hectic afternoon down in Denver—renting two cars, buying Stacy a new dress and me a wig and fake mustache, and finding a ground-floor motel room with a private entrance near the airport—we put it all together in time for a freshly scrubbed Stacy, looking sixteen in spite of the twenty-four on her driver's license, to be sitting in Tricky Dickie's topless bar on Colfax when Jackson came in after a day at the office. He was all polyester and smiles as he arrived for his vodka martini and his visual fix of female flesh. Just as I feared, though, he had a hired tough with him.

Stacy had been great—street-wise and tough. The bartender didn't want to believe her ID at first, and when she bullied him into giving her a drink, he wasn't sure he wanted a strange hooker in his place. She set him straight, then fended off the stag line until he believed her. When Jackson made his play, she held him off a bit.

"Listen, man, I'm looking for work," she told him, "not a party. No citizens, no johns, and no traveling salesmen, okay?"

"What sort of work were you looking for, honey?" Jackson asked.

"The same sort of work I was doing back East," she answered, "until the weather got to me."

"The weather?"

"The heat, man," she said.

"Oh, yeah," he said as if he had understood all the time, "right, the heat. What a . . . what sort of work was that?"

"I'm in the fucking movies, man," she said. "What did you think? Hanging paper, maybe? Boosting groceries? Get off my case and outa my face, okay?"

"Listen, babe," he said as he sidled closer while pretending to wave his empty glass at the bartender, "I've got some friends, some business associates actually, who sometimes make movies. Just for fun, you know."

Stacy sneered. "Fun and profit."

"You got it, kid."

"And I guess you'd like to check my moves before you put me in touch with these friends of yours, right?"

"Why not?"

"Right." She snorted. "Hit the road, man. You want a free sample, call the Avon lady."

"I, ah, don't mind paying," Jackson said cautiously.

"A hundred for a half and half," Stacy said quickly. "You look like the kind of john who'll need it."

"A hundred!" he said so loudly that the bartender and most of the patrons looked around.

"If you can't afford the merchandise, man, get out of the store," she said, then became very interested in her drink. I don't know how Stacy knew to play him tough instead of giving him the hooker's usual honey and promises, but it worked like a charm.

"Sure," Jackson said. "Sure, that's fine. Let's do it."

"Let's see the bread," Stacy said without looking at him.

The poor bastard had to cash a check and endure the bartender's sly grin when he brought the bills. He handed the money to Stacy and chugged his third martini.

"You hold it," she told him. "I just wanted to see it."

"My car's right out front," he said, falling over himself trying to be casual.

"My motel room's at the airport," Stacy said. "Let's hit it."

"Right," Jackson said, then turned to his hired friend. "Hey, man, let's go."

"Who the fuck's that?" Stacy asked, holding back against Jackson's hand.

"My driver," he answered loftily.

"Is he going to hold your dick, man?" she said.

"I'll be back," Jackson said, and his friend sat back down quickly and ordered another drink.

I brushed the curly-haired wig out of my eyes and followed them outside. This was the only part where I had told Stacy what to say. I didn't want her in Jackson's car.

"Hey, man," she said, "I got a rented car right there. Why don't you follow me?"

"I'll bring you back," he offered grandly.

"What if I don't want to come back here?" she asked.

"When I get through with you, honey, you'll follow me anywhere," Jackson insisted, ushering her into his Cougar.

I stood on the curb and watched them drive away, wondering where the hell Trahearne was with the other rented Ford. I kicked myself for trusting the old man to wait outside, for not having another ignition key for Stacy's rental unit. Five minutes later, Trahearne finally showed up, his big face flushed, a sorry smile twisting his lips.

"They took off, huh?" he muttered as I opened the door and shoved him from behind the wheel.

"Where the hell have you been?" I asked as I gunned the car down the street and made the corner in a four-wheel drift.

"Listen, son, we left the whiskey in the other car," he said, waving a pint of vodka at me, "and I knew we'd need a drink. We're too old to do this kind of crap without a drink. So I went around the block to buy a bottle. What the hell difference does it make?"

"He wouldn't follow her," I said as I slipped through a yellow light ahead of a bus. "She's in his car, and if they're not at the motel when we get there, if he took her home or someplace else, I'm gonna have your ass, old man, and have it good."

"Goddammit, C.W., I didn't know," he whined,

207

then he changed his approach with the sort of clumsy grace drunks think of as quick-witted. "What the hell, boy, that little lady can take care of herself. You can be damn certain of that." Then he slapped me on the shoulder again, hard enough to start the bleeding from torn stitches. I jerked the wig off and threw it on the floor at his feet. He picked it up and laughed, holding it out like a prize beaver pelt. "You looked like shit in this, you know," he said, then sat it on his head like a hat. "Of course, I look like a million dollars," he said, then laughed again. He reached over and ripped the phony mustache off and stuck it crookedly on his upper lip. "How's that?" he asked, grinning. When I didn't answer, he said, "Aw hell, come on, don't be so damned serious. Have a little drink and try to relax." He nudged me with the pint, and there didn't seem to be anything else to do. "They got my Melinda, boy, and I don't know what to do," he said as I handed the bottle back. "I don't know what to do."

"Try doing just exactly what I tell you to do," I said. "For a change."

"You're in charge," he said, "but it better come out right."

"Wonderful," I said, as I turned off Colorado onto 32nd through a service station.

When we got to the motel, the plum Cougar was parked in front of Stacy's room. I left Trahearne in the car, told him to wait, then went in through the other room and the connecting door. Jackson was already in the saddle. Stacy's eyes were pleading over his fat, pimpled shoulder. Before I could get his attention by sticking a silenced .22 in his ear, he grunted and moaned, trembling, and Stacy's eyes filled with tears. I clubbed him on the back of the neck with the automatic's butt, then jerked him off her onto the floor and kicked him in the stomach hard enough to twist my ankle. I started to kick him again, but Stacy jumped out of bed and grabbed my arm.

"It's all right," she said, "it's all right. It doesn't matter." Then she shook my arm hard. "It doesn't matter. Really."

"I'm sorry we were late," I said.

"It doesn't matter," she said again.

"It does to me," I said.

"My fault entirely," Trahearne apologized grandly as he came through the connecting door, "all my fault, honey, but it couldn't be helped."

Stacy took one glance at Trahearne, then one step, and she slapped him so hard she nearly knocked him down. "You drunken piss-ant," she whispered, then slapped him again.

"What did I say?" he wondered as she raced past him into the other room. Then he saw Jackson naked on the floor. "Lemme get my hands on that son of a bitch," he roared as he moved toward Jackson. I hit him on the point of the shoulder with the butt and he sat down on the bed. "Jesus Christ," he muttered.

"Just sit there and shut up," I said.

"Goddamn it, it's my wife they took, you son of a bitch, it's my wife," he said.

"If you don't shut up," I told him, "it's going to be your widow. I thought I told you to stay in the car."

"It's my wife," was all he answered, then he made himself comfortable on the bed, sighing, "I always fuck it up."

I took a roll of strapping tape and bound Jackson at the ankles, knees, wrists, and elbows, then I stuffed his dirty sock in his mouth and locked it there with a loop of tape around his neck. As I worked, I heard the sound of Stacy brushing her teeth and showering in the other room's bath. The noise of her toilet went on long enough to get Trahearne's attention.

"I never do anything right," he whined.

"I told you to shut up," I said. "Get off your ass and give a hand with this piece of shit."

"Yes, sir," he said, then giggled, covering his mouth with a finger. It was like trying to deal with a two-hundred-fifty-pound fifty-seven-year-old baby. I couldn't understand how Catherine or Melinda found the patience or energy. Hell, I couldn't even understand how Trahearne found the energy to be such a bastard. At least he got off the bed, grabbed Jackson under the arms, and before I could help, carried him into the bathroom and deposited him in the tub. "Was that okay, sir?" he said with a Gary Cooper smile somehow fitted on his moon face. Schizophrenia—that was the word I had left out. Trahearne sober and during certain stages of drunkenness was a sad old man with a hell of a load of character, but during other stages of his drunks, he was a two-hundred-fifty-pound fifty-seven-year-old schizophrenic child.

" ust get the hell out of here, okay?" I said.

"I'm all ¬ight now, he said. "I know I've been a fool and an idiot but I'm all right now. We've got business to tend to, I know, and I'll slow the drinking down, drink myself sober. I've done it before. So have you. You know what I'm talking about."

"Just stay out of the way, then," I said.

"Of course," he said, sounding as sober as Oliver Wendell Holmes. "This is your show."

"What now?" Stacy said as she walked into the bathroom, dressed in jeans and a black sweat shirt.

"Go back in the bedroom," I said.

"I signed on for the duration, man," she said, suddenly resolute, "and after fucking that creep, if you blow his brains out, I deserve to watch. I earned it. Shit, if you did it, that would be a ray of sunshine in my life."

"You are the sunshine of my life," Trahearne crooned, then sipped from the vodka.

"Let's have some of that," Stacy said as she jerked the pint from his hand.

I guess I grinned without meaning to and shook my head without thinking about it. When I saw Jackson's face, he looked like a man in the clutches of the Manson Family, and I didn't blame him.

"Are you going to tell me where she is?" I asked him, and he made the mistake of shrugging. "Get me the telephone book," I said to Trahearne.

"The phone book?" Stacy went into the bedroom and brought it back.

I lifted Jackson's feet and sat them on the thick book. His genitals had balled up in his crotch and they looked like some vital organ that had slipped from his body. I stood up and took the .22 out of my belt.

"You don't know where she is?" I asked. He shrugged again, and I said, "Okay." I let the automatic dangle from my hand as I waited for the sound of a jet making its final approach over the motel. "Last chance, " I said before the noise got too loud for him to hear. He shrugged again. "You know I'm not going to kill you, don't you?" I said. He shook his head, but his eyes smiled. He might be a piece of shit but Jackson had some balls on him. Either that or he was more frightened of his business associates than he was of me. That was a real mistake on his part. When the landing jet swept over the motel, I leaned down and pumped two rounds into his right foot. Blood splashed over the telephone book and the bathtub, as red as Jackson's face was white.

"Jesus Christ," Trahearne muttered as he sank onto the toilet. As he slumped, Stacy leaned over the sink and vomited with a single quick motion.

"I'm all right," she said, then she rinsed out her mouth. "Shoot the fucker again."

"You didn't have to shoot him twice," Trahearne said.

"Once to get his attention," I said, "and once to let him know I was serious." Then I looked down at Jackson. "I am serious, you know." Without waiting to see if he believed me, I jerked him up and shoved the telephone book under his butt. "You understand?" He nodded quickly.

"I don't like this," Trahearne said.

"Then get out of the room," I said without turning around. He didn't leave. Then I tapped Jackson under the chin with the silencer. "Now, the first thing you have to get straight in your mind is that you're through in this town. This part of your life is over. Either you leave this room dead or you leave it having told me where Betty Sue is, which won't make your friends happy, so give up this part of your life right now. Get your mind straight on that. We'll even buy you a ticket, but get this part out of your mind right now. Okay?" He didn't nod, he jerked his head up and down in a blur. "Now I'm going to take the gag out, and you're not going to make any noise at all, right?" As soon as his head quit bobbing, I took out my pocket knife and sliced the tape over the sock and tugged it out. He moaned with amazing restraint. I took the vodka from Trahearne and gave Jackson a quick hit off it. "Now can you tell us where she is?"

"Yes, sir," he whispered.

"Where?"

"This guy I work for, Mr. Hyland—I think maybe you met him up in Fort Collins once—he has a house between Evergreen and Conifer, a big red brick colonial on the west side of the road on a three-acre lot. You can't miss it. Up there it sticks out like a sore thumb, and he's got his name on the mailbox."

"She's there?"

"Yes, sir."

"What kind of security has he got?" I asked.

"Security?" Jackson said, looking very confused. I gave him another sip of vodka.

"How many men does he have guarding the place?"

"Guarding the place?" he asked. "Oh, yeah, well, when they're shooting—"

"Shooting?" I interrupted.

"Yeah, you know, making a flick," Jackson explained to me. "When they're shooting, Mr. Hyland has a guy on the gate and another dude walking the grounds. To keep the neighborhood kids away, you know—kids don't have any respect for private property anymore, so Mr. Hyland has Petey and Mike sort of watch things when they're shooting."

"What about the big Mexican?"

"Torres? He's Mr. Hyland's personal man and he's always next to him," Jackson said.

"Don't they know we might try to take her back?" I asked.

"I don't think they know who you are," Jackson said, trying to be as polite as possible. "I know I don't."

It didn't seem necessary to explain who we were, and as I glanced around the crowded bathroom, I wasn't all that sure myself.

"How did they know where to find Betty Sue?" I asked.

"Her daddy, you know, out in Bakersfield," Jackson said. "He knows some people we know and he got this postcard—we thought she was dead—I mean, that's what we heard a long time ago, and that's what you said after they roughed you up—so anyway, when her daddy's friends called about the postcard, Mike flew up to Montana and followed you down."

"Great," I said. I didn't even bother to turn around to give Trahearne a dirty look. He cursed under his breath and walked back into the bedroom. "Do they have Betty Sue locked up?"

"I don't think so," Jackson said. "They're shooting tonight."

"Tonight?"

"Yeah, they rent the equipment to use in the daytime at Hyland's ad agency, so they have to shoot at night."

"Cheap bastards," Stacy muttered.

"Has he got a fence around the place?" I asked.

"Yeah, a chain-link fence," he answered.

"Any dogs?"

"Dogs?"

"You know, guard dogs," I said.

"No, nothing like that," he said. "Hyland hates dogs."

That reminded me. "Did you go with them after Betty Sue?"

"I drove the car, that's all," he said. "I didn't go up the hill. I wouldn't shit you, man, not about that."

"It doesn't matter," I said. "Listen, I'm going to cut your hands loose, and I want you to draw me a layout of the grounds and a floor plan of the house, okay?"

"Could I have another hit of that vodka first?" he asked.

"Sure," I said, then cut the tape and let him hold the bottle himself. When he finished his drink, he held the pad on his knees and drew for me. "Do your best," I said.

"I'll try," he muttered, then wet the pencil lead with his furry tongue.

"Act like your life depended on it," I reminded him, and he applied himself to his task with renewed vigor. When it was done, he handed it to me. It wasn't bad. "Only three doors?" I asked. "Front, back, and garage? No patio doors or sliding doors or French windows?"

"Right," he said.

"Where do they film?" I asked.

"In this downstairs bedroom here," he said, pointing it out with the eraser.

"Okay," I said, "you've done great so far. Now I'm going to leave you here in the company of this young lady . . ."

"I'm not staying here for a minute," Stacy said.

"Like I said, I'm going to lock you in the trunk of our car, and if everything goes well, we'll put you on a plane in the morning."

"Couldn't you just take me to the hospital?" he asked. "I wouldn't call anybody."

"You jerked me around once," I said, "and you're sleeping in the trunk until tomorrow morning."

"I guess I can understand that," he said.

"Good," I said, then I cleaned up his foot. Both wounds were through and through, and the bleeding had nearly stopped when I went to work on his foot.

"You reckon it's fucked up pretty bad?" he asked as I wrapped gauze around it.

"You're going to limp for lying the rest of your life," I said. He nodded as if that were a system of justice he understood. "Will you get me his clothes?" I asked Stacy. She snorted but she went to get them, then tossed them on the floor and went back into the bedroom.

As I helped Jackson dress, I asked him, "Why did they go to all this trouble? Not over a five-year-old doctor's bill."

"That was part of it," he said as he limped into his pants, "yeah, but the forty thousand, that was what pissed them off."

"The forty thousand?"

"You don't know about that, huh?" Jackson said with a superior smile.

"Tell me," I said.

"When Betty Sue split, she hit the till for forty K, man, and Mr. Hyland, he had to make it up out of his

215

own pocket. He's gonna work Betty Sue until he figures he's made his bread back, then he's gonna dump her down a mine shaft."

"Nice people," I said.

"Just good business," Jackson said.

Instead of knocking a wad of his teeth out, I gave him two codeine tablets left over from my last visit to Colorado.

"What's that?"

"For the pain," I said.

"You know, it's amazing, but my foot don't hurt all that bad," he said as he gingerly pressed the ball of it against the bathroom floor.

"Take the fucking pills," I said, and he did.

By the time Trahearne and I carried him to the car and stuck him in the trunk with a blanket and pillow, Jackson was nodding away and calling us "Mummy."

"What's going to happen to him?" Trahearne asked as I slammed the trunk lid.

"If we're alive tomorrow morning, we'll give him a head start on his friends," I said. "But if we're dead or in jail or in the hospital, he'll probably die locked in that trunk. Hell, even if everything goes like it's supposed to, he's probably a dead man already."

"That doesn't bother you?"

"Not a bit," I said. "He's a piece of shit, man, and he lied to me. I gave him every chance I could, and he still lied to me, so fuck him."

"I lied to you too," Trahearne said, looking away toward the shifting lights of the airport.

"Yeah," I said, "but that's the difference between you and him."

"What's that?"

"He's worth killing and you're not," I said, then I went back into the motel room and left him standing outside.

15 ....

Like everybody in the world, I had seen too many movies. I expected Hyland's place to be a large estate, a fortress with high walls and a massive gate guarded by a brace of men with automatic weapons, but it was just a good-sized brick house on a suburban lot with a four-foot-high chain-link fence. A man stood beside the gate, but it was wide open, and he was obviously bored stupid as he slumped against a gatepost. In the flash of our passing headlights, I recognized him as a man I had seen drinking coffee in a truck stop in Sheridan, Wyoming. Even standing guard, he looked like a trucker with bleary eyes, swollen feet, and itchy hemorrhoids. I, on the other hand, had come dressed for the party, decked out like a mercenary in jungle boots and a tiger-striped fatigue uniform, even done up in blackface like a night-fighter, and armed to the teeth, a K-bar combat knife strapped to my calf, a .38 S&W Airweight in a shoulder holster, and the silenced .22 Colt Woodsman under my belt.

As we drove past Hyland's gate, Trahearne laughed and asked, "You loaded for bear, boy?"

"Be prepared," I said. "That's my motto."

He sneered. "That's for Boy Scouts."

Before I could answer, Stacy said, "He's just jealous

because he doesn't have a uniform." Which shut Trahearne up.

She dropped me around the first curve north of Hyland's gate, and I crept back up the ditch toward the fence corner. Once there, I vaulted it, then bellied slowly toward the back of the house, watching for the other guard. I found him peeking through a slit in the blackout curtains at a back bedroom window. Some guys just can't get enough of that sort of thing. Even though the mountain air was chilly, the air-conditioning unit was going full blast. I used the noise for cover and walked up behind him. It seemed a shame to spoil his fun, but I sapped him silly, then trussed him like a pig for slaughter. When I finished with him, I took his place at the window.

Banks of movie lights filled the large bedroom with white heat that seemed intensified by the huge mirror over the king-sized bed. A naked black woman sat on a stool, fanning herself with one hand and smoking a joint with the other. On the bed, a blond, tanned guy was being worked over by a chesty girl in shorts and a halter, her head bobbing at his crotch with an angry exasperation. Two guys stood beside the camera chatting and smoking dope, and a short, fat fellow paced around the room talking to himself. In the shadows beyond the lights, Hyland and Torres sat on a couch, flanking a woman with a ton of blond hair who wore a flimsy robe, a very blank expression, and too much make-up. Hyland had a tall, cool drink in one hand. The other was draped casually over the blonde's shoulders, where it kneaded her large, firm breast regularly, as if he were exercising it. Only when I glanced at the woman's face again, did I recognize Melinda, then I looked away as quickly as I could.

At the gate I was supposed to wait for Stacy to stop the car on the highway to ask the guard for directions, but when I went around the house to wait for her, he was off in some other world. I walked up behind him and put him to sleep too. When Stacy stopped the car, I stepped out of the shadows and waved her into the driveway. She cut the lights and pulled in.

"Just a second," I told her, "I've got to finish gift-wrapping this one."

She stomped on the emergency brake and followed me behind the shrubbery. As I leaned over to finish taping the guy's ankles, Stacy jerked the sap out of my back pocket, and before I could stop her, she had flattened his nose, crunched some teeth, and given him a lump as big as a walnut between the eyes.

"Jesus Christ," I muttered as I wrestled the sap from her.

"That'll teach the motherfucker to shoot dogs," she said calmly.

She went back to the car, and I had to rummage around behind his gag for fragments of teeth so he wouldn't choke to death, but it was a hopeless task. I cut the gag off him. His mouth was going to hurt so bad that he probably wouldn't make much noise. If he woke up at all. The knot between his eyes looked nasty, maybe fatal, and I knew that Stacy didn't need his death on her conscience.

It had been a long day, so I rode up the driveway on the car fender, then hopped off and removed the valve stems from the tires of the three-quarter-ton Dodge van and the black Continental. Sitting on four flats, the vehicles looked comic, but I was too tired to smile. As Stacy turned the car around to face down the driveway, I used the keys I had taken from the guards to try the garage door that opened into the kitchen, but it wasn't locked. I dropped the keys on the steps and went back to organize Trahearne and his shotgun.

"You stay outside," I told him as I checked again to be sure that he didn't have a shell in the chamber. "Don't come inside unless you hear gunfire, and if you do come inside, don't shoot anybody until you're sure who they are. Right?"

"Teach your grandma to suck eggs," he said.

"That's my line," I said.

He glared at me. "I had a platoon on the 'Canal when you were still in diapers."

"Just stay outside," I said, "and try not to think about it."

He grunted, and that sounded like the closest I could get to an agreement. I changed clips in the .22 so I would have three rounds of rat shot above six rounds of hollow-point hot loads, then I got a Browning 9mm automatic out of the car for Stacy, jacked a round into the chamber, and left the hammer back.

"If it happens," I said, "hold it like I showed you and aim for their kneecaps and keep pulling the trigger until it's empty." She nodded, breathing shallowly, her eyes wide. "You sure you want to do this?"

"Let's do it before I change my mind," she said, and followed me into the house.

As we eased through the darkened rooms, she covered me while I cut telephone wires, which I had forgotten to do outside. Every time I glanced over my shoulder, she was standing in a crouch, the heavy automatic clutched in her right hand, her left hand holding the right wrist, the pistol covering the rooms in long, smooth arcs. She seen too many movies too. I just hoped that she would pull the trigger if I needed her. After we had checked both floors and found all the rooms empty, we paused at the bottom of the stairs to catch our breath, then went down the hallway toward the bedroom where they were filming.

I listened for a moment at the door. Somebody was complaining about the working conditions, the late hours, and the dubious physical accomplishments of *some* so-called actors. "Have you ever had an erection?" the voice inquired as I opened the door, stepped in, and shot the top off Hyland's glass with the hollow point in the chamber. Just for the effect.

"Everybody be calm," I said as Stacy backed into the corner beside the door. "Be real calm."

It almost worked. Everybody froze for a second. Except for Torres. With one smooth motion, he stood and reached under his left arm. At seven feet, a round of .22 long rifle shot will pulverize a rattlesnake's head, and when I shot Torres in his right hand, it seemed to explode, but he didn't make any more noise than the silenced round.

"You'll have to hire somebody to wipe your ass and pick your nose," I said. He chuckled and let his hand fall to his side.

As if that were some sort of signal, the film crew broke out in a fit of small movements and aimless chatter, but as soon as Stacy swept the automatic across them, they all stilled and shut up. All but the chubby director.

"All right," he demanded, "what's going down here?"

"If he opens his mouth again," I said to Stacy over my shoulder, "blow the back of his head off."

He opened his mouth, then shut it quickly as he looked down the barrel of the automatic. He took another look, sighed, and fainted into a puddle.

"All you film folk," I said, "I want you lying flat on the bed, face down, with your fingers laced behind your necks. Right now." Melinda stared at me, confused, but when I jerked my head, she dashed for the bed and joined the scramble for a place.

"Now, you two gentlemen assume that old familiar position against the wall behind the couch," I said to Hyland and Torres. They were too tough to hurry but they got there anyway. "If they lift a finger," I said to Stacy, "start pulling that trigger and don't stop until it's empty." She nodded and moved to my left to cover the two men while I patted them down. Hyland was clean, but Torres had been reaching for a .357 magnum Colt Python with a six-inch barrel. "It'd take you a month to get this sucker out," I said as I unloaded it, but he didn't answer. He just leaned against the wall, watching the blood from his hand creep down the plaster. "Now, you boys just stay right there," I said as I stepped away and tossed the Colt under the couch. "We're going to have a little conversation."

"What do you want?" Hyland asked calmly.

"The girl," I said, "and a little satisfaction."

"Take her," he shrugged, "enjoy her to your heart's content, buddy, because you're a dead man."

Just to see if he was as tough as he acted, I skimmed him across the buttocks with another round of rat shot.

"Jesus Christ," he wailed, and broke into a slick sweat.

Torres glanced at Hyland with contempt, then at the .22 with interest. I fired the last round of shot into the row of bottles standing on a dry bar against the far wall.

"That's the last round of rat shot," I said, "and I don't know how far you'd get with a hollow point between the eyes, but you can try it if you want to."

He relaxed and leaned harder against the wall, but before I could start the conversation, Trahearne lurched into the room, shouting, "Where is she!" as he jacked a round into the chamber of the riot gun, then let it off into the ceiling. The large mirror exploded like shrapnel, a bank of lights flared, then went black. Hyland rolled over the arm of the couch to hide behind it, and Torres shoved off the wall, heading like a mad bull toward Stacy and the automatic. He didn't even glance at me and didn't hesitate. He didn't think the little girl would have the nerve to pull the trigger, and it was very nearly the last mistake he ever made.

Stacy fired five rounds as quickly as she could pull the trigger, holding low. But the automatic jerked a little higher with each shot. The first splintered the floor between his feet, the next two went between his legs, and Torres could see what was coming. He hit the floor in a headfirst slide. When he finally halted his skid, Stacy had stopped firing, and he glanced up. She held the pistol steadily pointed at his head. How she had missed him at that range with five rounds, I'll never understand. Torres couldn't either.

"Enough," he whispered, then crawled back to the couch. "You mind if I lie down for a minute?" he asked.

"Be my guest," I said.

He climbed up on to the couch and rested his head on the arm that Stacy had blown to stuffing and splinters.

"How the fuck did I miss?" she asked herself.

"Where's my wife?" Trahearne said. The gunfire had brought him to a dead halt too.

"I thought I told you to stay outside," I said, but he didn't even look at me. "She's over there." I pointed to the pile of people who had hidden behind the bed. Trahearne handed me the shotgun and went to get Melinda. "Get her out of here," I said as he helped her up, clucking like a mother hen.

As they walked past me, Melinda slipped the wig off and dropped it on the floor. Trahearne tried to kick it but he missed and would have fallen down if Melinda hadn't grabbed him. Even with her cropped hair and smeared make-up, she still looked worth a man's blood, maybe even his life. A line of red from a small cut ran down her smooth cheek, and as she glanced at me, I could see she was crying as they made their way across the littered room.

The film crew had moved off the floor back onto the bed, and they were examining their wounds from the flying glass. From where I stood, nothing looked too serious, just small cuts. The male star had the worst one, a shard of mirror about four inches long sticking through the loose muscle below his left shoulder blade. When he started whining about it, though, the black girl jerked it out and told him to shut up.

"Mr. Hyland," I said as I walked over to the end of the couch, "you can come out now." He didn't, though. When I looked over the arm, he was crouched in a puddle of blood. One of Stacy's rounds had blown the side of his head all over the wall. It was an incredible effort, the hardest of the whole lousy night, but I turned to Stacy and said, "Mr. Tough Guy's over here in a dead faint. Why don't you herd those other folks down the hall to the bathroom so they can clean up."

She nodded, then jerked the automatic at the people on the bed. The black girl had to slap the male star to get him going, and the head girl and one of the cameramen had to carry the director, but they got it together, finally, and trooped out the doorway.

"Is he dead?" Torres asked as soon as the room cleared.

"He's all over the wall, man," I said as I walked over to the dry bar and picked up a bottle of Scotch out of the broken glass. "Let's go to the kitchen and have a drink."

"That's the first good idea you've had tonight," he said, then rolled off the couch and stood up. "Maybe the first good one in your whole life."

I stuck the .22 under my belt and propped the shotgun across my arm. Torres shut up. As we left the room, I cut off the light and closed the door.

"Doesn't taste like Chivas, does it?" Torres asked as we lifted our glasses.

"Right now it tastes like shit but it tastes great," I said. On the way to the kitchen, I had locked the crew in the bathroom and sent Stacy outside to cover the front of the house. Just in case the gunfire had attracted anybody's attention, I told her.

"Hyland," Torres went on. "He buys four-ninety-eight Scotch and pours it into a Chivas bottle, then the dumb son of a bitch expects nobody to notice it."

"Nice eulogy," I said.

"More than he deserves," Torres suggested. "What happens now?"

"Depends on how you want to play it."

He took a long swallow of his drink, then stared at me. "Okay, let me lay it out for you," he said, then held up his hand wrapped in a bloody dishtowel. "I think my working days are over, man, and I'm used to living good . . ."

"All your days were nearly over," I interrupted.

"No shit," he sighed. "I still don't know how that chick missed me."

"I wish she had missed Hyland," I said.

"If you don't tell her, man, she won't know," Torres said, "and in a way she did both of us a favor."

"How's that?"

"He's the sort of dumb bastard who would have taken this personally," Torres said. "He didn't know when to cut his losses."

"And you do?"

"Right," he answered. "Look at it like this, man, Hyland was an idiot—I mean how dumb can you get, making flicks in your own place—and the uncle who got him into the business is no longer in business, if you know what I mean, so there are a few people who won't cry when they find out Hyland is out of it, you see."

"And you're one of them?"

"I know more about his business than he did," Torres said, "and with him out of the way, I can step in and run it right."

"So I just walk away with the girl? Clean?"

"Absolutely," he said. "Except for one thing."

"The forty thousand?"

"You got it," he said.

"That was a long time ago."

"Right. But everybody concerned knows about it," he said.

"I think you're jerking me around," I said, "trying to make a little profit on the side."

"Can you blame me, man?" he said, then grinned. "And I ain't kidding you, if I had that forty K, there would be a lot less heat."

"That's your ticket to the movies, isn't it?" I said.

"You got it."

"Not in my pocket," I said, "but if you'll give me sixty days, I'll do what I can."

"Quicker would help," he said.

"Listen, don't press me," I said, "not when I'm holding this shotgun."

"Aw hell," he said, then waved his bloody hand at me. "If you were going to kill me, man, you'd've done it right out of the bag instead of screwing around that dumb shit rat-shot bit. It's too messy, man—dead, I'm just more trouble than it's worth, but alive, I can clean up this end."

"Sixty days," I said, "and no promises."

"Okay, what the hell, it's worth it," he said. "Deal?"

"I've got to have an edge," I said.

"Like what?"

"Your prints on the piece that killed Hyland," I said, "and the account books out of his safe."

"Or what?"

"Or I'm talking to a dead man," I said. "I'll leave you in the room with Hyland, the Browning in your hand, the .22 in his, and take my chances."

"The pieces aren't registered to you, huh?",

"Out of Arkansas," I said, "as clean as whistles."

"You ain't exactly a model citizen."

"I'm no kind of citizen at all," I said.

"You get the piece, I'll get the books," Torres said calmly.

"You get the books, I'll watch."

"Right," he said, then knelt in front of the sink cabinet, opened it up and removed what looked like ten years of accumulated kitchen cleaning materials. He lifted the floor of the cabinet to expose a round safe sunk into the concrete foundation. He worked the dial, and paused before opening the door. "The first thing out, man, is a piece, but it'll come out slow," he said, then opened it up and lifted out a nickel-plated .32 automatic and handed it to me.

"A beautiful piece," I said as I unloaded it.

"Yeah," Torres said, "he must've paid at least twenty dollars for it." He laughed, then stood up and handed me a stack of narrow ledgers. "Can I ask one more favor?"

"What?"

"If you send me copies of these," he said, "it'll make the changeover all that much smoother."

"Okay."

"I almost believe you," he said.

"You mail me a receipt for a thousand-dollar contribution to the humane society," I said, "and I'll mail you copies."

"You got it, man," he said. "I'm sorry about the dogs. Hyland, he hated dogs and when this bulldog bit him on the ankle, he went crazy. I tried to stop him, really, but he—"

"Just shut up," I said as I leveled the shotgun at his nose. "You got it?" He nodded. "Now let's go get the Browning." I herded him outside, took the automatic from Stacy, then prodded him back into the kitchen. "Unload it," I told him, "and wipe it clean, then reload it." He did it quickly and professionally. I didn't even have to tell him to take each round out of the clip. When he finished, he found a large plastic bag and dropped the piece in it. "Now let's go down the hall and pick up those five pieces of brass," I said.

"You're a careful son of a bitch," he said as he handed me the plastic bag.

"That's what I'm doing here," I said, "practicing my careful act, scumbag."

"You don't have to insult me," he said as I followed him down the hall.

"I wouldn't know where to begin," I said, then stepped back as he opened the door and switched on the light. The five shell casings were clustered behind the door, and he picked them up and gave them to me. "Now get me the magnum out from under the couch," I said.

"Come on, man, that's my favorite piece," he complained. "Besides, it's registered to me."

"That's even better," I said, and he knelt down to reach under the couch. "Nothing personal," I said as he pulled the revolver to the edge of the couch and I clubbed him with the shotgun butt behind the ear. His face slammed into the floor, his back arched, and his feet tattooed across the rug. "Nothing personal at all." I picked up the .357 and stuck it in my belt, then drew my boot back to kick Torres in the face, but I knew it wouldn't help. I put my foot down. I had gotten Melinda out, but it hadn't provided any satisfaction at all.

When I got to the car I motioned Stacy behind the wheel, then climbed into the passenger seat and dumped my load of arms on the floorboard along with the ledgers.

"What took you so goddamned long?" Trahearne asked as Stacy drove us away. "We must have been sitting in the car for a goddamned hour."

"Honey," Melinda chided him in a whisper, "honey, hush. He got me out."

"Yeah, well, I'm paying him good money for it," he said.

Stacy slammed on the brakes, skidding across the gravel of the driveway, and turned around and shouted at Trahearne, "You old fat bastard, you shut up! No—you say thank you and then you shut up! You haven't done a thing tonight but piss and moan and fuck up, and if it wasn't for him, Melinda would be doing it under the lights with that good-looking blond dude, so you say thank you and then you shut the fuck up!"

"It's okay," I said.

"Stop making excuses for him!" she shouted at me.

"I don't have to thank the hired help," Trahearne huffed. That made Stacy so mad that she flounced back under the wheel and stuffed the accelerator to the floorboard. The car shot down the drive and fishtailed onto the highway.

Nobody said anything for a long time as we headed back toward Denver, the silence only broken by the whisper of tires, the gurgle and plop of Trahearne's bottle, and Melinda's sobs.

I had a long drink of water out of a canteen, then wet a towel to scrub away the camouflage paint on my face. When I finished and leaned back in the seat, Stacy reached over to pat my thigh.

"Thank you," Melinda said softly, "thank you so very much."

"Yeah," Trahearne grunted as nicely as he was able. "You want a drink?" He reached the pint of vodka over the seat back.

"Is that your answer to everything!" Stacy shouted, wheeling in the seat and nearly running the car off the freeway.

"Don't make him mad," I said as I grabbed the steering wheel, "or he won't give me one."

"Oh," she muttered, then settled back to driving. When I offered her a hit off Trahearne's pint, she cursed, but took a long swallow. "I don't know why you drink that terrible stuff," she said, spitting and coughing.

"It's the only way to get drunk," I said, and everybody laughed as if I had said something funny.

"I'm sorry," Trahearne said, and that sent up gales of laughter.

"You should be," Stacy said, giggling. "I can't believe I missed that son of a bitch," she added, then giggled louder.

"You couldn't've stopped that big bastard any quicker if you had blown his head off," Trahearne said, and they chuckled.

"Meaner'n a Marine," Stacy squealed.

"That's not saying much," Trahearne said. "My mother's meaner than any Marine that ever lived."

"No kidding," Melinda offered in a soft, shy voice. "She wouldn't have missed," she added, and they all laughed again, so happy to be alive that they would have laughed at a stop sign.

Back at the motel, we moved all the gear out of the car into the room, then I left them there while I unloaded Jackson from the trunk to the front seat. Stacy's driving had left him some the worse for wear. He wasn't bleeding too badly, but he looked like a man who had just survived a terrible auto accident. I drove him to the emergency-room entrance at Denver General and left him on the curb, a shoe in one pocket, a half-empty pint of bourbon in the other, assuming that he would work it out after I explained that Hyland was dead and nobody was looking for him. He nodded briskly, then hobbled toward the hospital, hopping quickly off his right heel.

"I'm sorry!" I shouted out the car window, but he waved his hand without turning around, as if to say it was all in a day's work.

When I got back to the motel again, it wasn't even midnight yet, and I found the troops sitting down to delivered pizza and room-service beer, and we ate and drank furiously until a flurry of fatigue swept over us like a tropical rainstorm, dropping us like sodden flies. Trahearne fell asleep with a piece of pizza in his hand moving toward his mouth, and as she helped him to the bed, Melinda tumbled down beside him with a quick, sudden snort like a woman clubbed in the back of the head. Within seconds Trahearne, flopped on his back, began to snore as only he could.

"Jesus Christ," Stacy whispered, "how can she sleep through that?"

I yawned. "She must love him."

"She must."

"I guess I have to sleep in your room," I said.

"Of course," she answered sweetly, then took me by the hand and led me through the connecting doors. Stacy was asleep on her feet, and as I collapsed toward the bed with her, I went under too.

But it was, as I knew it would be, a quick, uneasy sleep, dreamless, but broken by fits and starts of waking out of darkness into the unfamiliar room—like the first few nights back from the bush in the base camp at An Khe—a treacherous sleep. And the second time I woke up, around three A.M., I didn't want to go back into it. I untangled myself from Stacy's arms as gently as I could, but she woke up too.

"Every time I close my eyes, I see that room with the mirror exploding like knives," she murmured dreamily, "and I don't understand why I don't feel bad."

"The good guys won," I said, loosening her grip on my neck.

"Where're you going?"

"The john," I said.

"Come back," she whispered. "I don't feel bad but come back, okay? I don't understand why I don't feel bad."

"I'll be back," I said, climbed up and closed the

connecting doors, then went to the john. When I came out, she had taken off her clothes and lay naked above the covers, her hands holding her small breasts as if they were as painful as wounds.

"It's not like hers," she said quietly—she didn't have to explain who *her* was—"but it's all I'm ever going to have."

"You're lovely," I said.

"I know you want hers," she said, trying to smile and cry all together, "but make love to me."

I lay down and held her as the sobs rippled like convulsions through her slim body, held her until she cried herself to sleep. I covered her up and went to the bathroom to make a drink, meaning to drink until I could sleep again, but I heard a tapping at the connecting doors. When I opened them, I wasn't surprised to see Melinda waiting there.

"I guess we should talk," she whispered, then held her index finger up to her pale lips. Sometime during the night, she had scrubbed the make-up from her face, but even wrapped in a sheet and wearing a wan face, the beauty I hadn't been able to see at first was as clear as the troubled look darkening her eyes.

"I guess we should talk," I echoed her, then led her into the bathroom and closed the door. She sat on the floor, cross-legged, her elegant feet rosy in the harsh light. I sat down on the toilet seat in my classic thinker's pose. "I seem to be having a lot of conversations in johns tonight."

"I'm sorry," she said, as if she could reach back and change it all now. "I'm so sorry."

"Me too," I said, "but it's too late to do anything about it. Way too late."

"How do you know when it's too late to change things?" she asked with a sad smile. But she didn't want an answer. Not to that question. "What did take you so long after Trahearne and I left the house?"

232

"I had to clean up the mess," I said, "talk to Torres and Hyland about the details." It didn't seem necessary for her to know that Stacy had killed Hyland. I didn't want anybody else to know.

"What details?" she asked casually.

"Like what to do with your body if you don't come up with the forty thousand," I said, and she dropped her face into her hands. "You can't steal from those people," I added. "Didn't you know that?"

"I didn't have any choice." She raised her head to stare at me. For the first time since I had known her, I could see Rosie's influence on her features. She had the same patient eyes, the same cocky defiance in the tilt of her chin. "I just couldn't make another movie," she said. "I couldn't . . . couldn't do it . . . Hell, I can't even say it anymore . . . I couldn't fuck any more strangers. When I first started it seemed like a lark. I mean, it seemed like fun, you know, I was stoned all the time and fucking everybody anyway, so getting paid for it seemed like a great bonus. What I did with my body didn't matter. Only the mind and the spirit mattered, I thought. But I was wrong. Everything you do matters. Every action causes complications, repercussions. I learned that in jail."

"What happened?" I asked.

"Nothing all that dramatic," she said. "I went in thinking that I was Betty Sue Flowers—a little fucked up, right, and thirty pounds overweight, but still smarter and prettier than any of that trash in jail. I was wrong. I met a woman who was brighter and better-looking than I could ever hope to be, more talented, more promising in school. She was also the meanest, toughest person I had ever met. She beat me senseless the first night, and humiliated me every day and night after that, but the worst thing she did was tell me that in ten years I would be just like her. She was dead right, of course, so when I got out, I knew I had to change my life. The money gave me that chance, and I had no other choice, so I took it."

"What did you do with it?"

"When I left Selma's, I went to stay with a friend of hers in St. Louis, and she got me admitted to Washington University as a special student—."

"The great American dream," I interrupted, "finance an education with mob money."

"It seemed like a good idea at the time," she said quietly. "So I went to college until I discovered ceramic sculpture. Once my pieces started to sell, I came back out West. Everything was fine until . . . until all this happened."

"I don't know if all this was Trahearne's fault or mine," I said, "but I'll apologize anyway."

"That's not necessary," she said. "If it's anybody's fault, it's mine." She sighed. "What's going to happen now?"

"You have any of the money left?" I asked.

"I have about thirty-five hundred in the bank," she said, "and I can raise some more—maybe another three or four thousand—if I sell all my finished pieces. That isn't forty thousand, is it?" She chuckled. "Maybe they'll let me pay them back on the installment plan."

"Us," I said.

"Us?"

"I'm on the hook now too," I said. "I've bought a little time, but I don't have a big enough edge to keep them off our backs forever. They're really touchy about their money. They'll spend a hundred grand just to get the forty back, and then they'll cut off our hands."

"What can we do?" she asked tiredly.

"Borrow it from Trahearne," I suggested.

"He's so broke, I have to buy groceries on his BankAmericard," she said.

"How about Selma?"

"She's done too much already," she said.

"Ask Trahearne to borrow it from his mother," I said.

"I'd let them cut off my hands first," she said, then held them out in offering. The long, darkly red fake nails had been clumsily pasted over her own. As she looked at her trembling fingers, tears of anger gushed from her eyes, and she started tearing at the fake nails, scraping and biting, ripping nail and cuticle and flesh until the ends of her fingers were covered with blood, then she jammed her hands into the folds of sheet bunched at her lap. She stared at the stains and whispered, "I've made such a mess of things, and people I don't even know have to come to my rescue again and again . . . Maybe I should call Hyland and tell him I'll come back to work."

"I don't think that would work," I said.

"Why not?"

"He told me he never wanted to see you again," I lied.

"And I've probably made a mess of your life now, too," she said.

"It's always been a mess," I said lightly.

"You've done so much," she said, "and I don't even know why."

I didn't either but I reached for my wallet and took out her high school picture and handed it to her.

"I killed that girl a long time ago," she said quietly, "you've been looking for a ghost." She touched her face in the picture, smearing it with blood. She didn't sob, but tears coursed unbidden down her cheeks. "That cameo was my grandmother's, you know, the only thing she had left when they got to California— that cameo and seven kids and a husband with a cancer behind his eye," she said. "She raised them all, made them all finish high school. She ruined her feet and legs slinging hash in a truck stop in Fresno, and when she got too old to work she went to the county home. She wouldn't live with her kids, wouldn't trouble them that way. When I was a little-bitty girl, my mother would take me to visit her, you know, and I hated that dry stink of the old folks. They were so crazy with loneliness, they always came out of their rooms to touch me and fuss over me, and I hated it, just hated it.

"While she talked to Granny, my momma would kneel down in front of her chair and rest her legs on her shoulders and rub the varicose veins in Granny's legs, rub them until her hands began to cramp. Then she'd ask me to rub Granny's legs for a minute while she rested, and I wouldn't do it, wouldn't touch those veins like big ugly worms under her stockings. I couldn't make myself touch them, those legs she had ruined so her children would finish high school.

"Jesus God, why didn't I understand?" she moaned. "I didn't go to her funeral because I was playing at being tragic in *Antigone* . . . Playacting, my god, what a foolish child I was . . . a foolish child I have been." Then she stopped and stared at me, tears and blood smudged on her cheeks, like some ancient mask of grief. "Why?" she asked simply.

"I don't know," I said, and she tucked her legs under her, let her head fall into my lap.

"I haven't dreamed in ten years," she said, her voice muffled against my thigh, her breath hot against my skin even through the fatigue pants. "They say I dream and don't remember but I know I don't dream at all. My hands dream for me," she said as she rocked back on her knees and held her hands out again, offering them to some angry god. I reached for the hands, but she grabbed my face between them, clutched my cheeks and pulled me toward her, kissing me through the tears, whispering against my mouth, "Lie down with me, make me forget, please, please . . ."

With the last strength of my hands, I took her wrists

and pushed her away. As she rocked back on her knees, the sheet unwound from her shoulders like a shroud, and her naked breasts stood between us.

"You don't want me," she said, "and I can't blame you, not after all you know."

"It's Trahearne," I said.

"He doesn't want me anymore," she said. "He wants me gone, out of his life. I've know that for a long time but I chose to ignore it."

"He went to a lot of trouble for a man who doesn't want you," I said.

"He thinks I'm a slut," she whispered, "and he just wanted to make sure. That's all. That's not the same thing as wanting me. A woman knows. You want me, I can tell. I don't know why you won't lie down with me."

"I'm afraid," I said.

"Of me?" she asked, then twisted easily out of my grip.

"Of myself," I said, and she stared at me again, long and hard. "You love Trahearne," I added as I put my hands on her bare shoulders. She waited, as still as an animal resigned to a trap, waited for me to pull her toward me or push her away.

"You're right," she said, tilting her head so her cheek rested on the back of my left hand. "I'm sorry." She rose and wound the sheet around her body. "You think you're in love with me, don't you?" she said with her hand on the doorknob. I nodded slowly. "You don't even know me," she said, and I had to nod again. "It's very kind of you to care, but you don't even know me at all." Then she left, walking out of the sterile light of the bathroom and into the darkness. To my blurred eyes, the white sheet seemed to leave a drifting afterimage that glowed like swamp-fire.

When the connecting door clicked shut, Stacy got out

of bed and walked over to the door. "You missed your chance," she said quietly. I stood up and mixed another drink. "Men are such romantic old farts," she said, smiling. "Come on to bed."

We woke at ten the next morning, but Melinda and Trahearne had already gone, leaving me like some hired retainer to clean up.

16 ••••

I TRIED TO GET STACY TO GO BACK TO SELMA'S PLACE
while I tidied up the rest of the mess, but she wouldn't
hear of it.

"I've got my first new dress in five years," she said,
"and you're taking me out to dinner tonight, dummy."

"Right," I said, glad of the chance.

She waited at the motel while I ran errands. I
returned the two rental cars, had the account books
copied, sent the copies to Torres and stuck the originals
in a safe-deposit box along with a note explaining what
they were about. I made dinner reservations at a
Chinese place and bought two bottles of French
champagne, which we drank as we dressed for dinner.

"I've never had real French champagne." Stacy
sighed as she slipped her dress over her head. "But I
intend to have it again." Then she fell back across the
bed, laughing softly until she fell asleep.

I ordered dinner over the telephone and sent a cab
driver after it. When he brought the cartons back, I
paid him, then lay down beside her. Sometime during
the middle of the night, we woke up making love in our
clothes. After, we undressed and sat down to our cold
dinner, which we ate silently like two starving peasants,
then crawled back into bed.

"You know," Stacy said dreamily, "I must be well again."

"Why's that?"

"Here I am drunk on champagne, shacked up with a strange older man, the reek of gunpowder still fresh in my innocent young nose, and I feel absolutely great," she said. "How about you?"

"I've got these holes in my shoulder," I said, "a swollen ankle, Chinese indigestion, and nothing to look forward to but a champagne hangover and a long drive home."

"Isn't it wonderful," she whispered. "I'm gonna be a great horse doctor, you know, goddamned great horse doctor. When I grow up. Whadda you gonna be when you grow up?"

"Older," I said, but she was already asleep again.

The next morning, as I parked at the head of Selma's trail, I had to line up behind her pickup, a fence company truck, and Melinda's Volkswagen.

"You think she's still here?" Stacy asked.

"I think I'm back in the goddamned towing business," I said as I climbed out to look at the note under the VW windshield wiper. A key was folded up in the paper, which had one word written on it: *Please.* I shook my head, and Stacy and I picked up our tired feet and headed them up the trail.

Selma was sitting in the living room watching four young men struggle as they tried to dig post holes in the rocky hillside.

"I never thought it would come to this," she said as we joined her.

"You think it's enough?" I asked.

"I've ordered two guard dogs from a place in Broomfield," she confessed. " 'The world is too much with us, late and soon,' " she recited. "No one will ever

240

trespass here again," she added, then touched her bruised cheek. "Ever again."

"I hope not," I said. "I bought us some insurance, but put up the fence and get the dogs anyway. Just in case."

"You sound like a man about to make his goodbyes," she said. "You should stay a few days, should rest."

"Do," Stacy said, grabbing my arm.

"I'm too tired to stay," I admitted. "Why don't you all pack and head up into the mountains for a few days? Find a little lake and some air that nobody's breathed. I'm going to town to pick up a tow bar and my dog, then I'm going home while I still can."

"Perhaps you're right," Selma said. She glanced at Stacy, who nodded slowly and released my arm. "You're always welcome here, you know."

"Thanks."

"And if you need doctoring," Stacy said lightly, "give me a call. Any time at all." She gave me a quick hug and walked out of the cabin toward her own, her narrow back firm and erect.

"She's a lovely woman," Selma said, "and I think as terrible as all this has been, it has been good for her."

"She's a tiger," I said, "she'll be fine."

"Melinda told me," Selma said. "I always think I know my charges, and they always find some way to surprise me. You didn't surprise me, though."

"Why?"

"I knew that you would get Melinda back," she said, "and I want to thank you for it. You saved her life."

"If I hadn't been so stupid, they would never have found her," I said.

"One can't be blamed for believing lies," she said softly.

"I get paid for knowing the difference," I said, "but this time—"

"This time was different," she interrupted.

"Yes, ma'am."

"Will you do me one last favor?" she asked.

"Of course."

"Keep an eye on Melinda," she said, "check on her from time to time. I have this feeling that she's going to need a friend soon."

"I'll do my best," I said, "but I can't promise anything."

"Thank you," she said, "and please don't blame yourself for this last spate of her troubles. They began many years ago, and none of this was your fault."

"I'm not sure about that," I said, then left her there with her cats and her chicks and her shiny new fence.

But the really bad ones never end. They drag on like an endless litigation or a chronic jungle fever. I thought this one was over, though, except for the forty thousand dollars, which was mostly Melinda's worry. I had plenty of time to think about it, too, as I headed north one more time with Melinda's VW in tow and Fireball lying in a drugged stupor on the seat beside me. The bulldog was heavily bandaged to hold the drains in place. When I picked him up, the vets released him to me as if he didn't have much chance to survive. They had removed a portion of his stomach and resectioned his small intestine, so I babied him toward home as gently as I could. By the time we reached Meriwether, he looked so bad that I put him in the vet's while I towed the VW up to Cauldron Springs.

I had had a bellyful of the Trahearne family circus, so I left Melinda's car parked behind the hotel pool house, then went home to keep an eye on Fireball and tie up the loose ends. I sat in my office holding the telephone until it was slick with sweat, then I hung it up and dug up some postcards. It seemed a fitting form of communication. I sent one to Rosie with Trahearne's telephone number on it. Another to Melinda, telling her to call her mother. A third to Trahearne, which said simply: *You owe me, old man.*

As I left the office, I stopped by the secretary's desk and interrupted her as she buffed a higher gloss on her blue fingernails.

"If anybody calls," I told her, "tell them that I'm out of town indefinitely."

"How long is that?" she asked without looking up.

"Almost forever," I said, and she wrote it down.

I picked up Fireball, who was still hanging on, and drove him up to the cabin on the North Fork. His wounds healed slowly, but they healed. A fresh froth of white hairs grizzled his muzzle, he walked carefully as if trying to control his natural waddle, and he couldn't lift his leg to pee, but he survived. Finally I drove him down to Columbia Falls to have the drains and stitches removed. When we got back to the cabin, Trahearne's Caddy was parked in front and he was sitting at the table with a half-gallon of vodka and a jug of tonic. He didn't say anything as I picked up Fireball and carried him up the steps. When I sat him down, the bulldog walked toward Trahearne to sniff him, but halfway there he changed his mind and lay down to lick his scars.

"I suppose you blame me for that, too," Trahearne said casually.

"I guess I don't blame anybody for anything," I said.

"Must be tough being a saint," he suggested. He sounded sober but his eyes were red and drunk. A white crust of antacid flaked at the corners of his mouth.

"What are you doing here?" I asked.

"I couldn't work," he said, and hung his head.

"Maybe you're standing too far from your desk," I said.

"What the hell do you know about it?" he asked, his

anger changing to sadness in the middle of the question.

"Nothing."

"Then don't try to tell me how to do it," he said as he tried to pour vodka into his glass. It was too much trouble, though. He lifted the half-gallon and drank from the bottle, using the tonic water as a chaser.

"I don't think that's how you make a vodka tonic," I said.

"Fuck you." He belched painfully and had another drink.

"Let's start this conversation over," I said.

"Whatever you say," he mumbled. He stood up and staggered over to the edge of the cabin. He fell to his knees as if he were about to pray, gagged once or twice, then projectile-vomited a huge gout of blood off the side.

"Jesus Christ," I said. He did it again, and collapsed over the side, three feet down to the ground on his face. I went over and helped him to his feet and wiped his face, then hooked an arm over my shoulder and walked him toward his car.

"What are you doing?" he asked.

"Taking you to the hospital," I said.

"Lemme die," he muttered, "lemme die."

"You'd draw flies," I said as I stuffed him into the Caddy. As I went back to get Fireball, Trahearne laughed and gagged again. It took me a few minutes to throw some clothes into a knapsack, and when I stepped out of the tent, Trahearne had gotten out of the car and was stumbling toward the river. "Hey!" I shouted as I ran after him.

"Get away," he said as I caught him by the arm. When I didn't, he jerked his arm so hard that he threw me into a tree. Then he set off for the river again.

My first impulse was to leap up and knock the hell out of him, but I didn't want to break my hand on his giant jaw. This time when I caught him, I wrapped a forearm around his neck to choke him down. He thrashed and raged and bucked like a wounded bull, but I stayed on his back until he fell to his knees, then I turned him loose. He shook his great head, struggling for breath and oxygen for his brain, then rose without a word and took off for the river again. This time it was easier. The third time easier still.

"I can keep this up all day," I told him as he stood up the last time.

"You're going to have to," he whispered, still strangling on his words.

"To hell with it," I said as I turned away from him, then I swung around and hit him on the point of the jaw. It was like hitting a tree, and it felt as if I had broken all the bones in my right hand and wrist. "God damn," I said as I held it gently with my left hand. Trahearne stood upright for a moment, then took a step toward me and fell into my chest. We both went down, the big man on top, and I felt a couple of ribs tear loose. At least he was finally out, though. I crawled from under him and grabbed his collar to drag him to the car before the pain got too bad. But I couldn't budge him. I had to drive down to the Polebridge store to get help loading him into the back seat of the Caddy. By the time I drove to the hospital in Kalispell, Trahearne was snoring peacefully, and my right hand looked like a rubber glove full of water.

Two days later I went back down to visit him. When I walked into his hospital room, he smiled painfully.

"You're going to be the death of me," he said.

"I broke six bones in my hand, old man, and dislocated three ribs—trying to keep you alive."

I held up my cast.

"I guess I owe you again, huh?"

"Damned right," I said.

"Well, thanks."

"What the hell did you have in mind?" I asked as I sat down in the nearest chair.

"Who knows," he murmured. "Who the hell knows?" Then he paused for a long moment. "Melinda told me about the forty thousand," he said, "and I made the mistake of going to my mother to borrow the money."

"Mistake?"

"The crazy old bitch laughed at me," he said, blushing with shame. "I knew better than to ask," he added, "knew I had to work it out on my own."

"What did you do? Mortgage your house?"

"I would if I could," he said, "but the bank already has two overdue notes on it now. The only reason they don't kick me out is because my mother went down and guaranteed the notes. Goddamned crazy old woman. I've never understood anything about her, you know, nothing. Maybe she wants me around, but only on her terms. I don't know . . ."

"So she laughed and you hit the bottle, huh?"

"Not then," he said, "not just yet. I called my publisher and got him to give me a forty thousand advance against this new book—"

"What new book?" I interrupted.

"Whatever new book I write," he answered. "But I have to finish at least a hundred pages of it before he'll give me the money. That's why I came to see you."

"You want me to write it?" I asked. "Or just hold your hand while you do it?"

He nodded slowly. "If you could come up and keep me dry for a month, I could do it."

"You're kidding."

"Not at all," he said. "I know how much I owe you, C.W., but if you could just do this last thing, I'd . . . I'd do anything for you, pay you anything. I've just got to get back to work, you see, just have to . . ."

"For the forty thousand?" I asked. "For Melinda?"

"Yeah, right," he muttered.

"You son of a bitch," I said. "I'll do it, but not for you or your damned stupid book . . ."

"For her," he said quietly. "I'll take that. I guess that's more than I deserve."

"What's she think about it?" I asked.

"She doesn't know yet," he said. "She rented a truck and loaded up her pieces and took them down to San Francisco."

"Great," I said. "Why didn't you give her a hand?"

"She wouldn't let me," he confessed. "She said it was her trouble and that she'd handle it. But when I get the money, you can give it to them, and she'll be off the hook."

"Me too," I said, but he wasn't listening.

"It must be tough," he said softly.

"What's that?"

"To finish the grand quest and find the fair maiden sullied," he said, almost whispering.

"Only by you," I said, "only by you."

"That's what I meant, of course," he said, "to find the fair lady in love with the dragon, married to the shaggy, foulbreathed beast . . ." He stopped and stared at me. "You should have let me make it to the river."

"I thought about it."

"Why didn't you do it?"

"Because she loves you, I guess," I said, "though I don't understand why."

"Neither do I."

"What about you?" I asked. "Do you love her?"

He paused for a long time before he answered, then he said, "I'm not sure what that means anymore, but I know I can't live without her."

"You don't seem to live with her too well."

He paused again, even longer this time, then he said,

"You know, I used to look forward to the day when I got too old to give a damn about women. I used to think that when that day came, all that wasted energy I spent chasing them would go into my work. I thought I'd grow old and wise, sexless as an oracle, but it didn't work that way, son, not at all. It came on me sooner than I expected, it drove me crazy—or crazier. And when Melinda rekindled the fires, I was so grateful that I married her. Now I'm afraid to lose her."

"You don't need a detective, old man, you need a shrink."

"Maybe so, son," he said, "but you're all I've got. I'd rather give you the thirty dollars an hour anyway. At least you buy me a drink every now and again."

"But no more," I said. "The first drink you take is the last one I buy."

"I'll be as meek as a lamb," he said, and grinned. "You'll see."

As soon as the doctors could run a series of tests, they found out that Trahearne didn't have a perforated ulcer at all. Just an attack of acute alcoholic gastritis. They let him check out of the hospital the next morning.

"Put the top up," he said peevishly as he settled into the passenger seat of his Caddy. His face was so white that it seemed to have been painted with clown make-up.

"Shut up and enjoy the sunshine," I said as I wheeled away.

"Where are you going?" He sighed. "You're going the wrong way."

"I've got to get my pickup." I popped the top on a beer.

"I can't drive," Trahearne said, staring at the beer.

"I know," I said, "I've got a tow bar in the trunk. You just bought me one. I got tired of renting the damn

248

things. Almost as tired as I am of towing your damned cars back and forth."

"You're going to make me ride up that forty miles of gravel road?" he said. "All the way up and back?"

"And you get to watch me drink beer all the way, too," I said. "What the hell, if Fireball can make it, you can," I added, nodding toward the back seat where the bulldog slept.

"Sughrue, you're a mean son of a bitch," Trahearne said as he swiped at his sweaty face.

"You want two-bit sympathy, old man, or hundred-dollar-a-day efficaciousness?"

"How about six-bit words?" he asked, almost smiling.

"Uncle Sam bought me a pocketful," I said, "but I never have any place to use them."

Trahearne grinned until I made him open me another beer, then we drove north into the mountains. I drank and he watched all the way to the cabin, where I hooked our cars together again. On the way back down, I hit a couple of bars in Columbia Falls and Kalispell, then every one after that on the way to Cauldron Springs. The big man never complained. He just sat in the car sipping 7-Up and scratching Fireball's head. By the time I parked in front of his house, it was late afternoon, and I was drunk as a coot. When I opened the door of the El Camino, Catherine Trahearne nearly took it off with her Porsche. She locked all four brakes and slid to a stop in front of us, then leaped out and raced to help Trahearne out of the pickup.

"How are you feeling?" she crooned. "You should have let me come to the hospital, you know."

"I'm fine." Trahearne sighed heavily as she fussed over him. "Just fine. A little tired, though. Maybe I'll take a little nap."

"Is that *nap?* Or *nip?*" I asked as I climbed out. Trahearne gave me a sad, tired smile as he shook his head, but Catherine looked at me with such intense anger that it nearly sobered me. Nothing like a little naked hatred to get a drunk's attention. "Sleep tight," I added stupidly as she eased Trahearne up the stairs.

When they disappeared through the front door, I went around to help Fireball out. He nosed across the lawn slowly, looking for a bush. Not to pee on, though—to hide behind. Having to squat like a mere puppy embarrassed him no end. Finally, he found a bit of ragged evergreen shrubbery and he lowered himself behind it.

"What the hell are we doing here, dog?" I asked. But he didn't know either. He finished his business, then came back to curl up in the shade beside my feet. I leaned against my fender and went on with my beer.

Catherine came out of the house and walked down toward me, the short pleated skirt of her tennis dress fluffing as she bounced hurriedly down the stairs.

"You're looking particularly lovely today," I offered.

She was, too. The summer weeks of tennis had darkened her tan without drying her skin, and deep red highlights glowed in her cheeks. She smelled of perfume and lady-sweat, of coconut oil and sunshine.

"Damn fine," I added, hefting my beer can in toast as a warm flicker of old desire kindled inside my belly.

She stopped in front of me and slapped the beer can out of my hand. It clattered against the gravel driveway and spewed a froth of foam across the road.

"What the hell do you think you're trying to do?" she asked, breathless with anger.

"He's had all the tender loving care he can stand," I said as I tried to swallow my own anger.

"What the hell do you know about it?" she demanded.

"Almost everything there is to know about it," I said. "He hired me to keep him dry, and I just wanted to see if he's got the guts."

"Alcoholism is a disease!" she screamed at me. "It has nothing to do with guts."

"Well, he hired me, not you," I said.

"You're not even doing it for him," she said, "you're doing it for her." I didn't bother to deny it. "Oh, the goddamned bitch," she hissed. Rage flattened her lips and stretched the skin tightly across the bones of her face until they seemed to glow like a mummy's skull through parchment. Fine white lines glimmered hotly at the corners of her eyes, her temples, and along her jawline. She hissed a silent curse, stomped her foot, then ran over to her Porsche and roared away in a cloud of gravel and dust.

I went around and got another beer and watched her leave. She made the turn onto the highway with a very nicely executed four-wheel drift. Halfway back to town, her brake lights flared as she locked the wheels and skidded to a stop in the middle of the highway, where she sat for several minutes. Then, slowly and deliberately, she turned around and drove back toward the house.

"Please accept my apology," she said as she stopped the car beside me. "I'm truly sorry."

"Don't apologize," I said as she stepped out, "it's a sign of weakness."

Her anger came back in a single swift rush, but she gulped it down, and sweetly asked, "What?"

"That's what John Wayne says," I said. "I can't remember which movie but I know he said it."

"He's your hero, is he?" she said.

"Only fools have heroes," I said.

"I see," she said, smiling slowly. "I always make the mistake of underestimating you, don't I?"

"That's better than overestimating me, isn't it?"

"I'm not certain of that," she said, "but I'm certainly sorry."

"Forget it," I said. "It's a fool's errand, and I'm

probably doing it foolishly. It's the only way I know. Pride and guts—that's the only thing that will work for Trahearne."

"When the going gets tough, the tough get going?" she asked slyly.

"Make fun if you want to, but that's what character is all about."

"I'm sorry." She laughed and touched my arm. "I just couldn't resist teasing you. You were *so* serious, you know."

"Drunks are always serious at the wrong times," I said.

"Do you think you can keep Trahearne dry for a while?".

"If he really means it, I can help, I guess," I said. "It's worth a try."

"Perhaps I should come over later to prepare dinner for the two of you."

"Thanks," I said, "but we'll manage."

"I'm being, as they say, invited out?"

"Something like that," I admitted.

"Perhaps you're right," she said. "Come over for a drink after dinner."

"I'll see," I said.

"Of course." She reached up to kiss the corner of my mouth. "Take care of him for me."

"I'll do my best," I said, and she nodded as if she knew I would. She went back to her car and drove slowly around to Trahearne's mother's house. Once again I loaded up with our baggage and toted it up the stairs to the house.

Instead of napping, though, Trahearne was sitting in his shorts and T-shirt at his desk, idly working the slide of the .45 Colt automatic. A freshly poured glass of neat whiskey sat at his elbow.

"Don't worry," he said as I set the bags down in the living room, "I'm not about to blow my brains out. I prefer the slow suicide of drink." Then he lifted the glass of whiskey. "And don't worry about this, either," he said as he put it back down. "Its presence comforts me somehow." He picked up the .45 again and spun his chair to face me. The large automatic was almost dwarfed by his huge hand. He let it dangle from his fingers as if it were a broken wing. "You took that house down in Colorado like a good soldier," he said. "Were you?"

"It seemed like the only choice at the time," I said, "the best way to stay alive."

"That's the big difference," he said quietly, "between your war and mine. You kids knew that if you survived the tour of duty, you'd survive the war. We all knew we were going to be killed. That's the only way we could go on—we accepted out deaths in advance just so we could go on: But that's not the point, is it?"

"What's the point?" I asked as I sat down.

"What's the worst thing you did in the war?" he asked suddenly.

It wasn't a casual question, and I didn't have a casual answer.

"We were fighting through a village south of An Khe, a hole in the road called Plei Bao Three," I said, "and I grenaded a hooch and killed three generations of a Vietnamese family. Both grandparents, their daughter, and her three children."

"Were you a good soldier before that?" Trahearne asked.

"I guess so."

"And afterwards?"

"There wasn't any afterwards," I said. "I was in the stockade afterwards. A Canadian television news team was covering the attack, and I made the evening news the next day, so they had to lock me up."

"That's politics," Trahearne said, waving his empty hand at me, "not combat." After dismissing the central trauma of my adult life with a flip of his hand, Trahearne went on. "I'm going to tell you something I've never told anybody."

"Great," I said, but he didn't notice.

"When we landed at Guadalcanal, I wasn't much of a Marine," he said. "I mean, I walked and talked and fought like a Marine but it was all an act. I guess I thought I was supposed to survive the damned war or something—I don't know—but I was just going through the motions, trying to look good. Then we were dug in up on the Tenaru River, and the Japs pulled a night banzai charge. We held, we held and kicked the shit out of them, and I got some idea of what I was doing wrong. After it was over, though, I worked it all out in my mind.

"We were checking the bodies, the Jap bodies, and I found this Jap enlisted man floating face up in the shallows. There was just enough starlight to see that he was alive, enough for him to see me. I leaned over and shot him between the eyes with this .45.

"I guess I don't have to tell you what it looks like up close, I guess you know, but I made myself watch, made myself not flinch, and then I knew what the war was about. It wasn't about politics or survival or any of that shit, it was about killing without flinching, about living without flinching." Then he paused and tossed the pistol onto a pile of loose papers. "That's how I've lived ever since that night, and that's what's wrong. If you can't flinch, you might as well be dead."

"That was a long time ago," I said. "Maybe it's time to stop blaming yourself."

"Have you stopped blaming yourself for all those dead civilians?" he asked quickly.

"Some."

"You're lucky, then," he said sadly. "I can't stop. So I'm going to give in to it. Listen, I know what sort of sentimental nonsense my poetry is, and I know what

254

sort of macho dreck my fiction is—I'm as phony as my goddamned crazy mother—but I've learned something out of these past few insane months, and I'm through with all that other crap. And it's all your fault."

"It's always my fault," I said lightly.

"In the beginning, I wanted you to find out about Melinda so I would know—if Rosie hadn't hired you, I would have found some way to do it—but I watched you go after her for a smile and eighty-seven dollars, and you never judged her, not once, you forgave her without asking anything in return. When I was in the hospital, I thought about it all the time, and I finally understood it. All this time, all these years since the war, I worried about how tough you had to be to live, how I had to live without flinching, but when it came down to it, when it had to do with living instead of dying, I didn't have the guts to forgive the woman I loved. I couldn't cut it, son, not a bit." He paused long enough to pick up the .45 and shove the stack of pages off his desk. "So now I'm through with all that. I'm going to write a novel about love and forgiveness. Even if it kills me. And that's why I'm not about to blow my brains out with this." He tossed the pistol back on his desk. "It's nothing but a paperweight now."

"Good."

"I've pulled my last trigger, boy," he said, grinning. "Hell, I didn't even pull the trigger on the shotgun that night—I just jacked a round into the chamber and I was so drunk that I had the trigger back when I did it, and the son of a bitch went off. Nobody there was more surprised than me."

"Some of us were pretty surprised," I said, grinning back at him.

"Nobody more than me," he said, then he chuckled and handed me the glass of whiskey. "Now get out of here, boy, I've got work to do."

"Right," I said. As I stood up and watched him

gather his sharpened pencils and a fresh legal pad, I discovered an odd knot in my throat and a burning in my eyes, but I went off to do my chores before the old man noticed.

Trahearne worked until dinner, then he ate scrambled eggs and sausage at his desk, waving me away when I offered him more. Since he seemed locked in, I decided to wander outside to check on the bulldog. Fireball had eaten most of the baby food in his dish and had fallen asleep with his nose still touching the bowl. I left him alone and drifted over toward the creek. Catherine met me at the bridge. She was wearing a long knit gown that rippled across her body in the twilight.

"Were you coming for a drink?" she asked as she locked her arms around my neck and socketed her groin against mine.

"Something like that," I said as I slipped my arms around her firm waist.

As she kissed me, she murmured against my mouth, "We've no place to go, lover." It didn't seem to matter, though. She moved her hands down and quickly unfastened my Levis, then lifted the long folds of her skirt and gathered them about her hips so I could hold her naked buttocks in my good hand as I bent my knees.

When we were finished, I glanced over her shoulder toward Trahearne's mother's house. A curtain at an upstairs window wavered as if someone had just stepped away from it.

"I think the old woman was watching us," I said.

"To hell with her," Catherine said as she smoothed her skirt down finely muscled legs.

"Did it ever occur to you that we shouldn't be doing this?" I asked.

"It never occurs to me until afterward," she answered, then laughed prettily. "Tomorrow evening," she added, "same time, same place." Then she walked away from me into the fading dusk, walked away before I could say no.

But the next evening when I showed up at the bridge after dinner, Edna Trahearne was waiting for me. She was dressed, as usual, in her retired fishing clothes, to which she had added a knit Irish hat against the evening chill. As I walked out on the bridge, she snorted as if I were late for a fly-casting lesson.

"Try to contain your disappointment," she growled at me. "Catherine is still clearing the dinner table. She'll be along shortly."

"It's nice to see you again, Miz Trahearne," I said as I leaned against the rail beside her. "Fish bitin'?"

"Aren't you the polite one?" she sneered. "How did you get mixed up with all these mortal folk?"

"How did you?"

"A moment of foolish passion, boy," she answered, then broke out in a cackle, a rash, fevered laugh that split the evening like a loon's call. "What's your excuse?"

"I guess I don't have one, ma'am."

"You'd best find one, boy," she advised cheerfully. "You've stepped into a nest of vipers, and if you're here without a good reason, you got no business being here."

"A day's work for a day's pay," I said, and she laughed again. "You're in a good mood tonight," I added.

"Every time that little slut is gone it improves my mood considerably," she said, then smiled as she waited for me to rise to the bait. When she was convinced that I wasn't going to bite, she snorted again, then asked, "What happened to your hand, boy?"

"I hit your baby boy in the chops," I admitted.

"A fella in your line of work ought to know better than to hit a man that size with your fist."

"I knew better," I said, "but I did it anyway. Just for the pure pleasure of it."

"You're polite, boy," she said with a smile as twisted as her fingers, "but you're not nice. Not a bit."

"Yes, ma'am," I answered, and the old woman turned away to hobble toward her house, pausing for a moment to speak to Catherine, who was walking toward the bridge. I couldn't hear what Edna was saying, but Catherine glanced over her shoulder to smile at me, the sort of smile my mother used to call a snake's grin. When they finished talking, the old woman went on toward the house, and Catherine strolled toward me slowly. She wore the same long soft green gown and carried a tall glass in her hand.

"I understand that you aren't always respectful toward your elders," she said as she stepped onto the bridge, the smile still sly on her face.

"I'm always nice to you," I said.

"You find it amusing to remind me of my age?" she asked, the smile suddenly wiped from her face.

"Just a little joke," I said by way of apology.

"I am not amused," she said as she swirled her drink furiously.

"I'm sorry."

"Why don't you go back and play nursemaid?"

"You got it, lady," I said, then walked away from her.

"C.W.," she said softly, but I kept on walking.

17 ••••

FOR NEARLY TWO WEEKS EVERYTHING WORKED SMOOTHLY, and Trahearne and I lived together as pleasantly as two old impotent bachelors, much as we had during his long visit up on the North Fork. It was like a vacation for me. In the mornings I ran, then sat in the sun and read my way through a large portion of his library. After lunch, I moved my chair into the shade and picked up whatever book I had just put down. Trahearne worked all day, though, writing in his furious scrawl and muttering to himself. About five every afternoon, he would stroll out of the house, stretch and growl, "Scribble, scribble, scribble, eh, Mr. Gibbon?" then chuckle as he walked down the stairs for his daily exercise, whistling for Fireball.

The big man and the bulldog walked toward town every afternoon while I followed in the Caddy like a trainer watching my fighters do their roadwork. When Trahearne tired, I would pick them up and drive on to the hotel pool, where Trahearne lolled about like an old walrus until his head began to nod. Then I drove the two invalids home and fed them. After dinner they both went to sleep, and I went downstairs to drink beer and watch television until I, too, found refuge in sleep.

Every morning, while I was away from the house

running, Catherine brought Trahearne a sheaf of typed manuscript and picked up his pages from the day before to transcribe them. Once, though, she was late, and I was sitting on the porch, back from my run and breathing hard as she came up the steps. She nodded at me, then went on into the house. When she came out, though, she stopped.

"I suppose you find this odd?" she said, rattling the long yellow sheets at me.

"Nobody else in the whole world can read his handwriting," I said.

"I'm pleased to do what I can," she said huffily, then went away.

"Aren't we all?" I whispered to her departure.

Trahearne stayed dry, seemingly without effort, except for a sip of my beer the afternoon we toasted Fireball the first time he managed to raise his leg to take a leak.

"God, that's good," Trahearne sighed after he had swallowed the beer, "so goddamned good."

"The first one always is," I reminded him as I took my beer can back.

"Right," he said, then trundled off on his walk. Fireball followed dutifully, marking every bush and rock in sight. When they reached the highway, Fireball waddled across the road to the creek to fill up again, and on the way toward town, Trahearne fussed at the bulldog constantly, telling him to put his damned leg down and come on.

That night, as he lowered himself into the pool, Trahearne asked me why I didn't come in with him anymore.

"It's like swimming in somebody's snot," I said.

"Sughrue," he said softly, "Sughrue, you're the most disgusting human being I've ever had the displeasure to meet."

"At least I don't swim in—"

"My god, don't say it again," he cried, then buried his head under the water. As he bobbed back up, he faked a great sneeze and splashed water all over me. His laughter rattled around the large tiled room, filling it with the sound of breaking glass. Then he drenched me again, shouting, "Never again! Don't ever say that again!"

I reached out with a damp boot and shoved his head back under the water. He grabbed my ankle with his huge hand and jerked me off the side of the pool. We both came up laughing like kids.

Later that same evening, as I was watching television and letting my clothes dry, I heard a knock on the large picture window of the daylight basement. When I glanced up, Catherine was standing there, grinning at me. My pants were nearly dry, so I slipped into them before I went to open the door.

"Aren't you the bashful one?" she said, still grinning.

"My mother was an Avon Lady," I said, "and she taught me never to answer the door unless I was dressed."

"That makes perfect sense," she answered, then she sighed and her grin didn't come back. "Listen, I'm coming down with cabin fever. When I finished typing this evening, I decided that I needed to get out of the house. Why don't we call a truce, and you can take me to town and buy me a drink."

"Good idea," I said.

When the Sportsman Bar closed at two, I bought half a dozen drinks in go-cups and carried them out to Catherine's Porsche. As I balanced them and climbed into the passenger seat, she reached over to touch my cheek.

"Let's take a midnight dip," she suggested.

"Good idea."

She eased the sports car through the darkened town and parked it behind the hotel, then got out and unlocked the back door of the pool house. Inside, I lined the paper cups up along the edge of the pool as Catherine rustled out of her clothes. Then she came over to help me with mine.

"Shall we swim before or afterward?" she whispered when I was as naked as she was.

"During," I said as I grabbed her and we tumbled into the warm, slick embrace of the water.

Sometime later, we sat on the edge of the pool with our feet dangling into the water. Wisps of steam hovered across the rumpled surface of the water, and like a distant echo of thunder, the spring rumbled gently at the far end of the room. The last quarter of the moon ticked slowly past a skylight window.

"It's so odd here at night," Catherine whispered. "It's like the entrance to some underground world where it's always warm and silent. That's why I whisper. When it's closed up like this, they couldn't hear you over in the hotel even if you screamed."

"Don't scream," I whispered as I held my hand over her mouth. She giggled against my fingers. When I moved my hand, she screamed, a quick high note that shattered the silence and echoed around the walls.

"I'm sorry," she said quietly, then giggled against her hand.

"You're drunk, lady," I said as I fumbled for another drink. The ice had melted, but I gunned it anyway.

"Isn't it wonderful," she sighed, leaning against me. "I'll tell you a secret," she said.

"Then it won't be a secret."

"You won't tell anybody," she said.

"I'm too drunk to remember."

"In the wintertime, when I come down at night, I

climb out of the pool and dash outside and roll in the snow, then dash back into the pool."

"Everybody in town knows that," I said.

"Oh you," she hissed, then slapped me gently on the chest. "You should try it sometime. It's like being reborn."

"Rolling around naked in the snow is not my idea of a religious experience," I said.

"Sissy."

"That's what they called the brass monkey after he rolled around in the snow," I said.

"What brass monkey?"

"The one that froze his balls off."

"You're terrible," she said. "Except when you're being wonderful."

"That's what I always say."

"I'll tell you another secret, you terrible man."

"I already forgot the other one," I said.

"You're the first man I've ever come here with," she said, watching her feet as they stirred the water. "The very first."

"I'm touched."

"Don't be cynical," she said. "This place is very special to me." She sat up straight again. In the darkness, the strips of untanned skin glistened, and as she turned to face me, her white breasts were as luminous as small moons. She must have seen me looking because she covered them with her darkly tanned hands. "The plastic surgeon who does my work says it's nip and tuck from now on," she said lightly. "He also reminds me how lucky I am that I didn't have children. Trahearne wouldn't have them, you know." When I didn't respond, she added, "Considering how things worked out, perhaps he was right."

"Trahearne's all the children anybody needs," I said.

"Trahearne is a great artist," she said quickly, "and

if I've made sacrifices, they were offered to that greatness."

"Okay," I said, sounding, I thought, properly chastised.

"You don't sound convinced," she said.

"Look, I'm fond of the old fart," I said, "but I'll let the folks in charge of greatness and all that crap decide that for me."

"C.W., sometimes you exhibit an unbecoming smallness of mind," she said.

"Provincial, huh?"

"A goddamned redneck," she said, then laughed. "You damned phony," she added, "I know all about you. Trahearne has told me everything." I didn't have anything to say about that, either. If Trahearne wanted to talk to his ex-wife, she was *his* ex-wife. "I don't tell him everything," she said, "if that's worrying you."

"I never worry."

"I worry about Trahearne," she said seriously.

"Maybe it's time you quit," I suggested.

"No, he needs me more now than ever," she said. "You can understand that."

"Sure."

"You're not jealous, are you?"

"I don't think so," I said. "My needs are small, and if you want to baby Trahearne, that's between the two of you."

"Not exactly," she said softly.

"What?"

"Melinda," she whispered.

"Right."

"You know, I think I would hate her even if she didn't have my husband," Catherine said calmly.

"Jealous?" I asked.

"Only of her backhand."

"What?"

"Oh, when she first moved up here, back when I was

still trying to be gracious about all this, I asked her to play tennis one afternoon," Catherine said.

"What happened?"

"She humiliated me, on the court and in the dressing room later when we came in for a swim," Catherine said. "I understand that you've seen that body she keeps hidden under all those baggy awful clothes, and you can imagine how it made me feel when I saw it." Then she paused. "Not that she showed it to me. She did her best to hide it—I have to admit that—but I peeked into the shower. That was the hardest moment of many hard moments."

"You're a lovely woman too," I said.

"It's kind of you to think so," she said. "I suppose she's better in bed than I am, too."

"I wouldn't know," I said.

"Really," she said, sounding genuinely surprised. "I thought she was fairly free with her favors."

"You're not the only one who thinks that," I said.

"You're a little bit in love with her, aren't you?"

"Maybe."

"Trahearne thinks you are," she said.

"Maybe I am, maybe not," I admitted. "I don't know anymore."

"Damn it."

"What?"

"Are you sober enough for me to ask you something very important?"

"Sure."

"Do you think she would leave him? Under the circumstances?"

"I don't know about that," I said. "She loves him but she thinks that he doesn't love her anymore. She might leave, but I wouldn't know what the right circumstances might be."

"Think about this for a moment," she said. "In my purse I have three cashier's checks. One for forty thousand made out to the bearer. Another for twenty thousand made out to a Miss Betty Sue Flowers. And a third in your name for ten thousand."

"No," I said. I stood up and walked toward my clothes.

"Listen to me," she said as she followed, "hear me out. Trahearne is working now, he isn't drinking and he has a chance to live and work for the rest of his life. If she comes back to live here, he will die within the year. You must know that."

"No," I said, "I don't want any part of this."

"When she flies back from San Francisco, Trahearne will ask you to pick her up at the airport in Meriwether," Catherine said as she rummaged in her purse, "and all you have to do is convince her to get back on that airplane—or another airplane—and fly out of our lives."

"No."

"Please," she said as she handed me a long white envelope.

"Trahearne would just send me after her again," I said as I hefted the slim bit of paper. Seventy thousand dollars seemed as light as a feather, yet so heavy that my hand could barely hold it up. I tapped it against my cast, which was crumbling after being dunked twice that day. "He'd just send me after her again."

"But if you took a long time to find her, long enough for him to finish this new book," she said, "it wouldn't matter by then." When I didn't answer, she added, "I wish you could read the beginning of this new book. It's beautiful, and you would understand why this is so important."

"I can't do it," I said as I tried to hand the envelope back to her.

"Just think about it, then," she said. "Keep the money and think about it. You owe me that much."

"I guess I do," I said as I set the envelope down and worked into my clothes. "Whose money is it?" I asked as we finished dressing.

"Does it matter?"

"Maybe."

"Edna and I put up equal amounts."

"I'll think about it, but I know I won't do it," I said.

"If you don't convince her," Catherine whispered as she stepped into my arms, "Trahearne's a dead man."

"I can't," I said, then buried my face in her damp hair. Beneath the sharp mineralized odor of the spring water, the light flowery touch of her perfurme lingered.

"Everything would be so simple if you could," she whispered against my neck, "and it will be so awful if you don't."

"It's already awful," I said.

We rode in silence back to Trahearne's house, and when she dropped me there, we didn't even say good night. I watched her drive over to the other house and park her car in the garage on the far side, watched the progression of lights turned on, then off as she moved through the house. The light in the living room stayed on for several minutes, as if Catherine had spent time looking at Trahearne's war trophies again. Then the downstairs went dark and a soft glow lightened the upstairs windows, as if a hallway light had been turned on. As I turned away, both upstairs windows on this side of the house flared, and I could see the two women's shadows moving behind their separate curtains. The old woman had been sitting downstairs in the darkness among the remains of that old war. A shudder swept across my back, and I went over to my El Camino, unlocked the topper, then crawled inside to lock the envelope in the gun case in the bottom of my tool chest. I went on to bed before I could think about any of it.

Catherine was right about one thing, though: two days later Trahearne asked me to drive down to pick up Melinda so he wouldn't miss a day's work.

When she came down the ramp, I almost didn't recognize her. She wore a tailored, vested suit in a dark shade of peach, her hair was blond again, short still but smoothly cut instead of hacked into a rumpled mess, and she even wore light touches of make-up. When she walked briskly across the asphalt and through the terminal doors, everything came to a halt at the airport while everybody watched her. She wore a new pair of leather boots, too, with stacked heels, and she didn't have to reach up to give me the light hug and kiss with which she greeted me.

"How do you like the new me?" she asked, her smile so warm and dazzling that it nearly blinded me.

"Jesus Christ," I murmured.

"Thank you," she said, accepting the compliment as if she felt she deserved it. "How are you?"

"Overcome with desire," I confessed.

"Thank you again," she said calmly, then swung her shoulder bag around and headed for the baggage claim. Two matching leather suitcases came down the conveyor. She nodded toward them, and I picked them up.

"What the hell's in here?" I grunted.

"A new life," she said, still smiling.

I followed her out to the El Camino, hurrying to keep up with this new, confident stride. Even from the rear, she looked happy. When she swung open the passenger door, Fireball tumbled out to greet her. If he had been any more excited, he would have rolled over on his back and pissed on himself like a puppy. As it was, he bounced around and barked and slobbered until he ran out of breath.

"Old Fireball MacRoberts seems to have recovered," she said as she knelt to rub his stubby ears.

"Roberts," I said as I tossed her bags under the topper.

"What?" she asked.

"Fireball Roberts," I said, "not MacRoberts."

"Oh who cares?" she said joyously, and I had to agree.

"I'm almost afraid to ask what happened," I said as we drove away.

"Buy me a beer and I'll tell you all about it," she said as she opened the cooler between the seats and cracked two beers. She handed me one, then drank half the other in one long rippling swallow, the smooth muscles of her throat working fluidly. "How's your hand?"

"Still broken," I said as I pounded the ratty cast on the steering wheel.

"What happened?" she asked.

I had made the mistake of assuming that she knew, but it seemed that Trahearne hadn't told her. If he hadn't, I certainly wasn't going to.

"One of those things," I said.

"Well, if you want to be mysterious," she said, then laughed and attacked the beer again. When she finished it, she crumpled the can like tissue paper, tossed it behind the seat, and went after another. "You ready?"

"Not just yet," I said, hefting the nearly full beer. "What did you do down there?"

"I don't know where to begin," she said, "so many wonderful things happened. I found a gallery in Ghirardelli Square, and they liked my work well enough to arrange a show—which sold out in three days; can you believe that?—and I shipped the rest of my pieces to a place in L.A., so that's settled.

"Then I went to see all the old ghosts. Rosie and I got roaring drunk, had a terrible fight, then fell weeping and laughing into each others arms." She paused long enough to laugh giddily. "I went up to see

Mr. Gleeson, and he was a pathetic old fool. Then I dropped in unannounced on poor Albert, and it took him two Valium and a giant Scotch before he stopped stuttering. I forgave the bastard for being a bastard, and you know what he did?"

"No, but I can guess."

"He came on like Mister Smooth-action." she said, "and when I wouldn't have any of it—I laughed in the creep's face—he burst into tears and dashed upstairs to see his shrink. I loved it." She laughed again, then dug into her purse. When she jerked out a long white envelope, I occupied myself with the beer can, but she slapped me across the chest with the envelope. "Five thousand dollars cash money," she said. "Will you see that Hyland gets it for me?"

"All right," I stammered, then stuffed the money in my shirt pocket.

"A down payment on a new life."

"Melinda—" I started to say.

"Betty Sue," she interrupted quietly, "Betty Sue Flowers. It's a decent name."

"I've always thought so," I said.

"How's Trahearne?" she asked. "He didn't have much to say over the telephone."

"Nose to the grindstone, dry as a bone," I clichéd.

"He did mention that you were a great nursemaid," she said. "You'll stay, won't you? As long as he needs you?"

"I guess so," I said. "Unless you want to run away with me."

"Don't be silly," she chortled as she slapped me heavily on the thigh. "I've just come home again."

18 ••••

As soon as we got back to the house, Betty Sue tumbled out of the pickup and raced up the stairs toward the front door. Fireball and I followed slowly— I was trying to be polite and he was practicing his aim—but she met us at the doorway, her finger lifted to her soft lips.

"He's working," she whispered.

"Listen," I said as I set her bags down, "I think I'll go fishing this afternoon. You know, so you can be alone with the great man."

"Don't be mean," she said shyly. "And it isn't necessary for you to go away."

"I'm going anyway," I said, then told Fireball, "let's go kill a trout." But he was sitting stolidly beside Betty Sue's heel. "Will you keep an eye on the dog?" I asked her.

"He'll keep an eye on me," she said. "You have a good time."

"You too," I answered, trying to mean it.

As I walked to the pickup, beneath the heat of the late summer sun, a hint of cool, crisp air tickled my nose. Autumn soon, I thought, and another Montana winter waiting in the wings. Every fall I considered drifting south to San Francisco and renewing my California license, but I never went. Maybe this would be the year. But for now, I knew where there was a little roadside lake up in the mountains behind Cauldron Springs. Moondog Lake, where the trout had an affinity for worms, a place to waste an afternoon watching my bobber dance across the windy chop.

I drove down to the highway and turned right, away from town, but Catherine's Porsche caught up with me before I crested the first rise. I pulled to the edge of the road, parked, and got out.

"What did she say?" Catherine asked as she walked over to stand beside me. "Well?"

"We didn't talk about it."

"Why not?" she demanded flatly.

"This whole idea is . . . is terrible," I said. "You can't expect to pay people to do this sort of thing."

"Why not?"

"There's more than money involved," I said.

"That's why Edna and I are willing to spend so much money."

"Well, you're going to have to get somebody else to do it," I said. "Or do it yourself."

"You're the only one who could do it," she said, "and if you don't, whatever happens is on your head."

"Sometimes I get the awful suspicion that this whole thing has been out of my hands from the very beginning," I said, "so it can't be my fault. But even if it is, I'm not going to try to bribe her to leave the man she loves."

"If she loved him, Sughrue, she would leave him for free."

"Betty Sue doesn't—"

"So it's Betty Sue now," Catherine interrupted. "That's very interesting."

"That's her name."

"Fitting," Catherine sneered.

"Look," I said as I stepped behind the pickup to unlock the topper, "I'm going to give you those damned checks back and then wash my hands of this whole fucking mess."

"It's on your head now," she said, then ran back to her car and drove away before I could climb into the pickup bed.

"My ass." I coughed into her dust as I locked up.

I didn't leave Moondog Lake until full dark, so it was nearly midnight before I drove down the highway toward Trahearne's house. The lights were still on, so I went on into town for a drink, then drove back out to check again. This time the lights were out. I eased up the driveway, parked, and let myself in through the basement door. As I mixed a drink the household above was silent. I switched on the television to catch the late movie from Spokane by cable, hoping for something rich with romance and scenery. *The Hanging Tree,* maybe, or *Ride the High Country.* Instead I caught *The Rise and Fall of the Roman Empire,* which put me to sleep. Occasionally I woke for a barbarian attack, a Christopher Plummer screeching speech, or Sophia Loren's breasts nudging the small screen, then fell back into a confused sleep.

I woke to the sound of gunfire and the instant memory of a preceding scream. I glanced at the television, where an aggressive young man urged me to buy a new pickup from the thousands on his lot. Then another shot boomed through the house. Down the hallway, I heard glassware break in the basement bathroom. I dashed to my bedroom for the .38, then raced back and up the stairs to the main floor, listening to the grunts and thuds of a struggle. As I slipped through the darkened kitchen, another shot banged. I dove across the living room rug and rolled into a left-handed firing position behind Trahearne's lounge chair.

The desk lamp in the study was on, but it had been

knocked askew and it shined out the doorway directly into my eyes. Beyond it, though, I could see two shadowy figures struggling, wrestling for possession of the .45 automatic, which went off again. A shelf of books scattered into smoldering pulp. I fired a round through the ceiling and shouted *Freeze!* but nobody paid any attention to me. As I charged the door, I heard a fist strike soft flesh, and Betty Sue staggered toward me. I shoved her aside and crouched just outside the door. When Trahearne bulled his way through it, I slammed him on the side of the neck with the butt of the .38, then again as he was going down. As he fell, he swung the .45 toward me, but I clubbed it out of his hand with my cast. He hit the floor unconscious and belched a small puddle of vomit, which smelled like straight whiskey. I picked up the .45, unloaded it, and tossed it on his lounge chair.

"Is he all right?" Betty Sue panted behind me.

"He's alive," I said as I knelt to check his pulse, which beat along as strong as a bear's, "but he's dead drunk. Are you all right?"

"Just had the breath knocked out of me." She huffed and puffed. "That's all." She moved over to kneel beside me. "Help me get him to bed."

"Right," I said, stuffing the .38 into my belt. "Glad I didn't have to shoot anybody," I added. "I'm terrible with my left hand."

"Help me," she answered, and the two of us levered the big man upright and walked him toward the bedroom. As we dropped him on the bed, he woke up long enough to tell us that he didn't need our damned help, but he went to sleep before we could debate the point. "Thank you," Betty Sue said, still breathing hard and deep.

"What the hell happened?" I asked.

"I need a drink," she answered, then walked out of the bedroom.

"Me too." I said as I followed.

But she wouldn't talk to me in the living room, either. I poured whiskey into two glasses and handed her one.

"Can I have a cigarette?" she said. I lit two, and she grabbed one out of my hand and sucked a cough out of it.

"Maybe you better sit down," I suggested.

"Outside," she said, and I followed her again.

As I leaned against the door frame, she paced back and forth across the deck, hitting the cigarette and the whiskey until she finished them both. When I went back inside, I noticed that the lights were on in Trahearne's mother's house. I hoped that they hadn't heard the shots. Outside again, I handed Betty Sue a fresh drink.

"What happened?" I asked.

"I'm not sure," she said in a small voice. "When he finished working this afternoon, we went into town for dinner, and he started drinking—he said it was all right, a celebration, you know, because he'd just finished a section and I had come home. And it was all right. He was in great form, full of good spirits and jokes . . ."

"Until?" I said into her pause.

"Until we went to bed," she murmured. She blushed and hugged herself against the chill night air, wrapping the new yellow nightgown tightly around her body. "He went to sleep—finally—and I guess I dozed off too," she said. "When I woke up he was gone. I went down to see if he was in his study working—he does that sometimes when he can't sleep at night. He was there. He was . . . holding the gun to his head . . . He was holding the gun and staring me right in the eye . . . It was almost as if he was daring me to make him pull the trigger. I don't know . . . I remember screaming, then after that we were fighting for the gun. That's all I—"

"You better pull yourself together," I interrupted as

I saw the blue lights of a sheriff's car racing out of Cauldron Springs toward the turnoff to Trahearne's house.

"Why?" She was close to crying.

"Because the law is here," I said.

"What should I say?"

"Don't say a word," I said. "Just sit down on that lounge chair and whenever somebody asks you a question, you break into tears. All right?"

As if taking me at my word, she fell on the chair and began sobbing loudly. I stepped back inside the house and flipped on the porch lights, then stood empty-handed in their glare as the sheriff's unit skidded to a stop at the bottom of the stairs. The officer stepped out and leaned across the hood, covering me with his revolver.

"Shoot him!" came a wail from the direction of the creek. "He's killed my baby boy! Kill him!" The old woman floundered out of the shadows, dragging Catherine as she tried to hold her back. "Kill him!" she wailed again.

"Mr. Trahearne is perfectly all right," I said to the deputy behind the car. "No one's been hurt."

"On your knees, buddy," he growled, "and lace the fingers behind your neck." I didn't even bother to hesitate. As I assumed the position, he moved from behind the car and eased up the steps with his piece aimed steadily at my thorax region. "Tighter," he said as he stepped behind me. "I want to see white knuckles."

"The right hand and wrist were broken recently, officer," I said as he grabbed my fingers and a handful of hair. He patted me down, sighing in my ear as he jerked the .38 out of my belt.

"Stand up," he ordered as he cuffed my left wrist. As I stood up, he pulled it down behind me and grabbed the right and cuffed it above the cast.

"Easy," I said as quietly as I could. "I told you that nothing has happened. There's no reason to rebreak the wrist."

"Kill him!" the old woman screamed again as she scrambled up the stairs like a wounded crab. Catherine didn't even try to hold her back.

"Tell the old bitch to shut up," I said to nobody in particular.

"You shut up, buddy," the deputy said as he jerked the cuffs. "The sheriff will be here shortly," he added, then jerked the cuffs again as if the alignment of my shoulder sockets didn't suit him.

"Your baby boy is safe and sound, sleeping off a drunk," I said to the old woman as she hobbled up and bared her gums at me.

"I told you to shut up," the deputy said, then did his act with my arms again.

"Don't do that again," I said mildly.

He laughed and did. Some people never learn. Particularly country cops. They never get enough action to stay in shape. I grabbed the deputy's heavy leather belt with my left hand and tugged him closer, then stomped the instep of his right foot and cracked him on the nose with the back of my head and butted him with my ass. As he staggered backward, reaching for his holstered revolver, I turned around and kicked him in the crotch so hard that his feet came off the deck. He hit the floor in a fetal position, but I untangled his arms with my feet and knelt on them and sat on his chest.

"You didn't listen to me," I said to him. He rolled his head sideways and spit blood. I heard grunting and scrambling feet behind me. Catherine kept a good hold on the old woman, though. From the smile on her face, I assumed that Catherine had decided that after what I had done to the deputy, I was going to be out of action for a while. Betty Sue sat on the chair, her mouth open as if she had stopped in the middle of a sob. "Hey," I said to her, "get this dummy's keys and unlock the cuffs."

She didn't say anything, she just did it.

"He really is all right," I said to Trahearne's mother when Betty Sue got the cuffs off me. "He just got drunk and decided to redecorate his study with a .45. That's all."

"Really?" Catherine asked with a cocked eyebrow.

"Take his mother down to the bedroom so she can see for herself," I said as I lifted the deputy's revolver and unloaded it. The two women glanced at each other, then went into the house. "Hey," I said to Betty Sue, "could you get me a towel and a bowl of ice?" After she had stepped into the house, too, I stood up and released the deputy. "Did you hear all that?" I asked. He nodded and crawled toward the vacant lounge chair. "What kind of fool do you want to look like when the sheriff gets here?"

"You're the fool, son of a bitch," he muttered. "Just wait till I get you in a cell."

"You think you'll have a job ten seconds after the sheriff finds out a cuffed prisoner took your piece off you?"

The deputy sneered. "He's my uncle."

"But Roy Berglund's no fool," I said. "Nephew or not, he'll shuck you like a hot tamale. He doesn't get elected by hiring kinfolk who look like fools."

He thought about that for a minute or two, long enough for his pride and his family jewels to stop aching quite so badly, then he glanced up at me, asking, "What did you have in mind?"

"Watering the grass," I said, but he just stared at me. "It always gets those damned stairs wet and slick as owl shit."

"Goddamned stairs," he muttered, then grinned and wiped at the blood on his face.

Betty Sue brought a bowl of ice and two dishtowels. I handed them to the deputy, then went to arrange the lawn sprinklers. Afterward, we sat down to wait for the sheriff. Everybody except for Edna Trahearne. She went home mad.

Roy Berglund looked like a sheriff. He was tall, blond, with crystal-blue eyes and a craggy face. As far as I knew, he wasn't dumb or corrupt. But he was an elected official, more interested in how he looked than how he did his job. And he looked great in a uniform. He had taken time to dress in a fresh one before he picked up two extra deputies and a medical examiner. As he strode like a giant through the sprinklers and up the stairs, they followed like the mere mortals they were. Roy looked great until he stepped, with a leather boot heel, on the wet redwood landing. As he skated across it, his huge arms windmilled furiously as he fought for balance, and he felled a deputy with a backhand right. Betty Sue had to break into sobs to cover her giggles and the deputy on the chaise lounge snorted with laughter until his nose started bleeding again.

"Turn off that goddamned water," he shouted at the deputy lying on the ground. Sheriff Roy was angry. The most important citizen, the son of the richest woman in the county, had been foully murdered, and Sheriff Roy's dignity had been damaged. "Now, what's going on here?" he demanded.

"I'm afraid it has all been a terrible mistake," Catherine said as she stepped out of the shadows, taking charge with smooth assurance. "We—Edna Trahearne and I—heard gunshots and assumed the worst. We leapt to a hasty conclusion." Sheriff Roy looked both confused and disappointed. "My husband—my ex-husband, that is," Catherine said with a slight smile, "was cleaning his pistol when

279

it accidently discharged. No harm done, I'm pleased to say."

"Oh," the sheriff said, tugging on his thick lower lip. "Okay," Then he turned to his nephew. "What happened to you?"

"I was going down to call you on the radio," he mumbled, "and I slipped on them damned stairs."

"Oh," the sheriff said again. "Well, Miz Trahearne, I'm sure glad nobody was hurt, but I've got to make out a report. If you could drop over to the county seat sometime during the next few days, I'd surely appreciate it."

"Of course," Catherine answered before Betty Sue could.

"Let's wrap it up," he said to his courtiers, then, as if it was an afterthought, he added, "Why don't you walk down to the car with me, Mr. Sughrue?"

"Sure," I said.

The sheriff waited until everybody else had a head start, then he wrapped a heavy arm around my shoulder and led me down the stairs.

"Watch your step there, C.W.," he said pleasantly. Up close I could see that he had taken time to shave too. "Now," he said softly when we were at the bottom of the steps, "what happened? The old boy try to punch his own ticket, huh?"

"I was asleep," I said.

"It's all right," he murmured, drawing me still closer. "It's just between us."

"Just between us, huh?"

"Absolutely."

"Just between us, Roy, I was asleep," I whispered.

"Don't jerk me around on this, boy," he answered, "or I'll have your ass in a sling you can't begin to carry."

"It's your sling, sheriff."

"How about three to five in Deer Lodge for assault on a peace officer?" he said.

"I think it's two to ten," I said, but I didn't know either.

"Whatever it is, you won't like it," he said, but when I didn't answer, he tried another tack. "How come you didn't stop by my office to let me know you were working in my county?"

"I'm not working," I said. "I'm just visiting."

"Hope not for long, boy," the sheriff said, then slapped me on the shoulder and laughed as if he had just made a joke. "Don't you even throw a beer can in the ditch, boy," he added.

"You think knowing that Trahearne tried to blow his brains out will buy you anything?" I asked.

"A man who has everything don't need no presents," the sheriff said over his shoulder. "I know what happened and I don't care. I just hate to have a man lie to me."

"Me too," I said.

He laughed as he walked away. "See you around, Sughrue," he said, then climbed into his unit and had a young deputy drive him home.

Back up on the deck, Catherine stood at the head of the stairs and Betty Sue sat on the lounge chair. They were both watching me as I climbed tiredly toward them.

"Betty Sue, would you excuse us, please?" Catherine said without looking at her.

"Of course," Betty Sue answered, and went into the house.

"Let's talk about it tomorrow," I said as I lifted my foot up the last step. "Okay?"

"Tomorrow will be too late," Catherine said. "Talk to her now."

"I'm going to bed."

"I'll just bet you are," she said to my back.

Inside, I went to the bar for a fresh drink. I was in the middle of my second one when Betty Sue came back from the bedroom. She had changed out of her nightgown and into her old baggy clothes.

"I liked you better the other way," I said.

She didn't bother to answer as she stopped to lean against the frame of the study door. The glare of the tilted desk lamp fell harshly across her pale, worn face.

"Let him clean up his own goddamned messes," I said.

"I can't," she said. "What if you had felt that way about my mess?"

"That's different," I answered lamely, but she had already stepped into the study.

The angle of the light lowered, the line of shadow sweeping across the carpet toward the doorway, and the desk chair squeaked as if she were sitting down. I poured myself another splash of whiskey and went outside, switching off the deck lights as I stepped through the door. My .38 Airweight still huddled on the pad of the chaise lounge where the deputy had tossed it. I unloaded it and stuck it in my back pocket. A slice of moon like a hairline fracture opened the night sky, the dark bulk of the remainder clearly visible. As I stared at it, I heard Fireball whimper down on the lawn. I called him and heard his slow scuffle up the stairs. Up on the deck, he waddled over and climbed painfully up into my lap as I sat down on the lounge chair. His haunches were trembling furiously.

"That's okay," I said as I patted his head. "Everybody is gun-shy the first time." The bulldog whined as I rubbed his neck until he stopped shaking. Then I sat him down and went back into the house. He followed, his nose brushing my heels.

Betty Sue still sat at the desk, her head in her hands as she leaned over the pile of tangled yellow pages. Her eyes were dry, though, when she glanced at me. Fireball walked over to her, and she lifted him into her lap. I went over too and leaned against the desk.

"Are you all right?" I asked.

"What did I do wrong?"

"Nothing."

"Then why did he try to kill himself?"

"He can't handle it, I guess."

"Handle what?" she asked as she wiped at her nose with the back of her hand.

"Love and forgiveness," I said.

"I think I'm leaving him," she said softly.

"That's probably the best thing."

"For whom?"

"Both of you."

"You're probably right," she said. "It might be the best for everybody."

"Where are you going?"

She stared at me for a long time, then answered slowly, "I'm ten years late but I'm going home."

"At least I'll know where to find you," I said.

"Don't," she whispered, "please don't."

"Whatever you say."

"And don't worry about Hyland and the rest of the money," she said. "I'll take care of it somehow."

"Are you really leaving?" I asked.

"Yes."

"Wait a minute," I said, then went out to the El Camino to pick up the checks and her five thousand cash.

"What's this?" she asked, as I gave her the envelope.

"Look at it," I said.

"My god." She sighed as she pulled the checks out. "Catherine?"

"And his mother."

"If they want him back this badly, I guess I have to let them have him," she said, then handed me the checks and the cash. "Give the checks back to Catherine and the cash to Hyland," she said. "I pay my own way."

I folded up the checks and stuck them back into my pocket along with the five thousand in cash. "In the morning," I said. "I'm going to the bank to cash this one for forty thousand, then I'm driving down to Denver and put it in their hands. Catherine can have your five thousand and these other two checks back."

"Please don't," she pleaded.

"Listen," I said, "you're not the only one involved—my ass is on the line too."

"I'm sorry," she answered. "Thank Catherine for me—tell her I'll pay her back."

"You tell her."

"I'll be gone before daylight," she said. "I've got a few things to pack up in the studio and a few clothes, then I'm gone."

"I'll be gone before that," I said.

"Come here," she said, and I leaned toward her. She slipped a hand behind my neck and pulled my face toward hers. Our lips brushed lightly. "Thank you," she whispered. "Thank you for everything."

"Do me a favor," I said as I stood up.

"What?"

"When you go home, take that goddamned worthless bulldog with you."

"Thank you," she said again, a touch of laughter rising through a mist of newly born tears.

I touched her cheek with the fingers of my broken hand, then left her that way.

19 ••••

WHILE I WAS PACKING, I WENT INTO THE BATHROOM TO pick up my toilet articles and found the large mirror broken by the round Trahearne had fired through the floor. A large piece had fallen off it and crushed the slim vase with its burden of straw flowers and lonely women's faces. I reached into the tangle of glass and pottery to pick out a large piece with a woman's face upon it. I stared at it for a long time, then tossed it back on the counter and finished packing.

After I loaded the El Camino, though, I didn't have anyplace to go. I drove down the gravel track to the highway, anyway, then turned right toward the mountains again. When I reached the crest of the first rise, I stopped and got out, lit a cigarette and opened a beer. The Trahearnes' houses were dark, but a flood light spilled out of the studio up the hill from his house, and behind the windows, Betty Sue's shadow walked back and forth briskly. In the darkness of the valley, the studio seemed like a crystal island in a sea of black water. I finished the cigarette and the beer, then drove on up to Moondog Lake to wait out the rest of the night.

At dawn an early loon filled the far end of the small lake with his maniac gibber. I kicked out my poorly tended campfire and headed back toward Cauldron Springs.

When I reached the edge of town, I stopped at an outdoor telephone booth to call Torres to tell him that I had his money, then I eased through the waking town, searching for a cup of coffee. Everything was still closed, though. I toured the town aimlessly, the only person awake except for an arthritic old man shuffling from a cheap motel toward the hulk of the hotel and its hot spring waters. I stopped to offer him a ride, but he refused, cackling as he told me that he needed the exercise. I drove slowly on past the hotel and as I turned, I saw Betty Sue's VW parked in the alley behind the pool house and the tennis courts. Staring at it, I went past, then turned around and eased down the alley to park behind her car, which was stuffed with her gear.

The back door was unlocked, but when I went inside the pool house, the waters lay flat and empty, filled with a luminous viscosity from the underwater lights, a light as ashen as that seeping through the skylights. I walked over to the pool and shouted her name, but her naked body floated face down in the pellucid waters, her right arm draped over the small body of the bulldog, as if she had tried to protect him from the bullets. Three black holes clustered in the middle of Betty Sue's back, and another glowed like a coal behind Fireball's ear. Below them, the .45 nestled like a poisonous sea plant against the bottom of the pool, and a cloud of blood, undissipated in the still water, surrounded the bodies like a hazy halo around a dark moon.

It wasn't what I wanted to do, but what I had to do. I went back outside to open the hood of the El Camino and remove the air cleaner. I hid the checks and the cash inside the paper element of it, then went back inside and over to the hotel. The old man who had refused a lift and an even more crippled and older desk clerk were discussing their ailments. I let the conversation die a natural death before I told the desk clerk to call the sheriff's office.

The first thing Sheriff Roy did, of course, was arrest me. I spent two weeks and three days in the Logan County jail without saying a word to anybody except my public defender lawyer, and I only told him that I didn't have anything to say. If the Trahearnes didn't push, the county attorney had no case, so I kept my mouth shut, and they didn't push. They came once, though, Catherine and Trahearne, to visit me in jail. We sat at the end of a long table, my attorney at the other end. Trahearne looked downcast, but Catherine smiled as she told me that I wasn't going to be charged.

"Thanks," I said.

"We told them about those people in Denver," Catherine said, "but of course they all have iron-clad alibis."

"Those sort of people always do," I said.

"What happened to the money?" she asked casually.

"It's in a safe place," I said. "Do you want it back?"

"You've earned it," Catherine said, smiling.

"Right," I said.

Trahearne started to say something, but Catherine reached over to press her fingers to his mouth. I assumed that she was living in his house again, comforting him, protecting him.

"I hope it was worth it," I said, then stood up and went back out into the hallway to pick up my jailer.

That afternoon as I drove out of town, Sheriff Roy followed on the tail of my El Camino. He flashed his headlights at me, then when I wouldn't stop, switched on his spinning blue lights. I didn't even slow down, not even when he opened up his siren, and ten miles out of town, he cut it all off and left me alone. When he stopped to turn around, I stopped too and backed up. We both climbed out and met midway between our cars.

"You got a lot of guts, boy," he said.

"And you've got a lot of gall," I answered.

"I just didn't want you making the mistake of coming back up here to straighten things out," he said.

"What things?"

"Person or persons unknown," he said. "Leave it at that."

"They paid me more than you," I said, then headed back toward my pickup.

"They didn't pay me nothing," he claimed behind me, and I believed him.

In jail, I had missed the funerals, but when I got to California, I saw the graves. Betty Sue had been buried between her brothers in one of those modern, tasteful cemeteries, nothing but lawn and flat stones. It keeps the upkeep down. They can mow right over the headstones. Right over the rotting meat. Oney and Lester had dug right through the concrete and buried Fireball in front of the doorway of Rosie's place, then poured a new concrete plug upon which his name and dates were scrawled in a drunken scribble.

The afternoon I got to Sonoma, Rosie and I were sitting on the front steps, looking at his grave, Lester and Oney flanking us with the beers I had bought them.

"You boys go on inside," she said, and they did. "I thank you for all your trouble," she said.

"I'm sorry," I said.

"At least I saw her that once," she said, "and that's

better than nothing." Then she paused to hit on her beer bottle. "She told me about . . . about everything, " she said softly, "but I just don't understand why they had to kill her. She would've paid the money back, you know that, or if they could've waited, her husband would've paid it—he told me that when he came down with the body—they didn't have to kill her."

"No," I said.

Then she turned to me, saying, "I don't reckon I could hire you again to . . . to take care of those people out in Denver . . . would you?"

"No," I said, "you couldn't hire me, and it wouldn't do any good anyway."

"The man who killed her, he probably didn't even know . . . didn't even know her . . . didn't even know why . . ." she stammered, then dropped her head into her arms.

"That's right," I said, letting her think it had been that way.

"I won't cry yet," she said as she lifted her head quickly.

"Will you do me a favor?" I asked.

"What's that?"

"I've got some of Betty Sue's money," I said, "and I know she'd want you to have it." I dug the five thousand out of my hip pocket and handed it to her. I had already sent Torres his money. If he was afraid to cash the check, that was his problem. "Why don't you get on an airplane and go to Hawaii or some goddamned place? I could run the place for you."

"That's too much to ask," she said as she slapped the sheaf of bills against her thigh.

"Do it," I said, sounding angrier than I meant to.

"You sure?" she asked.

"Dead sure."

"I'd rather fly back to Oklahoma to see some of my kin," she said quietly.

"Stay as long as you like," I said, and finally Rosie turned loose the tears. When she stopped, she went back to the trailer to pack, and Lester and Oney used my pickup to take her over to San Francisco and the airport.

While she was gone, I tended the bar, ran the place, and spent my days waiting for him to show up.

It took him a week, but finally, on a Thursday afternoon, Trahearne showed up, rolling through the front door like a drunken bear. He paused long enough to exchange boozy condolences with Lester and Oney, then he ambled back to the far end of the bar, where I waited. As he shuffled onto a stool, I walked back down the bar, cracked two beers for the boys and a third for the old man.

"How you doing, boy?" he said as I sat it in front of him.

"Better than you, old man," I said.

"How's that?"

"My conscience is clear."

"Yeah, I know," he mumbled. "If I hadn't been so broke, none of this would've happened. That Hyland son of a bitch!"

"Who?"

"Hyland," he answered. "That son of bitch down in Denver."

"He was dead when we left the house," I said.

Trahearne didn't say anything for a moment, then he said, "You don't know that. He might have talked his way out of it or something. You don't know that."

"I saw the body, old man."

"Then it must have been that big ugly son of bitch," he said.

"It was a big ugly son of a bitch," I said, "but he didn't have the guts to pull the trigger."

"What's that?"

"He got his ex-wife to pull the trigger," I said.

"I don't understand," he said.

"She pulled the trigger," I said, "but you put the gun in her hand. And all for nothing, old man. Betty Sue was gone, already gone."

"Oh, come on, boy, you've got to be kidding," Trahearne said, then laughed hollowly. "Let me buy you a beer, boy, before I take off? I've got to get home, you know, get back to the old desk. Like you said, I've been standing too far from it. So get yourself a beer, boy."

"Go home," I said as I jerked his bottle out of his hand. "Get your ass home, old man."

"Come on, boy, gimme my beer," he whined.

I threw it on the duckboards beside me.

"Okay, if you feel that way, boy, I'll take off," he said.

"When you get home," I said, "I want you to do me a favor."

"What's that?" he asked as he stood up, drawing himself up like a wounded man.

"Wait for me."

"I don't know what you mean," he said, confused, rolling his head.

"Go home and wait for me," I said. "I've got a brand new elk rifle, a 7mm magnum, old man, and some afternoon, some afternoon, you're going to step out on your front deck after a day of scribble, scribble, scribble, and I'm going to put a 175-grain hunk of lead right through your gut."

"Always with the jokes, Sughrue," he said as he stumbled back from the bar.

"Go home, old man," I said, "go home and wait for me and try to work, old man."

"Come on," the big man pleaded as he banged into the pool table.

"You're dead," I said. "Go home before you start to stink."

I guess he did. The last I saw of him, he was hurrying out of Rosie's place, stumbling over Fireball's grave.